KILL THE DEVIL TWICE

KILL THE DEVIL TWICE

An Italian Memoir

EDWARD PIACENTINI BERNARDI

Kill The Devil Twice

978-0-9988561-1-7 (sc)
978-0-9988561-0-0 (hc)
978-0-9988561-2-4 (e)

Cover Design by Peggy Swanson

Publisher's e-mail address: bernardinovels@gmail.com

PRINTED IN THE UNITED STATES OF AMERICA

AUTHOR'S NOTE

My original novel, *The Reluctant Patriot*, began as Mussolini, through rhetoric, chicanery, force and audacity, consolidated his position and brought his ideas of change and law and order into every little hamlet in Italy.

This second novel, *KILL THE DEVIL TWICE*, is set in the last days of World War II and its aftermath. Days of pestilence, cruelty, regret and despair; Benito Mussolini's everlasting "gifts of change" to his countrymen.

While most of the events are based on historical fact, the characters and their actions are fictitious.

TABLE OF CONTENTS

PART TWO

REVENGE AND PEACE: 1946-1948

MAIN CHARACTERS

Beatrice Martinelli Carboni .... Matriarch

RELATION TO BEATRICE

Giovanni (Gianni) Carboni .... Only son
Nilde Carboni Pasqua .... Daughter
Emilio Pasqua.. Son-in-law
Michelle Pasqua.. Grandson

Gina Martinelli Carboni.. Sister
Domenico (Mico) Carboni.. Nephew
Giovanna (Gio) Carboni .... Niece

UNRELATED TO BEATRICE

Carla Berti Grandi.. Gianni's Lover
Lorenzo Grandi .... Carla's Husband
Bruno Nasciente.. A Brazilian "Friend"

Tulio & Vaccaccia.. Partisans

INTRODUCTION

IN THE APENNINES 1944-45

"Victories, like the taking of Rome and the storming of the Gothic line, will keep their names thru the centuries." Author Eric Linkletter

"The Battle of the Apennines is a famous page in German military history." Field Marshall Kesselring

Late in 1944, Adolph Hitler ordered one of his most important generals, Field Marshall Kesselring, to build and defend, at all cost, a formidable defensive line to run one hundred seventy miles along the Apennines, splitting the Italian boot from the city of Pesaro on the Adriatic to La Spezia on the Mediterranean. The Germans named it the "Gothic Line".

Over 1,200,000 soldiers were involved in fighting a war of attrition in one of the hardest battle fronts of the entire war, including the savagery during the fight for Monte Casino. Further, those who fought on "The Gothic" also endured the ravages of a most tempestuous winter of cold, heavy snow, wind and ice.

Allied attempts to mount an offensive were thwarted for many weeks, resulting in a virtual stalemate. Kesselring's success in holding the line was so critical to overall German military strategy, that Hitler rewarded the Field Marshall with the command of all German armies on the western front.

As the snow began appearing at the mountain heights, the Americans, who had transferred thousands of troops from Italy to southern France, and having failed to make any headway up the mountain sides, decided to wait out the winter to recommence their attacks.

The winter of 1944-1945 would be one of the coldest winters of the war in Italy. A winter the gods sent down to punish both defender, invader and, sadly, innocent civilians.

Our story begins as the snow begins to melt in the small Apennine town aptly named Sasso:

The Rock.

PART ONE

IT'S NEARLY OVER: 1944-1945

CHAPTER 1

FINDERS KEEPERS

Late in March 1945, after a four-month lull in the fighting between the opposing forces, the Allies accelerated preparations for a renewed assault on the enemy. The American base at Cutigliano, a beautiful Tuscan town situated at the base of the soaring Apennine Mountains, bustled with activity. Replacement troops, machinery, weapons, hospital cadre, Italian run-aways, ordinary citizens and various partisan groups all crammed into every building still standing from the past summer's bombardments.

The accommodations may have been wanting but, thanks to the Americans, in exchange for various small services, rations were readily available for those the GIs dubbed "tourists". Importantly, the "tourist" also knew they were relatively safe and they would survive the war.

After having lived through five years of hell!

However, the situation on the German side of the "Gothic Line" was chaotic. The folks living in the little town of Sasso *(The Rock),* located in the high Apennines about twenty miles above Cutigliano, heard starvation's knock on an everyday basis. There was little food, most of the chestnut trees had been cut for firewood and the four legged creatures, who would have provided sustenance, were more intelligent than their two legged brothers and had, long ago, departed this hell hole.

Michelle Carboni Pasqua had a few shells for his Lugar. The young man hoped to shoot a hare, maybe even a wild boar or, at least a bird of some sort. He was walking just below the high Apennine mountain peak called "*Il Cimone*". He was at about three thousand feet with winter still in residence.

Michelle was now fourteen years old and, even at this young age, had more than his share of the war. His father, Emilio Pasqua, was one of the poor souls Mussolini had sent to the Russian front. He had not been heard from since the battle for Stalingrad in 1941; he was presumed killed during the carnage and blood spilled in the cruel Russian winter.

A year earlier the lad was nearly sent to the concentration camps; saved only because a German Lieutenant, a frequent visitor to Michelle's Grandmother Beatrice's house, intervened. The boy was taken off the north-bound convoy at the last moment. His uncle Gianni wasn't as fortunate and was shipped north, escaped and was now with the partisans somewhere in the mountains on the other side of the river. The lad was eager to join his Uncle Gianni, cousin Mico and the partisans, but both his mother and Nonna Beatrice forbade his even talking about "this idiotic idea". Michelle sneered at the thought he was too young and awaited the opportunity to ask Uncle Gianni about joining the partisans.

He found nothing. Not a sighting. Nearly four hours and not even a squirrel! Disappointedly, he trudged towards his home, where he and his mother and grandmother would need to endure yet another meal of plain chestnut polenta. Worse, he knew his mother, Nilde, would be incensed if she found out he was carrying a Lugar on his person.

The lad had stolen the weapon from the body of a dead German officer the partisans ambushed while driving his vehicle a short distance from *La Rimessa.* Michelle witnessed the event and when he saw the partisans running away up the mountain side, he approached the body, saw the soldier was dead, rolled him over, took the man's Lugar and ran. Had he been caught, he would have been executed immediately.

The entire scene was witnessed by a neighbor who yelled at the boy as he was running from the scene. The villager later told Nilde about her son's actions. She, of course, fumed. Not only did Michelle steal a weapon from a dead German officer, but she feared the witness might tell the entire town about her son's actions and there would then be hell to pay. The Gestapo would accept no excuses and, fourteen years old or not, their verdict would probably be death for the boy.

Michelle gave no thought to the neighbor or the Germans; he itched to shoot at something. He wanted to shoot "just for practice" but, with only four shells for his weapon, he decided not to waste ammunition. The boy looked at his prized Lugar, lovingly caressed the weapon saying, "We could meet some Germans or partisans on the way down; one never knows where they are hiding. We sure don't want them to know I adopted you. Right?"

He gave the weapon another pat, dropped it into his deep jacket pocket and began his return home.

The huge house sat right on the main road between the cities of Modena and Florence. The Carboni clan, using the area's plentiful rock supply, erected the formidable structure to serve as a horse exchange and rest stop for travelers. Built over two hundred years ago, she had withstood brutal winters, an earthquake, invasions and, so far, the ravages of the current war. Today, the big house was home to four individuals and, since Mussolini's downfall in 1943, also housed German officers and troops from time to time.

Michelle approached the house and saw a German officer's vehicle parked next to the house. His first inclination was to run, thought better of it, opened the huge wooden door and entered the house. His Nonna Beatrice's back was to the door, facing a German officer warming his hands at the fireplace. Michelle cringed, closed the door and approached the fireplace.

"What happened? What's wrong?"

Beatrice clenched her fist, her fist urge was to pummel one of her favorites, her "little boy".

"Where is that damn gun you stole?"

"I didn't..."

"Don't lie to me! You were seen stealing the weapon."

The officer leaned forward, a vicious tiger ready to pounce.

A hesitation.

Beatrice, "Damn it! Tell me right now where is the weapon? Give it to me!"

The officer was about to speak, Michelle looked at the man and whispered, "I don't have it anymore. I got scared and threw it into the river."

Silence.

"Michelle if you are..."

The officer interrupted, "How many partisans did you see? What did they look like?"

Quietly, "I saw three. There may have been more. I heard shots and saw the car crash into the tree. I hugged the ground."

"Then what happened?"

"Three men in civilian clothes ran across the road towards the jeep. I was really scared."

A hesitation, "I didn't raise my head so I don't know what they did."

"Did you hear any more shooting?"

"No. The next thing, I heard them running; I looked up and saw them cross the road and into the shrubbery."

"Then what did you do?"

No reply.

Beatrice began to speak, the officer interrupted and grabbed Michelle's collar, "Boy! I asked you a question. What did you do?"

"I started to run home, passed right by the dead soldier, saw the gun in his holster and took it."

"How did you know he was dead?"

Michelle lowered his head, whispered, "He was face up; his jacket was covered with blood", another hesitation, "and one of his eyes was gone."

The officer turned to Beatrice, "Madam, you have been good to us. We value your friendship but one more incident, just one more, and you will be reported to my superiors. Understand?"

The officer loosened his grip, "I'm not going to report you. You are lucky I am not SS or Gestapo. They could already be swinging you from the tree outside your front door."

A humble, "Thank you, sir."

"The war is ending; don't be a damn fool. Your grandmother's friendship won't save you again."

A click of the heels, a turn towards the door, a military salute and he was gone.

Beatrice Carboni, nee Martinelli, had many anxious and frightening experiences in her first sixty-plus years of life. Just before the dawn of the 20th century, her husband, Mario Carboni, freed his gambling obligations by hanging himself from a barn rafter. The beautiful, statuesque widow was left with a life-time of tears, debt, two little girls, and half ownership in an old two story house they shared with her brother-in-law and her sister, Gina.

Brothers had married sisters and the arrangement eased the work load for all and created a strong family relationship. A most important family tie Beatrice would call upon in the years ahead.

Two years after her husband had committed suicide, she had a short affair with one of the town's wealthiest men and, a year later, gave birth to her son, Giovanni (Gianni).

The news of the illegitimate birth echoed from the hills to the big mountain and back to the hills! "Illegitimate! She has a lover. Who is it?" The local black-clad widows were particularly condemning as they waggled their sharp tongues in the strongest condemnation possible, the ultimate denunciation, "The Carboni widow had committed a mortal sin!"

Beatrice persevered, surviving the small-town gossips and difficult times, raising her son and two daughters from her marriage as best she could. She and her family had faced and lived through the difficulties of the first World War and now they were trying to survive through the present occupation.

Near starvation, Germans, ex-Fascists, partisans kept knocking at her door, but she protected her own, often at personal risk, and the family persevered. She was truly the embodiment of mother-hood.

However, at this moment she was livid, "This stupid grandson, who thinks a rope around his neck is the same as wearing a tie at Christmas, scares the *cacca* out of me!"

The lad's sole response was a silly grin, further angering his grandmother.

"Damn you Michelle! Where did they store your brains?"

Nilde, Michelle's mother, entered the house at that moment, "What is all this screaming about?"

"Ask your son?"

A mother's consoling smile for an only son, "Michelle, what did you do this time?" She couldn't help showing great pride in her tall handsome offspring.

Silence.

Nilde, seeing her mother's continuing stern, humorless composure, "Will one of you please tell me what this is all about."

"Your son is volunteering his life to star in a German opera ending with a rope around his neck and his death at the final curtain. A German officer was just here; your son was seen taking a pistol from the body of the soldier ambushed and killed yesterday."

Nilde began to shake, wobbled towards the dearest thing in her life, opened her fist and, for the first time in her life, slapped someone. She was speechless.

Tears flowing, anger and fear both rising to the surface, "Michelle! Michelle! It is bad enough we lost your father in Russia, that your *Nonna* and I going crazy worrying about Gianni with the partisans and you going stupid." She reached up, grasped her son's shoulders and began shaking the boy, "What am I going to do with you? What are we going to do with you? Why do you do this to me?"

Michelle backed away. "OK! OK! I'm sorry. It won't happen again. I'll be careful."

The lad hugged his mother for a long while, then turned to his grandmother, "I'm sorry *Nonna*; it won't happen again; I promise."

The lad then stepped back, "I'll be careful but for now", he reached into his jacket, showed the Luger and, with a mischievous smile, asked "where should we hide this?"

The two women were left speechless.

CHAPTER 2

ESCAPE!

Gianni Carboni smiled as he entered the wooded area. He was alive! He could go home to Carla. He would live to see his child. He would see his mother. He would see his house, *La Rimessa*, again. His cousin and best friend, Mico, had not fired the Luger.

Gianni hastened his pace down the mountainside towards his home. His dance with death was over. Despite the cutting Apennine wind, perspiration trickled down his side, sliding down his arms; a fear driven contradiction of hot and cold. His head cleared and realized he had not heard a shot; neither the one intended for him nor the one meant for his half-brother, Lorenzo. "They must be conjuring a brutal death for Lorenzo", he mumbled to the stars. A mishmash of mixed emotions raced through his mind; death for Lorenzo was justified revenge and Carla would never again suffer from his threats and humiliation. More importantly, a dead Lorenzo meant Carla would be Gianni's to love and hold.

He kept plodding down the steep mountainside. He had to get to his house. With the Germans retreating on the main road, Gianni did not think cousin Mico, whose partisan *nom' di guerra* was Ivan, would send a search party in pursuit. He hoped Mico would let him go; that he would not search the house and upset the family, especially Gianni's mother, Beatrice. He was confident Mico would not vent his anger on his own aunt or other family members if they happened to be at the house.

He was wearing long underwear under two pair of heavy pants, a heavy brown woolen sweater knitted for him by his mother, as were the sweat laded heavy woolen socks. A black poncho gave some protection from the mist, while an old black cap covered his head. A three-day old beard added to the ominous appearance of the handsome Gianni Carboni. He smiled, "…and I don't smell too good either…I could easily pass as a vagabond or, perhaps, as a phantom from the long ago."

A dead branch scrunching under his boot altered his thought process and, disturbingly, his half-brother came to mind once again. He felt a sense of guilt but, nevertheless, shouted to the snow laden pine trees, "I don't give a damn how they do it; I just hope they killed the bastard."

He walked on thinking about his outburst for a moment, "Maybe I've become like the rest of the others", he stumbled, caught himself, "Better watch where I'm going instead of arguing with myself about right and wrong. For the present, dignity and respect are words from a distant time; a different world."

He felt not a trace of guilt for wishing his half-brother a speedy death.

He approached the highway, saw smoke emanating from a few roof tops below. He stopped for a few moments, stomped his feet, adjusted the blue scarf around his neck. Saliva had frozen against the woolen material. His heavy boots were soaked and the wind, despite the heavy clothing, fought for his attention. "Damn it's cold", a chuckle, "but it should help keep the hard heads inside."

Gianni reflected upon his months with the Mico-led partisans; the savagery, loss of dignity, hunger, fear, the bitter cold all mixed into a recipe of destruction heaped on poor Italy by Germans, Fascists and the partisans, themselves. Five years of war; two years of brother killing brother had turned insanity into the commonplace. You killed, looted your own and sang praises to unknown deities hidden in their safe-houses.

He had made the right decision; the war was now one of attrition. There was no glory watching brother killing brother. Worse, was the brutality some these "patriot-partisans" heaped against old men, women and children; innocents, unwilling pawns in a war seemingly without end.

It was madness.

He coughed, "Whatever happens, I made the right choice. I may die because of it, but at least I'll be alive while I live. I won't be a dead man pretending life."

Mico, his cousin, friend and a leader of the partisan band had commanded Gianni execute the Fascist traitor, his step-brother, Lorenzo. He remembered how the pistol lay cold in his stiff hand; it would have been so simple, so just. The man deserved to be killed ten-fold but, even at the risk of his own death, Gianni could not pull the trigger.

He knew he would pay the price for his defection, but in the bitter cold of an Apennine afternoon he also knew it was the only choice he could make. He was sick of war. He was sick of the political reasoning justifying brutality, revenge and actions no sane human being would ever consider. He smiled thinking about his cousin Mico's "*nom de guerre*"; Instead of a nice Italian name like "Domenico", Mico had become "Ivan", a Communist marionette.

Just a short hour before, Mico gave Gianni a hand gun and ordered him to kill Lorenzo. Unable to act as an executioner, Gianni had dropped the weapon and began walking away from the group of *partigiani*.

He had heard Ivan's snarl resonating, "Stop, Gianni, or you will be the first to die." His heart beat had rushed at such a pace that, despite the frigid air, perspiration had soaked his shirt. He had continued towards the woods at a slow pace, expecting death as each step crunched the thin layer of snow. He had been ready to die.

But the explosion never came. The shot never arrived! He was alive! His cousin and boyhood friend did not pull the trigger. He was alive!

Gianni stumbled, pushing the naked branches aside, as he tumbled down the mountain side. His body ached, panting, he managed a smile. Through the shrill whistle of the cold wind, Mico's words resonated again. He remembered his exultation as he entered the protection of the heavy trees. No shot had been fired. His friend could not pull the trigger; war or no war, he had let Gianni live. He laughed, inhaled the frigid air, and laughed again.

However, he was now on the run. His failure to carry out his superior's command put him at an additional great new risk. The Germans, the Fascist and, now, his own partisan comrades were all enemies; he had no allies. He now had to hide somewhere and wait out the war. But, first he had to get to his house. He was sure the partisans would not come after him until morning so he had time to rest and, then, time to consider his options for the days ahead.

It was now dusk; the clouds hid whatever effort the sun was making to prolong this, one of the most excruciating days of his life. He was about to exit the wooded slope when he heard the familiar growl of a German patrol car approaching. He hid, face down, in the mud and let the car zoom past. Since the Germans no longer dared single vehicle movements, Gianni remained hidden in the prone position and awaited additional traffic.

He heard no further movements. The eerie quiet unnerved him. He started shaking, not knowing if the cause was the cold and wet ground, the Germans, or both. He remained hidden as his battle field senses re-awakened and he began thinking like a combatant again. Despite the cold, he conquered the urge to move with the enemy still on the highways. He knew it would be best to await the silent black of an Apennine night. No sense taking a risk and running into a German patrol, partisans or Fascist sympathizers. The Germans would either kill him or place him back on a truck headed for the northern concentration camps. Better frozen feet than being invited to one of those Nazi work camps; he had escaped the "long ride north" once; he would not be so fortunate a second time. He would await nightfall.

He sat up, coughed, embraced himself and began the wait by reliving the incredible experiences of the past few days. It was all madness! The big war was nearly over. For days now the entire area could hear the rumble and roar of Allied long guns fifteen miles to the south. Each day brought increasing activity on the highway as the Germans rushed equipment and men to the north, towards the Modena rail terminals.

"There is no reason to continue the war, thought Gianni. It's over. Let the hard heads go home. And, for Lord's sake let's stop these acts of revenge among our own!" He laughed as he realized the reality of the moment; his nose was running so he used his sleeve as a handkerchief. So much for happy thoughts and wishful dreams.

He stretched his legs and laid down on the ground curling himself against a huge pine tree that somehow had managed to evade bombs or axe. The wind was now whipping little snowflakes in a frenzied dance across the road below. His mind drifted again; he was so tired "Can't fall asleep, they'll find a frozen plank; stay awake, Gianni. Think. Move your legs. Rub your face."

But, he counter argued, "Why am I hiding? No one is about in this cold. The chance of being caught is small. Admit it! You faced a gun and now you are afraid of crossing a road? I can nearly see the house. There is no better place to be. Nowhere in the whole wide world! And that place is but a couple of hundred meters away. Think, Gianni. Just a bit more and you'll be with Carla, Beatrice and the rest of the family."

Just a bit more. But, he didn't move. He wiped his nose with a gloved hand and scolded himself anew, "I'm being too cautious. I'm going to chance it!"

He stood, leaned against the tree and pulled the black wool hat down over his ears "So, let's go Gianni-boy! Let's go!" Every bone in his body ached as he slowly crept towards the road. He imagined he could already feel the warmth of the big fireplace at *La Rimessa.*

He was about to cross into the open but, once again, heard approaching vehicles. He dove back into the brush and lay still. Three military cars, heading north, roared by at high speeds. He remained hidden, his heart bursting. A few moments later, a second roar of heavy motors approaching. Clutching the cold ground, he peeked towards the south and saw a caravan of German vehicles. He counted eight two-ton personnel carriers and concluded, "The hard heads are removing soldiers from the front! The bastards are beginning a night withdrawal!"

Then silence again! Not a whisper. In a matter of moments, a complete calm enveloped the area and stillness became the new enemy. He couldn't believe his bad luck. He couldn't believe his good luck. Both, arriving within moments of each other. Were the gods working for him or against him? He fought the urge to cry and tried to reassure his "*Grugno*", a name he had given to that gnawing feeling one discovers during stressful moments, "We've been through worse; we are practically home. Let's wait it out. Let your body freeze but we remain hidden 'til dark. No more chances Gianni boy. No more chances."

Darkness, his one true ally, finally arrived and, under its cloak, he ran across the road, slithered through the trees and crept down a slight slope and cautiously approached the front of his house. His wet clothing clung to his body, he felt terrible. He stomped his feet as he drew near a side window. He could see a dim light escaping from the wooden shutter imprisoning the warmth of the big room's fireplace; he shivered, turned back to the front and softly rapped on the huge door.

No response. He gently rapped again; no response.

He clicked the handle, found the door unlocked, slowly opened the huge door and quietly entered the dark room. Low embers flickered from the huge stone fireplace; a snore accompanied the murmur of the pirouetting embers.

He chuckled at the sight of his mother, Beatrice, asleep in the huge sofa chair. The old girl had a knitted brown blanket wrapped around her shoulders, a bottle of *"the red"* cradled in her arms, stockings rolled down to her ankles and feet propped upon the fire place ledge a few feet from the low flame. He reasoned his sister Nilde and nephew Michelle must be asleep upstairs.

Gianni slowly liberated *"the red"* from his mother's lap, and pensively looked at this exceptional lady. Feeling an emotional sob, he stroked her hair as he remembered some of the challenges she confronted throughout her life. Her life story was one of truth, love, hard work and endurance. For her, each day was a new beginning. She never gave up.

He touched his mother's shoulder, shook his head at the irony of life. He re-called that just a few years ago, he discovered his father was Rolando Grandi – whose legitimate son was Gianni's lifelong nemesis, Lorenzo Grandi.

Mixed emotions of jealousy, loathing and regret pulsed through his mind, "Lorenzo Grandi, my half-brother; my enemy. A Fascist who threw neighbors and relatives into German hands. The Fascist devil who stole my love, Carla, and then treated her maliciously."

He looked at the wine bottle, took a swig of *"the red"*, said "Enough of that" and walked up to his bedroom. He removed wet clothing and shoes, rubbed his feet for a few moments, medicated with the remainder of the wine and was asleep under a pile of knitted covers before his head found the soft, hair-filled pillow.

CHAPTER 3

DID ABEL EVER LOVE CAIN?

Mico stood speechless as Gianni walked away from his duty, his obligation, but he could not pull the trigger. How could he shoot his friend, his cousin? He faced the squad of partisans knowing this failure to act had immediately diminished his authority over the troupe. He had shown a weakness he never would have tolerated from his men. An order was an order; you followed without question. A soldier was only a straw in the wind for the greater good of the country and, most importantly, for one's comrades in arms. One followed commands without question; to obey was a soldier's sacred duty.

There were no outward expressions of disappointment among the men. However, each knew if they had failed to act, as their leader had just done, they would have been subject to the harshest penalty, including death.

The men quietly walked back to their fires mumbling, looks of disgust passed from one face to the next. Their brave, fearless, intrepid leader known as Ivan, had failed. Mico had lost the respect of his men; he no longer was their leader; he was merely a foot soldier like the pig Vaccaccia or any of the other ragged misfits belonging to this band of *"partigiani"*.

Despite his past heroics, until he proved otherwise, big Mico's reputation as a leader fighting for a great cause had vanished in a matter of minutes. In the men's eyes, he was now no better than his cousin Gianni, who had shirked his duty by disobeying a battlefield order in exchange for the warm embrace of his mamma.

Mico knew his four years of risk-taking and obedience to the cause, no longer mattered. Friendship and blood line had clouded his soldierly responsibility. There would be a price to pay and it happened immediately.

Mico ordered the youngest of the partisans, known as Ricardo the Terrible, to take the Fascist coward, the prisoner Lorenzo Grandi, back to the shed and tie him securely. They would deal with Gianni's step brother later. The young man hesitated and didn't follow Mico's order until the commanding officer, Capitan Tulio nodded his approval.

Mico immediately approached Tulio, "Captain, permission to carry out a mission?"

A smirk, "Permission to do what?"

The big man was wrapped in a heavy knee-length black coat and had the appearance of a huge black bear. He looked down on the officer and in a heavy raspy voice said, "Captain, I made a mistake and the only way I can regain your respect is for me to go after Gianni, bring him back to the camp and force him to execute the prisoner."

Tulio listened to the request, frowned, fingered his holster and sneered at his adjunct, "and what if you don't return?"

The men, especially Vaccaccia, barked the same question.

The Captain, a delay and then with a suspicious smile, "Alright, I agree. Tomorrow morning take a couple of men and go after that coward cousin of yours; bring the weakling back."

He turned his back on Mico and addressed the group, "Men, as you have just heard, Ivan is asking permission to go after his dear cousin and bring him back to carry out the order to execute Lorenzo."

It had become dark but light from the campfire flickered and one could see and hear the men's responses. Sardonic smiles, "show me grunts" and *sotto voce* murmurs greeted Tulio's remarks.

Vaccaccia, the worst of the lot, stood, spit out a wad of tobacco juice and asked with a chuckle, "Hey, Captain, what if Mico doesn't come back?"

There were mumbles among the men; an evil, sinister sounding burble of discord. Vaccaccia, "the ugly cow", tobacco spittle on his 3-day old beard, "You can't trust him; blood is thicker than duty; Captain, with respect, how do we know he won't run, along with his cousin, Mr. Gianni Carboni?"

The man punctuated his comment by spitting tobacco juice into the fire.

Mico turned his back on the blabber-mouth and addressed the others, "Isn't it strange; you bastards are more intent on hurting my cousin, my own brother-in-war than you are confronting the real enemy. You make me want to vomit."

He turned, "Tulio, for over two years we have been through many battles together; you know I have served the cause as well, better and longer, than anyone in this rag-tag bunch you have appointed as my jury. You are the leader; you are the one who gave the order to kill. Why does someone like Vaccaccia, who has shirked his duty since he joined you, have a say?"

The Captain didn't respond; only the sizzle of the campfire could be heard Mico stood and faced the group, "So heroes, who is coming with me to make sure I return?"

"You, Vaccaccia? You son of a bitch; you haven't been worth the food we've given you and now you play the fearless warrior, the kind of scoundrel every partisan unit is dying to enlist! Right?" Mico scowled at the weakling, "Come on hero, let's go down and get Gianni."

Vaccaccia lowered his head, put a new chew in his mouth; not a word in reply to the insult.

"Any volunteers among you wanting to make sure I return to camp? You, Ricardo?"

The youngster scratched himself. Vaccaccia, eyes down, head buried deeper into his overcoat, mumbled, "You were always the big hero, continually on us as if we were useless."

Seeing a few approving nods from the men, Vaccaccia sat up and raised his voice, "Our so-called second-in-command screwed up and now he wants us to put our asses on the line to help him." In an act of bravado threw a salute at Mico, "Go yourself big hero, you don't need us." A derisive sneer, "We'll stay right here and have a good laugh on the Carboni boys. Right men?"

Mico stood, walked toward Vaccaccia, grabbed his collar and half-raised the agitator to his feet, "You chicken-shit-good for nothing, stand up and ..."

The Captain, poking his index finger into Mico's back, interrupted, "Enough of this crap; you go alone and this time I expect you to obey my order; if you desert us, we will come after you, war or no war. Bringing Gianni back to carry out the order to execute Lorenzo is your responsibility. Do we understand one another?"

Addressing his men, “He goes alone; if he doesn’t return we will go down and burn his mother’s house and, I swear, I’ll never stop looking for him.” He turned and faced Mico with a petulant snarl and asked the men, “Everybody in agreement?”

Mico pushed Vaccaccia down unto the ground and freed his grip, Vaccaccia looked up, “I’ll never forget this, Mico. One way or another you are going to eat your words!”

Mico’s stomach was churning. Anger, humiliation in front of his subordinates; Tulio’s abrasive, condescending tone gnashed his ego and pounded blood through his arteries, painting his face in a deep red. His past contributions, his leadership in difficult combat situations, his bravery was forgotten. Until proven otherwise this man, who had sacrificed so much for “the cause”, was now an outsider.

Tulio pulled Mico away from the men and in a firm, officious manner, snarled, “You leave for La Rimessa at dawn. Gianni is sure to be there. Where else can he hide? ”

When out of earshot of the others, the big man addressed the Captain once more, “Tulio you seem to forget who I am; what I have done for you, our cause and the entire group. Don’t the past couple of years mean anything? Am I now the enemy? I failed to kill my cousin, but I told you I’m going to bring him back, isn’t that enough for you after all we have been through together? What am I now; a piece of crap? Am I the new enemy?”

Silent for a moment, Tulio blinked but his voice said it all, “I’m ordering you to leave early tomorrow morning, get your ass down there and bring your cousin back. If you don’t, you’d better keep walking yourself. The men, rightfully so, will no longer have any use for your leadership. You expected so much from them; asked them to lay down their lives for our cause and now….” he hesitated, slowly took a cigar out of his pocket, licked the outside, plucked one of the campfire twigs and lit the curly stub of tobacco. He coughed, “Hear me well, Mico. Tomorrow morning you go down and bring your cousin back. He is going to kill Lorenzo whether his moral code condones the action or not. It is now a matter of obedience to one’s senior commander. I repeat: Gianni disobeyed a direct order given on the battlefield. His action was treasonous!”

He stared into is subordinate’s eyes, “and the same goes for you Ivan, you have a direct order, now carry out your assignment.”

A voice from deep within burst a response, "Treason? Being ordered to kill your own flesh and blood was a battlefield matter? Why are you being so cruel, Tulio? Couldn't you have one the others, Vaccaccia for example, do the deed? What are you trying to prove by forcing Gianni to be the executioner? Who in the hell is the enemy, anyway?"

Tulio drew on the cigar again, calmly responded, "You bring him back or we come after you both. Of course, if you don't come back, the Germans would love to entertain you; Ivan would be a great catch for them."

The two men, brothers in war, glowered at one another as Mico responded, "You know Tulio, I assume you know your name means one who leads; but there is also a second meaning, it is another name for dizziness."

Mico broke into a sarcastic smile, "And I think you have heard one too many explosions; you are another casualty of war; the only problem is you don't know it."

A steely glare was his Captain's only response.

The big man had a sleepless night. For the first time since he escaped the Fascists a life-time ago, he began to question the beliefs he had fought for, been willing to die for. He tossed on the make-shift cot as he thought about those political beliefs that, for an eternity, had kept him from his little family in far-away France.

In the early days of Mussolini's rise, Mico ran away from home and his Fascist father; he failed in his effort to enter the United States and was returned to Italy as a criminal. After a few weeks, he escaped his Genovese jailers, went into France where he met and married his Suzi.

Shortly after France fell in 1940, at the suggestion of his new father-in-law, he joined the *Et Eclaireurs Israelites de France*: EIF, The Jewish Scouts of France **(i).** By 1943 he was deeply involved with the movement, giving needed assistance to escapees from Nazi cruelty. In the spring of '43 he was assigned the task of delivering messages and instructions to Communist cells operating in the nearby Italian provinces. Then, when the Allies invaded the Italian boot, he was assigned to a partisan group near his hometown, Sasso.

(i)See Author's Notes: The Jewish Scouts of France)

He was a zealot risking his life for the good cause of his people. He never questioned the means used to reach the party's objectives. It was a moral crusade and he had been willing to remain away from his family, live in great discomfort and risk death for his principles.

And now, on this cold night, those beliefs were being questioned. Had he been wrong? Had he fled one bad situation for something as bad? Tulio's brutal command against one of his own men and Gianni's brave reaction, stirred a potpourri of confused ideas. Questions came to the surface, triggering inner turmoil, raising doubts about his core beliefs.

He tossed, pulling a dirty, damp blanket over his shoulders, "Are my political ideas so fixed that I will go down to Aunt Beatrice's house, tear away her son and then command him to execute his half-brother? And, once I get Gianni back to the camp, why would he, with a life-time of reasons for shooting the pig Lorenzo, kill his flesh and blood the second time around? A killing he already had refused to carry out under the threat of death."

Whispering to himself, he continued, "Why would Gianni act any differently now? Gianni will disobey again and Tulio will order me to put the Luger to Gianni's neck and ..." He gazed into the darkness, "… and, that bastard Tulio insisting Gianni be the executioner; why not have one of the other partisans execute the traitor Lorenzo and just get it over with? Tulio's orders were perverse; pig-headed orders to make a point, a command to show superiority, not because it was the right thing to do."

The rumble of distant artillery resounded down the valley, disrupting his contemplations. He shivered again as the rolling thunder rained steel slivers indiscriminately over the Apennine landscape. He was sure the Americans were advancing, preparing their way with a random rain of death delivered under a charade called "liberation"; a pretense of killing Germans and Fascists but, at the same time, maiming or killing dozens of innocents. It was lunacy.

Torn by conflicts of allegiance, loyalty and duty and to the staccato accompaniment of the Allied firepower grumbling throughout the mountains, he pondered the question; "The Allied forces will arrive soon; the war will end and in the last hours of battle I am asked to kill my own cousin", he shivered. "If I bring Gianni back to Captain Tulio, how will I be able to face my mother and my Aunt Beatrice, whose name my own daughter carries? How will I be able to face my sister, Giovanna? How will I be able to face myself?"

It was two o'clock in the morning, he closed his eyes and said a bedtime prayer, "Vaccaccia, you no good son-of-a-bitch, I should have broken your nose."

The prayer brought him to the cusp of his second epiphany.

CHAPTER 4

IL CUORE D'UNA MAMMA

Gianni awoke to the downstairs babble of his mother and sister, Nilde. He dressed, went down the stairs and was lovingly greeted by the two women. He dunked a small piece of hard, three or four-day old bread into a cup of *orzo***.** A crumb fell to the wooden table, Gianni wet his index finger, daubed the ort and brought it to his mouth saying, "When I came home last night I found the door unlocked and you asleep with a half empty bottle of *the red* on your lap; seems to me you were living a bit dangerously."

Nilde, thin as breadstick, jutted out her sharp chin and grumbled, "I keep telling her, Gianni. She won't listen. Whenever you leave she is into *the red* all the time."

"Oh, shut up. Living with you is enough reason to take a lot of medicine. She flits around the house like a frog chasing flies."

"Listen to her, Gianni. I have lost a husband to the Russian front. My boy wants to join the partisans. It'll be just a matter of time before Michelle takes his war prize, disobeys me and heads for you partisans. And this one solves it all by opening yet another bottle. She is driving us crazy."

"What war prize?"

A hesitation, "My son stole a Luger from the body of an ambushed German, then faced questioning about the incident, all the while hiding the stolen weapon in this coat pocket!"

Nilde, with an avalanche of words, ran on and on recounting the prior day's incident, then asked, "Gianni what am I going to do with him?" A sob, "he is going to get himself killed!"

The handsome family idol, chuckled, "Stop it. Both of you stop it. Nilde, leave Mamma alone; what she has lived through entitles her to take whatever medicine she wants." He finished his orzo and continued, "...and, since, there no longer is a pharmacy in the entire mountain area, it seems to me the *red* is as good an antidote as any."

A broad smile, "Meanwhile, I'll talk to Michelle. Frankly, it's something I might have done myself."

The two women were stunned by the comment; Beatrice began to respond, but Gianni held up his hand, looked at the two women and in a measured, low pitched voice, "I need both of you to help me. I have a major problem that must be solved right now or we may all be in trouble. He put his hands on his loved one's shoulders, drew them into a big hug, "...and your squabbling isn't helping matters."

He released the two, sat in a chair, poured wine into a second cup of hot orzo and explained what had transpired. A gasp from Beatrice; Nilde, for once, remained silent; transfixed.

"The war is nearly over; it's just a matter of surviving the next few weeks, a month or two at most. The Americans are at Cutigliano; dozens of towns between us and the front have been eating their shrapnel for many days now. Their long-range guns poured hot steel on Rio del Sol last night I am sure they will be bombarding Sasso before too long. Last evening I saw German vehicles heading north – the flow will increase. The Allies are on the move; and, ladies, the Germans are going to be downright mean to anyone standing in the way of their retreat, especially able bodied males like me."

He was quiet for a moment, then in a sad voice, "Mico, or Ivan, as the partisans call him, is a major problem. He and his men will be coming after me. I've got to get out of here. I've got to risk going over the mountains towards the American lines."

"Gianni, Gianni you can't......" Nilde's plea was interrupted,

"I considered several alternatives. Mico and his men are probably on their way. Maybe, because of all the German activity, they may wait until dark but I can't take that chance. I'll hide somewhere until dark, then cross the Rio River, walk up Mt. Cimone, take the old mule trail towards Mt. Lancino to Melo. From there I'll cross over to the American side at Cutigliano."

Nilde, voice quivering, "There are German patrols all over the Rio area.

How are you going to get across? And, if you do get near Cutigliano, how are you going to get through the German lines to the American side?"

"So, what should I do Nilde? Hide here? Give myself up to the partisans? Do you think if I go back and kill Lorenzo all will be forgiven? These men are ruthless. Their days of revenge and retribution are soon coming to an end. They want to feast now while sacrificial lambs are still to be had. They are coming after me; at this moment, they probably want me more than the hard heads. No, this is as good a solution as there is. I go tonight."

Beatrice looked at her son. He had bathed, shaved and changed into clean clothing and stood before her. A mother's eyes saw him as the real Adonis, "Your decision is easier for me than the one you made when you went to *L'America* so long ago. If you hide here at *La Rimessa*, Mico will immediately find you. I don't think he will force you back but Lord knows what he will do. If you try to hide elsewhere the Germans will find you and kill you as a partisan traitor or send you to the concentration camps. Stay here and the Germans will eventually grab you."

He took a deep breath, "No sense playing games now. I must tell you that Carla Grandi is pregnant with my child and I can't risk seeing her before leaving. Nilde, you must do me a great favor; I would like you to bring Cousin Giovanna to me. She visits Carla frequently and she will easily be able to deliver my message."

Beatrice had not moved. She studied her son, peered into his eyes with admiration and love. She hesitated, "I've known about you and Carla for quite a while, tell me …"

Gianni interrupted, "You heard. Carla is pregnant with my child and …"

"She is married…"

"Lorenzo is dead..."

"I think you should…"

Before Beatrice could continue they heard the roar of several German vehicles passing by. They remained quiet, Gianni easing towards the back door leading towards the woods. The vehicles' movement was a loud, slow grumble.

Gianni, "They are towing heavy equipment towards the north, away from the front."

The vehicles rolled past, the roar fading into the purr of a household cat.

"Nilde, don't make it more difficult than it is. Please, just go and get Giovanna for me."

"Gianni", a slight hesitation, "take my Michelle with you."

He was startled. He could not believe his sister would suggest he take her son out of her sight.

"Gianni please take him. I know he is getting ready to run away to the partisans. I think he risked stealing the Luger for use as a partisan."

Nilde took a deep breath, "Pete Morri, the street sweeper, saw my Michelle run out of the woods, roll the body over, steal the weapon and run! I'm sure Morri reported the incident and who is to say the Gestapo or the SS won't be back for more questioning. Gianni, I'm scared. Really terrified!"

The poor woman began crying. "If the hard heads had found him with the pistol, they would have shipped him to the camps or executed him on the spot. Such stupidity!" she paused and continued in an exasperated voice, "… and he still has that damn Luger hidden somewhere. He won't give it back."

Gianni looked at his mother. Without a word, Beatrice turned and walked towards the kitchen. She knew this was a decision only Gianni could make. She also knew the Carla discussion could wait for another time.

Nilde placed her hand on her brother's forearm and in a plaintive voice whispered, "Please, Gianni, please take him with you; he is driven to become involved in this madness and I can't control him any longer."

Gianni looked at his sister but did not respond.

Nilde wavered for an instant and continued. "In fact, the Germans seized the three Pucci brothers a couple of days ago; the little one is younger than Michelle; one way or another, it is only a matter of time before something dreadful happens."

Nilde looked at her brother with pleading eyes, hesitated again and, when her brother did not respond, quietly said, "Write your note to Carla."

He patted his sister's shoulder, quietly asked, "Where is Michelle anyway? Go find him and bring him home. When you return you can bring my note to Giovanna. Meanwhile, I'll think about taking Michelle. Now go!"

She put on boots and her heavy coat. "Write your letter, Gianni, I'll find Michelle."

A cold breeze rushed into the warmth of the room as Nilde went out the door. Beatrice looked out from the kitchen, returned to her chair near the fireplace, opened a bottle of *the red* and poured herself a glass.

Gianni shivered, checked the watch he had taken from the body of a German officer the month before. It was a beautiful Swiss masterpiece with five different dials. Gianni noticed one dial told him it was eight in the morning in a free Paris. The larger dial indicated it was nine in the morning in war torn Sasso. Gianni said nothing.

As he drew the heavy wooden bench to the table to write his message to Carla, he thought about his sister. Always the nervous type, she had lost a husband to the Russian front, and night and day she had to worry, as did all the neighbors, about the ever-present Germans who were no longer allies.

Gianni could not fathom the anguish she must have suffered arriving at such a decision. Yet, she showed her strength asking he take her only treasure through enemy territory. How horrible her options.

And, to make matters worse, Beatrice's looking to the bottle for strength, Gianni sympathized with his sister. She had every reason to be anxious and worried about their mother and the *red*. He sighed, "...and now, Michelle's leaving will cause new stress and new worries for her."

He pushed back his coal black hair with his right hand, "It will be a difficult task moving alone. Taking the lad will make the journey more difficult. Who knows how the boy will react to any challenges we might encounter?"

His old friend, *"Il Grugno"*, reappeared and the tightness hidden somewhere in his psyche tugged and wrenched as the war between fear and duty waged far within. He looked at the ceiling, "But, how can I deny Nilde? I've got to take him with me. There is no way I can reject her request."

He gazed fondly at his mother as she poured herself another glass of *the red*. "Lord, help us", he sighed. Then, to his mother, "I'll take Michelle with me; it will make the trip easier. Michelle will give me an extra set of eyes when we cross over."

He hesitated, "Ma, I love Carla and she loves me."

Beatrice stared at him, took a sip of the wine. She appeared to be about to reply, instead she slumped in her chair, faced the fireplace, not responding. Hesitatingly, "Ma, you should take it easy on *the red;* they say, vino is a friend that becomes an enemy."

"They also say picking your own nose is nobody else's business."

End of conversation.

With the stub of a pencil that must have been manufactured before he was born, Gianni began to write on the back side of what had been a German "Verboten" poster. He paused as his eyes moistened thinking about Carla, the love of his life, who soon would give birth to his child.

He returned to the task at hand and resumed scribbling:

Carissima, I am running tonight. I do not want to
put you and the baby at risk, so I leave without seeing you.
I know you'll understand. We won't be apart long, I can hear
the Americans' footsteps. It will be over in weeks; we'll be
together long before the cherry trees blossom.
I love you Carla. I always have loved you.
I will always love you, Gianni

He wanted to say more. But, what else was there to add? He folded the piece of paper and awaited Nilde's return. Beatrice remained slumped in her chair as Gianni climbed the old wooden stairs to his bedroom, plopped down, and closed his eyes wondering when he would next have a warm bed. He was asleep before finishing the thought.

He stirred, looked at his watch; he had slept for nearly two hours. He was about to rise and start packing a sack for the journey when he heard his sister contently jabbering with someone.

A very familiar voice responded to Nilde's pleasant "yacking". She yelled "Gianni, its Mico. Come down."

Bristling, "Mico? What in the hell is wrong with her? Damn her stupidity. Didn't she hear what I said this morning?" Blood rushed to his head, hands trembling, angrily repeated, "What in the hell is the matter with her?"

He leaped from the bed, grabbed his pistol and hid behind the bedroom door. Overwrought, he took the safety off the weapon, his hand shook as his mind went whirling into a gray, divisive sadness, thinking, "If I couldn't kill Lorenzo how in the hell can I shoot Mico?"

He never had sensed such an emotion.

CHAPTER 5

NEL ROSSO, VERITÀ

"Gianni, I'm joining you. I'm not going back either", Mico called to the stairwell.

No response.

"Gianni, come down. Let's talk. I'm unarmed, I gave my pistol to Nilde. I'm here to help."

"Bullshit! Get out of here, Mico. You come up these stairs and I'll kill you. So help me, Mico, I'll put a bullet through your head." His hand was trembling.

"Nilde told me you are going to go over the mountain. I understand she asked you to take Michelle with you. I'll join you. I'm not going back to the partisans, Gianni. Damn it, listen to me. I'm with you."

"You come up the stairs and they will be laying you next to your buried father."

"I'm coming up. My hands are in the air. I'm not armed."

He started to climb the dark stairwell, reached the mid-way point and stopped. Gianni was at the top of the stairs. The big man kept climbing, arms held high.

Gianni retreated to the doorway, "That's far enough; start talking. Let's hear your love-of-country bullshit and keep your filthy hands above your head."

Mico, in rapid fire dialect, explained what Tulio had ordered and said, "I'm through, Gianni. You are right. This war within the war is stupid, especially with the Allies a few weeks away. I can't bring you back any more than you could kill Lorenzo. How could I possibly bring you back? Tulio would order you to kill Lorenzo and you would disobey the order. You would be tried, sentenced and I would be the one chosen to carry out the order!"

Gianni looked at his cousin, the man he had known a life-time appeared changed. The young, jovial "let's have another glass" Mico had disappeared years ago, and now, in his place, stood a hard looking, old, tired warrior. For the first time, he noticed that Mico's big mop of hair had receded and streaks of grey were elbowing their way for attention. But his tired eyes were twinkling, belying the seriousness of the moment.

"Let me tell you what your favorite partisan, Vaccaccia, said …"

Although his head was spinning, he showed no emotion. Gianni lifted the pistol, a bemused smile, "I don't give a crap about anything any of your comrades said; just keep talking."

"Alright. Let me ask you, if I couldn't shoot you the first time, how could I do it this time? How in the hell could I possibly kill you? I would be killing a part of myself. I would be killing one of the few people I truly love, Gianni. Gianni, believe me, I am with you."

No response.

"You couldn't kill Lorenzo and he is your devil; your hell on earth. Gianni could a brother kill a brother?"

No response.

"And how in the hell do you think you could kill me?"

A long, long pause, "Don't give me that crap, Mico. From the beginning of time brother has killed brother. Now you want me to drop my weapon so you can take me out in the field just as Cain invited Abel before he killed him. You are so politically biased; I wouldn't trust you as….."

The front door opened, Michelle came running into the house yelling, "I've got meat! Meat for everybody! Nonna, Zio Gianni…. Mamma, where are you?"

Mico turned and started walking down the stairs. Gianni remained frozen; unwilling to move.

"Mico! You're here, too", shouted Michelle. "Look, I have a full hind quarter of a young horse! The American strafed the gun position and all he hit was the horse lapping up water down river…. a bunch of us cut ourselves slabs of meat…. we were like the Texas piranhas you told me about, Uncle Gianni!"

Gianni lowered his gun, descended, gave Mico a quick glance and approached his nephew, "Michelle, piranhas are in South America, not in Texas."

"Well, Texas or wherever, we have a feast on our hands", came a response from the fireside.

Beatrice, who had heard the entire repartee between her son and nephew, rose and approached the group, scrutinizing Mico and Gianni with a derisive sneer, "You two, go do something useful, see if you can scrounge some wood without the Germans finding you first."

A rejuvenated Beatrice adjusted the blanket covering her shoulders, "Michelle, you go down to Zia Gina's house and tell Giovanna and Zia Gina to come up here. I'll prepare the meat for our Easter meal."

"Easter Sunday was last week", the youngster replied.

"So was April Fool's Day", countered Beatrice.

Michelle, who had become as quick of tongue as his grandmother shot back, "Is that why we didn't have anything to eat for Easter?"

Beatrice hid a smile, "That was the Lord playing an April Fool's trick but He was remorseful; He sent manna from above in the form of American bullets and now we can celebrate. We'll have our Easter thanksgiving today."

"Ya, well He must have done it by blurring the pilot's vision. He missed the German position by a half-kilometer."

Beatrice, so proud of her handsome grandson and his quick-wit responses, smiled and grabbed Michelle by the arm, "Now, to make our day complete, I want to know where you hid that damn gun. Where did you hide the Luger? Give it to me before you have us all killed. Give it to me! Right now!"

The boy was about to reply, saw critical stares from everyone in the room and said nothing. He pulled the pistol from his pant belt and gave it to Gianni saying "Here you can have it; I haven't any shells left, anyway."

All his mother could say was, "Jesus help me!"

The others laughed as Beatrice gruffly commanded, "All of you get your asses out of here! And, damn it, if you see any soldiers, go the other way. We are going to have trouble should someone smell the roasting meat."

Throwing the huge hunk of meat, caked in dried blood and shreds of pale grey skin, on the table, she reflected a moment, "I can't believe Easter and April Fool's Day on the same day. What a strange coincidence."

Always a bit superstitious, she tried to find significance in the happenstance of the two calendar events falling on the same day. She sipped a bit of the red and mumbled to the oven, "Would their belated Easter meal auger the tricks of a belated Fool's day. Would the day deliver some sort of evil trick? Would this be her little family's last meal together? Perhaps, their Last Supper?"

She finished the wine, re-filled her glass, scolded herself, took another sip and began trimming the windfall. A bit of red was always worth a giggle or two, "Last Supper, or not, we finally have an abundance to enjoy. The American pilot's bad aim provided us with manna from heaven."

She giggled again, "The April Fool's joke was played on the horse!"

She stifled a laugh, realizing the others had been silently watching her, put the wine aside, began to scrape the carcass, looked up and wiped her hands on her apron, "Well, why in the hell are you all standing around? Are you all deaf? Get out of here right now! I don't need you hovering over my shoulders like four dirty, hungry buzzards. Get out of my kitchen! Let me prepare our Easter dinner!"

Beatrice, once again, had risen to the challenge; she was in charge; she gave the orders.

The group smiled, Nilde took Michelle by the arm and went out the door. Mico and Gianni remained standing near the door.

"What are you two waiting for? Get outside and talk to each other like the friends you are. Put this political bull-shit in the manure bin and come to your senses! Think about us. Think about how fortunate you are to be like brothers. Use your brains, if you have any left after all that has happened. Gianni, you may be my son and, Mico, you may be my nephew but neither of you is an angel and, certainly, neither of you is very intelligent if you continue with this vendetta talk. Now, get out of here!"

Mico, unarmed, immediately strode out the door, walked to the back of the old house, away from the highway. Gianni followed hands at the ready. Mico sat down on the old wooden bench his father had made years before. "Gianni, I usually am pretty good with words, but I haven't anymore to use. So, I'm repeating, I'm with you; I'm done with the Communists, the partisans and the war. I want out, just as you do. It took you a while to make your decision, but I was in deeper, it took me a while longer. When you walked away from my weapon, you showed bravery for the right reason. Your belief in what was wrong with our partisan group, your love for Carla and your hope for a better tomorrow gave you the strength to challenge me. In every sense of the word, yours was a true act of bravery."

Gianni didn't reply.

Mico, shuffling his feet, continued, "As I said, it took me a while but when Tulio ordered me to bring you back, I knew this stupid war was over for me, too. It's over!"

A bemused look but no reply.

"Now, for Christ's sake, put that damn gun away and give me a hug. Let's figure a way to get Michelle, you and me out of here."

Gianni was gazing into the nowhere. Mico, stomach tightening and wondering if his cousin was listening, continued, "We've been shelled by the Americans for a couple of weeks now, the weather is a bit improved; they probably have already started their move towards us. Our group and probably other partisans have been ordered to accelerate the destruction of bridges and roads. We were instructed to do everything possible to muck up the German withdrawal."

Gianni remained silent as his cousin, Big Mico, spluttered, "The Germans have been pulling out equipment; we don't want to be here when they make the main withdrawal. They'll leave the women alone but you, Michelle and I will be dog meat. I didn't want to say it in front of the others, but the aroma of cooking meat will be an invitation for every hungry hard head in the vicinity. We will be lucky beyond luck if they don't show up for our "Easter" dinner. And, damn it, we both know, the longer we stay here, the more we endanger our families."

If Gianni had any kind of a vocabulary he'd say the situation between the two cousins was a true oxymoron. Can a man love a friend and yet dislike him? He was so confused, at sea with his emotions. Here stood a man who had been a lifetime friend, closer than any brother could be and yet....

Mico, head down, sat motionless.

After an eternity, Gianni turned to his cousin and whispered, "Animals kill over territory, mating dominance, food. I understand those reasons. I can also understand why man goes to war and kills over a piece of land, for food or minerals, for a waterway, an ideology. I don't think it is right, but I can understand the motives; there are purposes, evil or not."

Mico was silent but content; his cousin was talking.

Gianni continued, "But many men, unlike the animal, sometimes kill and brutalizes for some sort of sadism I assume must breed within. They want their prey to suffer, to agonize before striking the mortal blow. It is not in the killing they find pleasure, but rather it is the sadistic pleasure seeing and hearing the enemy's aguish that overwhelms them."

Gianni sat down next to Mico, quietly asked, "After you had beaten the crap out of Lorenzo, why did you and Tulio, with smiles on your faces, insist I finish him?"

He paused and stuttered, "Why did you find pleasure in being so sadistic?"

Any contentment Mico felt a few moments before disappeared, "After all the harm Lorenzo had done to you over a lifetime, I figured you'd want to have the pleasure…."

"The pleasure? You wanted me to have the pleasure of killing someone?"

"He was responsible for killing who knows how many of our people, he would have killed you in an instant and he sure would have given you a good going-over before doing so."

"I hear you. I tried but, as much as I hated him, I could not brutalize him, or kill him. Did this mean I was a weakling, a traitor to your cause? So much so, Tulio sent you after me for the sole purpose of bringing me back to murder my own flesh and blood? Can you explain this?"

Mico didn't reply.

Gianni raised his voice, "You don't have an answer, do you? Well, let me enlighten you, dear cousin. There are bands of partisans out there helping to end to the war. But, Captain Tulio's order for me to kill my own wasn't a command from one fighting for his country; it was an order from an officer seeking some sort of sadistic pleasure. And, dear Ivan, that is why Tulio's band is no longer battling for a great cause, the liberation of the country. Their purpose now is about harvesting as much sadistic pleasure as possible before hostilities end. They don't want peace, they want loot," a hesitation, "they want blood."

"Some factions of the magnificent partisan movement have become as ruthless as the Germans and their Fascist brothers-in-arms. Like the Nazis and Fascists, they encourage atrocities of all sorts; including rape, public executions, displaying corpses of those murdered and on and on. And our poor peasants are caught between the rock of the Germans and the hammer of these renegade partisans. The Nazi's punishing, at random, these poor souls for "aiding the enemy" and partisans like your group stealing food and robbing anything else of value the peasant possesses; including live-stock, clothing and house hold goods. Tell me, are those the actions of people you'd call patriots?"

Gianni gazed up towards his beloved Cimone; a beautiful mountain now looking down on its landscape denuded by strangers. He felt a sense of true loss as he saw that "his" mountainside, a poor but idyllic garden of friendship and sharing, had become a cesspool of brutality and fear.

An audible sigh, "Mico, you followed a political agenda while I fought because of my family."

He hesitated, "Since the last war I have had a huge disrespect for all sorts of authority; I don't need some political god, pointing out the way. I want to be my own man; I sure don't need a Tulio explaining right from wrong."

He looked Mico in the eye, "Nor did I need you to force feed me Soviet political indoctrination; better known as political bull-shit. Your eastern masters are no better than the Fascist who wanted us to die in Africa, Russia, Germany, Albania, Greece or France…"

His hands were trembling, "And for what purpose, Mico? Tell me how we Italians made the world better leaving our families and homes and going thousands of kilometers to kill someone in Africa, Russia or any some-place?"

Mico felt a huge angst, lifted his head, looked at his cousin. He wanted to remind Gianni about the situation in France where evil threatened his family and thousands of others. He wanted to remind Gianni that his sacrifices were not just about politics. But, Gianni was talking; this wasn't the time for reminders; he didn't respond to the question.

Gianni picked up twig, moderated his tone, "But even worse, if we weren't sent to foreign lands, we remained close to home and killed our own. We killed our own in the name of some political ideology." A nervous giggle, "We killed because a braggart in a black shirt told us his friend with the funny moustache told him we would rule the world together."

The quiet one was on a tear, "And you, Mico? You fought the good fight to oust those fiends, but you did it because of the corrupt ideology of another tyrant; one with a bigger moustache."

He lowered his voice and slowly said, "Yes, Mico, you left your family, risked your life to help get rid of the poison only to find yourself drinking one with a different label."

Mico stood, also looking towards the snow-capped mountain, turned and put his hands on his cousin's shoulders, slowly and sadly, "I'm sorry. You are right." A hesitation, "Gianni, I love you, man!"

Gianni remained stoic, backed away.

There wasn't much else he could say. His shoulders slumped, tears formed. The war hero was crying.

The two looked at each other, Mico, tears streaming down his cheeks. Gianni, unexpectedly started to sob. relented, turned and hugged his cousin.

The two men stood motionless for an eternity when Mico, repeated an old joke from their long-ago trip to *L'America*, "Gianni, we are going on a long hike, so if you need anything for the trip, you just go ahead and buy it. OK?"

Gianni began giggling, tears now also running down his face. The world was suddenly a better place and both knew their tears were expressions of a love beyond definition.

The late morning sun smiled through a thin layer of clouds as the two cousins re-entered the house. Beatrice, ignoring the men, kept massaging the meat with an ointment of some sort. Her heart thumped blood through her body, hands quivering, body and soul responding to the realization the two men had been reconciled. Perhaps there was some hope left in this crazy world. Just maybe, decency and love did conquer...at least, occasionally.

Without turning said, "What are you two looking at? Get busy and pack for tonight's hike. There isn't much food, but there is cold polenta in *la cantina* and, thanks to my little goat, Matilda, you'll also find some cheese I made. Thank the Lord, neither your partisans nor the Germans have been able to find her or we wouldn't even have her milk. Now get moving; you don't have much time."

Ignoring the threat of possible German patrols, the entire family sat together for the first time in months. Nilde and their cousin Giovanna, who had been tending to the horse meat roasting in the outside fireplace, carried in the extravaganza; the aroma filled the room and mouths watered at the thought of the coming feast. Beatrice's sister, Gina, gave the final twirls to Beatrice's chestnut flour polenta simmering in a caldron hanging in the fireplace. Michelle had set the table with Beatrice's fifty-year-old dinnerware; the beautiful china, for fear the Germans confiscation or partisans' seizure, had been hidden in the dark wall of the *cantina*. It would be used for this occasion, Germans or no Germans.

Beatrice said grace, everyone earnestly listening and feeling the depth of her words, each grateful for the bounty, a welcomed miracle at the gates of hell.

Gina went to her coat and took out a bottle of *il rosso.* "This is from the red we made in '39. We had the bottle hidden; I've been saving it to celebrate the end of the war, whatever century that will be. Beatrice, sister dear, you have been drinking that watered-down poison, it is about time you have a glass of real *vino*."

Gina walked slowly around the table pouring a half glass to each. She reached Michelle, poured the lad the *red*, and said "You are a man now, Michelle. You are going over the mountain tonight and we expect you to bring Mico and Gianni back to us before too long."

She smiled, hesitated, tears forming, "Here's to us! To all of you, a Happy Easter in this ongoing hell; let's eat for who knows when we will eat again."

Never, had Gianni heard his quiet, unassuming aunt use the word "hell" nor speak with such strength and conviction.

The love of family gave a glow to the room; and for each, the meal of horse roast and chestnut polenta was as eloquent and as tasty as the pre-war delicacies Beatrice once prepared. The joy of such a meal and the exultation of togetherness sensed by all, reached the indescribable. The conversation was uplifting as the dove of peace flitted from shoulder to shoulder; for a moment, the war stood in the cold outside the massive front door of the house.

Gianni lovingly gazed at his family and wondered if the scene before him would every happen again. He held back a tear, and fought his old nemesis,

"*Il Grugno"* who was attempting to resurface. He swallowed a small sip of the precious *red* and the devil crawled back into his hiding place somewhere deep in the inner roads of his mind.

The three men could have demolished seconds and thirds, but no one said a word as Beatrice cleared the table, bringing remnants of the meat and polenta into the back room behind the fireplace. "We'll save the leftovers for tonight's walk towards the east. Now, I have a little surprise for you..." She went into the kitchen and returned with a bowl which everyone recognized as *zuppa inglese (English soup-a dessert made with ladyfinger biscuits, pudding and liquor).*

Gianni, "How in the world did you...."

"Never mind how", she replied with a huge smile as she gave each a small dishful. She circled the table and trickled a few additional drops of her home-made cherry liquor into each serving. With a huge smile, she then raised the bottle and in a deep-felt melancholy said, "To our family, it is the only thing that matters; it is the only thing each of us has left!"

She then took a deep swig from the bottle and sat down and in an instant, came to her feet as the screeching brakes announced the arrival of trouble.

Gianni, Mico and Michelle immediately jumped from the table, ran into the small back room, through the door and into the woods behind the house. Nilde and Giovanna quickly gathered dirty dishes and brought them down into the *cantina.* Gina fluttered around in panic; her help consisting of repeated laments including "Lord, have mercy. Lord, have mercy."

CHAPTER 6

UNWANTED GUESTS

A sharp light rap.

Beatrice opened the door and greeted a German officer wrapped in a heavy gray coat, the brim of his officer's cap reflecting a morsel of sunshine peeking through the somber grey now covering the blue sky of Italy. The officer's Luger was holstered but two heavily armed soldiers stood near the vehicle, carbines at the ready.

A shiver raced through Beatrice's body as she wiped her hands on her apron. She extended a hand in greeting, "Ah, Kommandant, welcome to our home. To what do we owe this visit? We haven't seen you for quite a while now."

Over the past year, the officer and some of his junior officers had slept and eaten at *La Rimessa* from time to time. Beatrice was well liked by the Germans as she could be relied upon to turn monotonous food provisions into delightful taste experiences. He was a friend; the same officer who managed to free Michelle from the clutches of the Gestapo the previous summer. The Lieutenant, did not accept the handshake, walked past Beatrice into the house and scanned the room. "Where is your grandson?"

Nilde, entering the room, heard the question, immediately started shaking and in an anguished tone asked "Why do you want Michelle? What has he done?"

"Where is he?"

"We don't know. We've been looking for him?"

"That is a lie. I suggest it be the last one you tell. Do you hear me?"

The four women stood moribund.

"We know Michelle and his four friends stole German provisions; a horse, to be exact", said the now smiling grey uniform as he walked towards the kitchen.

"And, my dear ladies, what do we have here? Roast beef? No, it's veal? No. *Ach du lieber*, I do believe it is a side of horse; well, at least it was a side, but it appears someone with an enormous appetite has been nibbling. Wouldn't you say so?"

The officer took a knife and cut himself a slice of the meat. "Very good, Beatrice; with your culinary skills, you once again have managed to turn coal into diamonds."

He turned, "But the coal was German property and your young man and his friends stole much needed supplies from our troops. In doing so, he has collaborated with the enemy."

"No. No." the women cried out.

Beatrice turned to the German, "The Americans killed the horse, we are near starvation and Michelle brought some home so we could have something to eat besides chestnuts. How does that help the enemy, Captain?"

The man didn't reply, went to the door and ordered his guards to take the food to their car. They immediately stomped through the front door, went into the kitchen and gathered everything in sight; even the pots and pans Beatrice had used to prepare the meal.

"Now, where is Michelle?"

"He ran out the back door when he heard your car arrive. I am sure he is running up the mountain."

"To the rebels, I am sure. Your grandson is a partisan. I heard he stole a Luger", a sneer, "stolen from the body of an officer assassinated by your criminal partisans!"

"He is fourteen years old! He did something stupid and we have punished him. Your investigating officer accepted the boy's explanation. He is no more a partisan than you are!"

"You have been a friend, Beatrice Carboni. Your meals added much to our wanting comfort; you have been a friend to me, personally", a wry smile, "but I am having doubts about his innocence. Frankly, I think you are lying to me!"

Hands trembling, she charged the officer, “No. No. He has been with us every day. And if he were a partisan, what would he be doing in the village taking horse meat in the middle of the day?”

She stopped, pulled a handkerchief from her apron pocket and forcefully blew her nose.

Pointing the handkerchief at the officer she sarcastically continued, “You know damn well that’s not the partisan way!” She withdrew her hand and continued, “Kommandant, he was stealing for us, his grandmother, his aunt a mother whose husband, Michelle’s father, died fighting side by side with German soldiers at Stalingrad.”

The man was taken aback, he was in awe as she continued the tirade, “And you even take pots and pans right from our kitchen. The same pots I have used to cook for you and your men… and you steal them from me? Shame, yes shame on you and the entire German army!”

Nilde, Gina and Gio had been ensnared between dread and admiration as Beatrice challenged the officer. They went into panic mode as Beatrice, tightened her apron and continued undaunted, “the horse was not stolen from you. It was in the middle of the field. It was dead!”

She stopped, a calm descended upon her, she smiled at the officer, “Take the damn meat for all I care, but give me my pots back.”

The handsome warrior stepped back, with his forefinger tilted his cap backwards, looked at Beatrice for a long moment, then smiled, “Well I’ll be damned; you sound just like my mother.”

He turned to the two guards, “Take the meat and that bottle on the table and give the lady back her pots. Men of the 114th Jaeger don’t steal from its friends.”

The men did as they were told and walked out the door. The officer followed, turned and said, “Arrivederci, Beatrice, tell your grandson to remain well hidden”, he looked towards his guards, stepped back inside, “regarding the Luger incident, they will be back to question your grandson. As a friend, I repeat, keep the boy well-hidden.” Another salute and he was gone.

The three women were flabbergasted, not knowing whether to laugh or cry. They chattered in disbelief as no one ever could, or would, address a German officer in such a manner. In one brief moment Beatrice had taken them from the depth of fear to the heights of elation.

Beatrice sat down, visibly exhausted, looked up and said, *"In vino verità, mio culo. In vino corraggio!* (In wine, truth my butt. In wine, courage!). I already had finished the liquor; wait 'til the Captain finds out the brandy bottle is empty."

Within an hour of the German's departure, the three men returned from hiding and slipped through the back door into the house. Hearing of Beatrice's actions, the men could only shake their heads in wonderment. Conversations were muted and subdued and Gianni, nerves frayed from two days of excruciating challenges, plus the added worries of the imminent departure, said nothing to his mother.

Mico broke the mood, "So, Zia Beatrice, that German s.o.b. polished off the last of your schnapps?"

"No, I beat him to it. He left with an empty bottle."

"Yes, an empty bottle", her sister Gina chimed in, "those last drops gave this nut the audacity to scold a German officer! We could be on a wagon headed for his beloved Deutschland."

Beatrice offered her sister a broad smiled as a peculiar and loud "Garumph!" emanated from her throat.

Gianni shook his head and allowed that strength can be found in many places; a good red, not an exception.

CHAPTER 7

"IL PONTE DI SPERANZA"— THE BRIDGE OF HOPE

Evening arrived without sight or sound from the partisans. But, not wanting to press their good fortune, they wanted to hasten their departure even though it was not yet dark. Gianni was particularly nervous awaiting his mother's return from her last-minute trip to the cellar.

Beatrice returned and handed Michelle a knapsack, "Here, this should hold you for a few days. There is a big slab of cold polenta, a hunk of goat cheese and a half-moon loaf of bread. It is the best I can do."

Gianni softened, hugged his mother "Thanks, Ma. You are the best. Don't worry, we will be back in a short week or two. If the partisan gang shows, tell them we left and are headed toward the American lines." A smile, "That will give pause to their desire for our blood; a good test of their bravery."

After tearful goodbyes and multiple prayers, which even Mico recited, the trio began their long journey upward and into the unknown.

Low lying clouds could be seen through the tree branches as Michelle eagerly and stealthily led the way down the darkening path towards the river. Gianni and Mico each bore a great responsibility for the boy's safety, so, while they enjoyed and appreciated the boy's enthusiasm, both wondered how the lad would react to danger. It was a concern they didn't need.

They drew near Carla's house as night began to conquer the sky. Gianni's stomach churned knowing Carla was ousted from her house for the benefit of German officers, including the one who had reclaimed the horse meat. Worse for Carla and Gianni, the local Fascist authorities then forced her to move back into her husband Lorenzo's house, saying, "It is the proper thing to do."

The situation tore at Gianni but there was no questioning the authorities; she did what she was ordered to do. Mico tug at his jacket, gently pulling him down the path. Gianni was sure his cousin understood.

They were near the old favorite tree, *La Faggia.* He could see the branches of the gentle giant guarding the waters of the river caressing the stones in their eternal search of a resting place. Gianni smiled as he remembered making love to Carla in this small paradise.

He reflected, "Such a peaceful spot; beautiful to sight and sound", he shook his head, "Why does man always manage to wreck a good thing?"

Mico, now leading the way, suddenly stopped and drew his Lugar. In the semi-dark, they saw a small form emerge from behind the tree. A low soft voice, "Gianni, it's me, Carla."

The first response was Mico's, "Oh! Shit!"

Carla rushed into Gianni's arms as another figure stepped from behind the tree.

"Are you insane?" Mico's loud whisper hissed as his smiling sister, Gio, wearing boots and carrying the old family hunting shot-gun, smiled a quiet "We are going with you."

"The hell you are!"

"Mico, keep your voice down. We are going with you and you can't turn us down; we've said our good-byes and …"

"She is four months pregnant and you think she can cross the river, climb up the mountain and traverse the summit in this cold and in the face of German patrols? You are both insane!"

Carla left Gianni's arms and walked a few steps towards Mico, "Mico, the most difficult part will be crossing the river; Giovanna and I will walk over the bridge, looking normal. If the Germans stop us, they'll merely send us back home. I'll make sure they see my little bundle proving I am pregnant. I'll tell them I don't feel well and Gio is accompanying me to see Dr. Mucci or to see Signora Saili, my mid-wife. They'll certainly know of the officers living in my house. They will be impressed, I am sure."

She hesitated a moment, then added, "My German is pretty good, you know."

Mico, "I don't care if you teach German, you aren't coming with us! That is final! Period! Go back right now." The snarl was vicious, the sound of a hissing snake.

Gianni stepped over to the group, told Michelle to start walking towards the river, and calmly said, "Mico, Carla is coming with us. I won't allow Carla to go back home now. She is willing to chance it; I think she'll be able to handle the climb. She will be my responsibility. You can go on your own. If Michelle wants to go with you, it'll be fine with me."

Gio, "and, dear brother, I'm going, too. Why shouldn't I be able to take the risk? Is it because I'm a woman? I'm stronger than some of those idiot partisans you were leading. And, I'm sure smarter than most of them."

Mico stood transfixed. He was dumbfounded as his sister started back down the path whispering, "Now let's get moving before we all are hanging from tree branches."

The two men looked at each other, Gianni smiled, shrugged his shoulders.

The leader of partisans, the veteran soldier who had given the commands to men at war, shook his head, lips quivering, could only answer, "Well, I'll be a *sonavabitch*!" and followed his sister and Carla towards the river.

The five reached the old shack at river's edge where they could see the bridge several hundred meters to the south. Gianni and the two women sat on an old bench outside the hut while Michelle and Mico sat on the stumps of two felled trees. No one said a word, each transfixed at the sight of the bridge and the challenge it posed.

Then Michelle chirped, "When I was a kid, I played "*piatta-cutta*" (hide and seek) up there."

Gianni had an urge to tease the lad about his age but remained silent. The others responded with loving smiles and returned their attention to the bridge. Michelle then said to the ladies, "It looks like there are three guards up there; are you sure you want to chance the crossing?"

Thankful she was wearing her winter mittens because her hands were trembling, Carla boldly answered with greater conviction than she felt, "Whether they are Italian or German, I can handle the guards."

She knew Gianni would be hurt but she continued, "If they are Fascist, I'll tell them I am the great Lorenzo Grandi's wife. If German, I'll inform them about their officers staying in my house", a smile, "and I'll do it in their language. For additional convincing, I will also make sure they see I am with child. Getting past the bridge guards will be the easiest part of our journey."

Gio interrupted, "Carla and I will cross the bridge and go up the slope past the burned house; we'll wait for you there. If we are not at the house when you arrive, assume we were stopped, wait for a half-hour and immediately go on your way."

She turned to the young lad, gave him the old shot gun, "Michelle, I'll want this back once we meet on the other side of the road. If the hard heads stop Carla and me, the gun is yours. It is clean, oiled and loaded with two shells. Here take these; you may need a few more rounds."

Michelle glowed as he accepted the weapon and the extra ammunition.

Mico stood, brushed his sleeve one more time, "*Per Bacco"* (for Bacchus' sake) you'd think we were out on a pheasant hunt. In days, the war will be over, I've managed to live through years of blood-letting and now I'm going to get my ass shot full of holes because I'm crossing enemy lines with a teen ager, a love-sick Romeo, a pregnant woman and a sister who thinks she is Julius Caesar."

Gio giggled, jumped to her feet, gave the Roman salute and hissed, "I am Julia Cesare!"

A scowl directed at his sister, "Insanity! I've got to laugh. Crying would ruin the comedy. All right, damn it, let's go. I'm with you." He playfully kicked the stump, "Although, beyond any doubt, we are all out of our minds!"

Carla smiled at Mico, gave Gianni a kiss on the cheek and, without saying a word, wrapped the dark wool shawl around her shoulders and started towards the bridge. Gio poked her index finger into her brother's belly, giggled and followed Carla down the rocky path. They were out of sight in minutes.

Mico, exasperated, stood and grumbled, "Gianni, damn it, this is crazy. We are all going to get killed. Why in the hell didn't you say anything to those two mad women?"

"As I said, you two can go on alone; Michelle, if Mico approves, you can go with him."

Michelle interjected, "You saved me from the Germans once Zio Gianni; I owe you. I won't be a burden. Mico, I'm sorry but I'm staying with Gianni."

Mico hunched his shoulders, scooped and slowly released a handful of dirt. He then rubbed his hand on his jacket sleeve and looked towards the bridge, "For nearly three years, my men accused me of being crazy. I thought I was being brave. You know, this proves they were right and I was wrong. I am zany; in fact, I've completely lost my senses. Logic doesn't work; basic intelligence is lacking; and I'm completely sober!"

The three men started across the river, jumping from rock to rock as the gentle stream lapped at their boots. It was nearly night fall; the risk of slipping was high. They remained close to one another, Mico, leading the way, held out his hand for Michelle as he balanced his way. Gianni came across last, turned his ankle and swore as he stepped onto the hard ground. He followed Mico and Michelle, limping his way to the main road. Gianni didn't mention the ankle was throbbing.

They hid in the bush near the road and watched as the two women crossed the bridge, heads down, plodding into the light breeze singing its way down the mountainside. Two German soldiers and a man in civilian clothing sat smoking as the women neared the bridge.

Carla sotto-voce, "Having the hard heads living in my house for so long has some advantages. Let me do the talking." Giovanna nodded her approval saying, "the little guy in the black overcoat is either Gestapo or one of our dear Fascist friends, be careful."

The three men stood as the women approached. The two soldiers raised their weapons, in broken Italian the taller one ordered, "Halt! Show your hands! What in the hell are you doing out here?" He looked at his watch, "you have five minutes to curfew."

Their stomachs were churning and nerves popped electricity through their bodies but neither woman showed any outward fear as they raised their hands and slowly approached the men.

In German,"I am Carla Grandi from *La Casa Berti*. I'm pregnant with child and my cousin is accompanying me to Dr. Panevino's house; I don't feel well."

They continued walking toward the three men.

"Carla Grandi? Is your husband Lorenzo Grandi?", asked the civilian in a Tuscan accent.

She nodded affirmatively. The man was probably one of Lorenzo's functionaries; a lackey whose time was coming to an end, thought Carla.

"You can pass into the village but, for your own protection, there is no way you will be allowed back until morning. Is there a place where you can stay for the night, Signora Grandi?"

"Well, if the doctor can't house us, we can borrow some pillows and sleep in the church. However, I am sure the good Padre will accommodate Lorenzo Grandi's wife."

She stared at the black coat, "Right?"

The Italian hesitated, turned to the soldiers, "I know the lady's husband; let them pass."

Addressing Carla, "Signora Grandi please go straight to the rectory, this is not a good time for you to be out and about."

Turning to Giovanna, "And you, too, young lady, get inside; the thump of those boots you are wearing", a giggle, "sounds like you are marching into combat!" Gio didn't laugh at the comment; she turned towards town and like a trooper on parade, stomped past the sentries.

Carla shook her head, shrugged, smiled and flippantly addressed the Italian, "You should see her dance wearing those boots", then strode away and followed a scowling Gio.

"I'm sorry Gio; I was making a joke; blame it on my nerves."

"Yea, Carla; a joke."

"Good Lord, we are about to get ourselves shot and you are offended about your looks!"

"Yea, I'm offended; you get by because you are pretty. As always, the prettier the woman, the more she can turn weaknesses into assets. If you are ugly and wear boots, they shoot your ass off, rather than wanting a piece of it."

Carla stifled a laugh, "Look, Gio, let's talk about this later; more importantly, we are past the first hurdle."

CHAPTER 8

A WALK IN THE MOUNTAINS

The three men edged up the embankment and watched as the two women walk past the guards. The ladies had done it!

Now it was their turn to cross the road.

A half-moon peeked over the mountain as they lay on the ground and awaited complete darkness. Thunder roared from the south as the American long guns greeted the night. More innocent deaths, more misery reaped on these poor mountain folks for the sake of peace! A conundrum, to say the least.

Gianni's ankle throbbing, said nothing about the pain.

"What did you do to your leg?"

"What leg?"

"Your leg, *stupido*!"

"I twisted my ankle. It's the same leg that has bothered me in the past. But I'm ok."

"Your ankle is not as twisted as your head, allowing Gio and Carla to come with us."

"No. it's my ankle. My head feels just fine. Anyway, I didn't' invite them; they told me they were going along."

"Horse manure!"

Gianni smiled to himself. The old relationship between the two had been reborn.

"Well, if your head is ok, let's see you walk the mountain upside down. Let's abort the entire idea and find someplace to hide. Maybe we can get to one of the upper mountain shepherd huts and rest there for a day or two. I can hear the Americans breathing; they are close, it won't be long..."

"I'm ok. I can walk. It's dark, time to get across the road. The Americans might be on the other side of the mountain looking for Germans, but I see hard heads up there on the bridge looking for people like us and I sure don't see any Americans."

Mico couldn't see the smile as Gianni whispered, "So, let's get the hell out of here."

Mico grunted his displeasure as they crawled to the edge of the road, hunched over and quietly crossed. No one noticed. They were safely across, hidden in the trees.

The three men immediately walked towards the house the Germans had burned in a reprisal the year before.

"Bastards!", erupted Gianni, remembering the incident of the four unfortunates, whose house and belongings had been ransacked and burned by the German troops. "Those poor souls whose only sin was to own a house on the main road, an easy target for a revengeful enemy."

"Shut up. You want to get us all killed. What the hell is the matter with you?"

"Right. Sorry Mico, just reacted to that long ago bad scene."

"There were a lot of bad scenes. Let's not make another one."

The night air was crisp and wafting the wet aroma of burnt wood as they arrived at the rendezvous point. Gianni sat on an old concrete bench near the front door framework. In the dark shadow, he rubbed his ankle, hoping the others didn't notice.

To the east, orange glows periodically invaded the night; faint thunder interrupted the stillness of the mountains. Gianni thought, "Gabriel's horn saluting those who will die or be maimed in the last minutes of the war. Unfortunates who had lived through years of war only to be killed in the last minutes. Cruel!"

He turned to his nephew, "You did well boy; but this was a first step, the route ahead is going to be harsh; between frantic Germans, trigger-happy partisans and Americans thinking we are enemy, we have quite a checker game yet to play."

Michelle took off his gloves, blew into his hands, clenched his teeth and with a scowl, "I'm no boy dear uncle and one of these days you are going to realize it!" He turned to Mico, "You wanted me for your partisan group; you know I'm up to whatever you ask of me. I'm ready and able for combat! Right, Mico?"

Mico, realizing he was treading in dangerous waters, "Well, right now you are as important a soldier as any one of us; especially with our responsibility for Gio and Carla, not to mention your uncle here with an ankle inflating to the size of a bocce ball. So, whether you are combat ready is not the question; the question is if you will help us all get through to Cutigliano; and regarding that, I am happy you are with us."

"Sorry Michelle", Gianni said quietly, "guess I was speaking for your mother and grandmother. You certainly are not a boy any longer and I'm also grateful you are with us. You give us a better chance of reaching the Americans. But, don't be so eager to find combat, don't be so impatient. You don't need to kill just to prove you are a man."

The three men sat in silence for a few moments. Michelle felt for his ocarina and thought about playing a tune, realized the absurdity and, instead, put on his gloves and started talking again, "When I was a little guy my mother brought me to the piazza to see the sendoff of the older kids to Il Duce's military training camps. I remember hearing the drum rolls followed by a trumpet's call to arms as the *Ballila* (Fascist Youth Organization) entered the piazza in perfect step. Everyone yelled and clapped; I wished I was old enough to join them as they marched towards the busses taking them to the camp."

He hesitated, "Ma told me thousands of *Ballila* from all over Italy, were going to camps, all at the very same time. It sounded so wonderful. I can still hear the children shouting, "Viva il Re! Viva Il Duce! A Noi (The Fascist Battle Cry)!"

Gianni grumped, "In those early days Italians gave their gold, their hearts and then, their children, to serve the new Italy." He pointed toward German soldiers on the bridge, "And there we see the return on our investments of gold and lives."

Michelle, "Gianni, you mentioned we should worry about Germans, Americans, partisans but you failed to mention the possibility of running into the Fascist; don't they exist any longer?"

Gianni chuckled, "Ya, they seem to be disappearing by the day; before this war is over I'll bet there will be but a handful of Fascist left; you won't be able to find a black shirt anywhere."

Mico chimed in, "The color black will be spat upon and the Americans will wonder where all the *Fascisti* have gone...."

Michelle absorbed this, picked up a twig and began drawing a circle on the ground, "How", he asked, "did they get so strong in the first place? How did the country come to believe Mussolini's speeches as if it were the word of God?"

The two cousins looked at each other, Gianni picked up a twig and began drawing his own circle, then with a smirk and a sly smile turned toward Mico, "It's your turn, after all, you are the political one."

Mico stretched his foot and erased the circle Gianni had drawn, "Well, it's a long story with many twists and surprises that shouldn't have been surprises. Your uncle here, came home from the war Christmas of 1918. He soon went to work in the Sasso cemetery and never heard of Mussolini until our Duce interfered with his love life.

Gianni, "Come on Mico, enough of that..."

"Well, it is true, isn't it?"

Michelle giggled, "What do you mean, Mico?'

"Your Uncle Gianni was from the class of '99; they were the last to be called into the Great War. He spent a few months pretending to be a soldier near Torino, was discharged and came home to tell us his greatest war-time achievement was that he and his buddies ate a cat; although at the time he was told it was rabbit; my great hunting partner didn't know the difference."

"A cat!"

Mico, "Yes, a cat."

Gianni began drawing another circle, "We were so damn hungry we would have eaten it even knowing it was a cat. The authorities treated the military grunts terribly, in all sorts of ways. Worse, when our fighting men came home after the war, many civilians who had been against the war took it out on the veterans. Our valiant men, who spent years on the front lines, came home to criticism for having risked their lives instead of thanks and appreciation for their efforts. The Socialists, particularly those who were against the war, were the worst. They hurled insults and ripped off hard-earned battle medals from men who had endured and suffered greatly for *La Patria.* I saw it with my own eyes; but I came home to Sasso, worried about our daily bread and said to hell with all of that. I wanted no part of the political crap."

Mico interrupted, "Ya, not much to eat in the mountains either but in the cities, besides the lack of food, all hell was breaking loose. No work, a weak government, major strikes throughout the country with many on the left wanting to follow Russia's lead and become a Communist state. Others formed vigilante parties and mounted physical attacks against the Socialist. It was bedlam. Mussolini and his thugs, with acquiescence of the church, veterans and the monarchy, took advantage of the situation. In a few short years, Mussolini, a small-time newspaper man, became a cult figure, a semi-religious icon, and Italy's savior from a bad government; in a short span of time he crowned himself supreme dictator."

He hesitated, spit on the circle, "Yes! Like our people in the plaza you saw waving their children off to military camps, the entire country embraced him and truly believed he was Italy's savior, no less!"

Mico was hyperventilating, "The newspapers of the world heralded the arrival of a liberator who proclaimed a new day for Italy. A redeemer who offered hope and change and soon most of the entire world shouted, "Halleluiah!"

Talking rapidly now, "Nearly everyone but the Socialist swooned and gave to the man of the hour. He asked, and Italian mothers had more babies for "Il Duce!" He asked and we gave; wealthy, poor, Catholics, Jews, everybody gave their gold and their sons; unions, teachers, priests and landowners believed and gave from their hearts to the new Cesare! If you were a true Italian you gladly gave to the new Italy and with great pride shouted, *"Viva L'Italia!"*

Quietly now, he continued, "Ya, we got change, didn't we? Now we have a new Italy, don't we? We've been had, Michelle. Once again, we placed our lives on the line for some damn politician who lied and cheated. A man who promised his way into the hearts of the poor while his minions, his cronies, profited in every conceivable way."

Gianni, who had been listening intently, erased his drawn circle with such force the twig snapped, interrupted, "Right, Mico, but there is more! Where is that optimism now? What price did we pay for those promises?

You want to know about Mussolini, Michelle? You lost a father at Stalingrad, so I'll answer your question with a question of my own. Who do you think killed him; the Russians or was it our beloved Duce?"

The lad did not respond.

Gianni considered mentioning Mico and his ties to the Socialist/ Communist, thought better of it, angrily threw the stub of the twig on the ground. He looked up and saw the outline of the mountains; black sentinels watching the sun trying to escape from the thunder and orange glow; its getaway to a peace it might find in far off lands.

He moved his foot and said into the night, "Michelle, hope is a glorious and magnificent word but it can be used to camouflage bad intensions and when that happens, the first victim is a virtue called "truth". Through centuries gone and those yet to come, the word masters send their prayers from the altar of propaganda. They proclaim they are the harbingers of "The Real Truth"; that they, themselves, are the hope of their generation."

A pause, "And the masses shout, Amen! Amen! We believe! We believe! There is no other You!"

Gianni hesitated, looked at his nephew and quietly said, "Time passes, history repeats and, once again, the masses say Amen over the carcasses, not only of those who first believed the lie, but, sadly, also for poor fools like you and me who really never understood why we risked our lives."

He hesitated, audibly sighed and touched his nephew's shoulder, "Michelle, we live in a stupid world and I'm afraid we will never learn."

CHAPTER 9

LADIES' NIGHT OUT

Carla and Gio headed towards the town center in a casual, unconcerned manner, hoping no other obstacles would present themselves. Both women were excited having fooled the guards and Lorenzo's Fascist friend. There was a certain glow of victory but they also knew the race for freedom had just begun.

The day had ended and the chill of the long night arrived. They continued walking down the dark village street. Gio, a few steps ahead, was lost in her own thoughts. Carla, feeling the chill, hugged herself and felt the little bulge under her coat. Caressing her stomach, she sensed an incredible contentment. Everything will be well. She was going to bear Gianni's child!

A dark thought interrupted her moment of bliss. Releasing her hug of the little bulge, she shivered and thought, "Thank God this is Gianni's child and not Lorenzo's."

Gianni had told Carla about Lorenzo's capture by the partisans and as the two women walked away from the guards, she reflected upon her husband's fate. She hated the man but, nevertheless, felt a smidgen of compassion and hoped the partisans had not brutalized Lorenzo before his death. Yet, somewhere from within, a voice echoed, "he deserved whatever they gave him."

As she continued following Gio down the cobbled street, Carla thought of her deceased father; a good man but one who had made a terrible mistake; an error in judgment nearly ruining his daughter's life. A rash emotional decision forcing his greatest treasure to live a life in hell; a life married to Satan personified.

A shudder quaked through her body as she fell back into those years at the close of the First World War; days of youth, love and laughter followed by agonizing years of discontent, regrets and distress.

Carla Berti, the educated daughter of one of Sasso's most prosperous individuals, fell madly in love with the uneducated Gianni Carboni. The lad had no social standing and owned little except handsome looks, a good singing voice, a guitar, an engaging personality and a calm, honest disposition.

The two had been secretly meeting for several months when, on a beautiful Sunday afternoon in September, storm clouds gathered and a ferocious bolt of lightning ended the couple's time in their earthly paradise.

Pietro Berti, humming the first few bars of *"Eri Tu"* from Verdi's *"Ballo in Maschera"*, happily walked into one of his barns, heard giggles and noticed strands of straw falling from the hay loft. The world stopped its rotation, tombs opened and the ghosts of long departed ancestors screeched into his bursting eardrums. He had caught his most precious treasure, his life's joy, making love in his own hay loft. Signore Berti went wild!

As the couple descended, Berti, who, in his lifetime, never hit anyone, grabbed his dearest jewel and threw her against a horse stall post. Then, dark eyes glistening, he turned, picked up a pitchfork and, with a maniacal scream, charged Gianni!

The younger man grabbed the weapon, held it firm and tried to reason with Berti; expressing his love for Carla.

"Love? I'll give you love! Get your ass out of here! Get out now or, if I don't kill you first, I'll have you put in jail for twenty years."

"Gianni please leave", begged a sobbing Carla.

"Carla, let me..."

"Please! If you love me, please leave", she moaned.

Gianni tore the fork away from the old man and, without another word, threw the pitchfork on the ground. He backed away, stood there for a moment, every nerve ending urging him to intervene and protect Carla.

He started back.

A scream, "No! Oh no! Gianni! Please go! Please, Gianni! If you love me! Please Gianni!"

He melted. All emotions drained, Gianni stopped his advance towards the old man. He knew it was finished. No more songs to be sung, no more kisses, no love poems from the heart.

He stood still, looked at Carla, thinking, "It is over. I only thought she was mine. It was a dream. It was not reality. It's all finished. I would only hurt her now. Love and respect for her father would ensnare her in a guilt trap for a life time…and no matter how much I loved her, guilt would always cloud our sun."

He knew Carla would never walk away from her father. He also knew he had lost a treasure. He turned and walked towards town.

Carla also remembered that, as Gianni left, her father grasped her shoulders and began shaking and berating her, "This is why I sent you to Modena to learn from the nuns? This is the reward you give me? This is the respect you show your deceased mother?"

The tirade went on for an eternity and ended with a hard slap across the girl's face. It was the first time she had been hit by anyone, let alone her father. Carla remained silent and accepted the reprimand. However, with his final words, "Get to your room, whore! I'll deal with this quickly!" Carla was crushed. Devastated. She knew her life would never be the same.

The punishment was speedy and brutal. Her marriage to the only son of the town's wealthiest family was quickly arranged. Absolutely no consideration was given to the beautiful Carla or that the man chosen for her was a carouser; the very spoiled and very difficult Lorenzo Grandi.

She had been thrust into a worldly hell to be controlled by the personification of Satan, himself.

Carla patted Gianni's child again. She smiled even as an all too familiar shiver streaked through her body; the lingering apprehension Lorenzo might still be alive. Mercifully, the bitter contemplation was interrupted, "Come on, Carla, we are almost there. You doing okay? Where in the hell have you been?"

"I was visiting a 1939 dream."

Gio understood.

"I'm fine, but slow down a bit! The hard part is over; we don't want those three to show new interest in us. Slow down, act natural!"

"Act naturally my butt, let's get into the woods before some wine-laced hard head starts singing *Lilly Marlene* to you", Gio responded.

Carla returned to Gio's comment about beautiful women, "Did any Germans ever make a pass at you?"

"Well, my boots and red hands were obstacles, I guess."

"You mean during these long years, no one gave you a pinch?"

"Well, there were a few winks, a couple of "can I touch the merchandise?" smiles. After all, I may not be the prettiest thing, but I do have some nice oversized tomatoes, don't you think?"

"You are very pretty. It's just that you dress and act like a mountain girl more than you do a church-going member of the choir."

"What is me, is me. I am a *montenaro's* daughter. My hands are rough from tilling the rocks, chasing sheep and yanking on cows' teats. I haven't the social skills you learned with the nuns in Modena. I was lucky to learn how to read and write. Three years of schooling isn't very much, you know."

"But, you are a lady; you are a flower, Gio. School and nuns can't turn an onion into a rose and though you may have a few thorns to protect you from the aggressive Romeos, you are a beautiful flower." She put her arm around her friend's shoulder as they continued walking,

"When we get past this, we are going to throw your boots away and buy a pair of those fancy, high gloss shoes like Mussolini's girlfriends once wore."

"I'll break an ankle...."

A deep voice, a heavy German accent, "Halt! Who goes there?"

Terror! Carla grabbed Geo's hand and responded in German to the dark shadow approaching, "Giovanna Carboni and Carla Grandi, Lorenzo's wife."

The gray uniform, lit cigarette in hand, stomped in front of the two ladies. "And who in the hell is Lorenzo? And what is Lorenzo's wife doing on the main street after curfew? And who is this lady? Does this Lorenzo have two wives?" The smell of *grappa* was strong enough to douse the man's cigarette.

Carla saw the uniform and addressed him, *"Oberfeldwebel"* (Sergeant First Class), I am pregnant with child; my friend is accompanying me to see the doctor in the village. The guards at the bridge allowed us to pass."

"There is no doctor in this village!"

Carla wanted to correct the man but instead replied, "I meant my midwife, Signora Mazzi. She will deliver the baby when my time comes."

The man stood well over six feet, red-faced, field cap tilted to one side, "Well, the guards at the bridge will be severely reprimanded. We cannot have civilians wandering the streets after hours. There are partisans everywhere and for all I know you two are out here to help those bandits."

"No, no, my sergeant. My husband is "*un pezzo grosso*" in the party, your officers live in my house, we are huge supporters, and we are at risk ourselves to the partisans."

"And what about this lovely young lady?" he asked in a subtle manner indicating he wasn't really interested in politics.

"She is an old farm girl, a bit slow of mind but she takes care of me. Please sergeant, let me get to the doctor."

The sergeant offered a bottle to Gio, she took a swig and walked away towards town.

"Stop, my beauty."

"She doesn't understand German and she does not like men, if you know what I mean."

The man roared in laughter, "You mean I just wasted a gulp of good *grappa* on a ….."

Carla started walking away from the sloshed giant, "It wasn't a waste Herr Sergeant, maybe we will see you tomorrow. *Gut nacht*, Sergeant."

"See, you've found your *liebhaber*", Carla teased as she walked briskly to keep pace with Gio.

"What's a *liebhaber*?" Their pace slowed as they looked back and then turned into an old path leading towards the old burnt house where the second act of the drama would begin.

In a sing-song manner, "Your lover. Your meteor in the sky. A hero who loves women wearing boots!"

"He smelled of engine oil and used cabbage and the grappa tasted like petrol. And leave my boots alone."

Carla chuckled and gave Gio a push from behind.

An hour later, having assembled at the burnt house, the group began its long walk toward freedom. Mico led the way followed by Gio, Michelle and Carla; Gianni, his ankle throbbing, trailed the group as they ascended the old mule path.

For more than a century, the well-worn upward path was used by mule skinners, hunters, mushroom pickers and shepherds. The wide path wound through what had been a beautiful green expanse but was now a landscape of mutilated trees and ragged stumps. Three years in survival mode had turned villagers into thieves, as they hacked and stole a forest of trees, changing the scenic mountainside into an ugly wasteland.

The Germans were now owners and frequent users of the path. There most treasured, and most effective modes of mountain transport, were mules stolen from mule skinners and the poor peasants. They certainly would be using the path during the retreat. Mico and Gianni understood the possibility but did not mention it to the others.

After a steady two-hour climb, Mico stopped and pointed upward toward a small hunter's shelter, "We'll rest there for a bit.'

Upon reaching the shed Gianni immediately limped towards a tree trunk and sat down.

"Gianni, you doing OK?"

"I'll be fine. Let's not dally; at this height if the Germans don't find us, we'll likely run into a stray band of eager partisans."

Mico gave a condescending smile, bent over and felt Gianni's foot, "Let me see that foot of yours." He took off Gianni's sock and shoe, "You are not fine. Your ankle is the size of a bocce ball. We are soon going to be going downhill towards *Monte Lancino* and it will be an impossible descent for you."

He tenderly tapped his cousin's shoulder, "Let's go back. At least Carla and Gio would be safer."

"Sure. And, if the hard heads capture us, we'll all be either on our way to Germany or we will be joining Lorenzo in the lower streets of hell."

Gio interrupted, "Dear brother of mine, have you forgotten the promised visit from Captain Tulio and his band? Wasn't that the primary reason we ran so quickly?"

Mico, a growled response to the two women, "We? I ran. Gianni ran.

Michelle ran. We had to run! You two ...."

Gianni glared, "Mico, you were free to run or stay in Sasso; no one is holding you now."

He stood and limped towards the shelter, Carla following.

"It gets so stupid, I feel like I'm starring in a bad comedy", chortled Mico, "might as well laugh, shedding tears over you would be a waste of water."

With a false laugh and to no one in particular "Let's go my gallant band of super heroes; let's hurry so you can soon find your Maker!"

Gio quickly and harshly responded. "Oh! Shut up!"

She did not see her brother smile.

After a brief rest the group continued its climb and about an hour later arrived just below the *Mount Cimone* summit. It had been a difficult climb but Mico knew the decent would be more demanding. The downward slippery slope of rocks, roots and mud would be a formidable challenge, especially in the dark. He was particularly worried about Carla and was sure there was no way Gianni could continue.

Mico, "There's the old shepherds' hut. We made good time. We'll rest there before we start the decent towards *Mt. Lancino*."

Not sure he was back in Gianni's good graces, Mico continued, "Gianni, remember when we were attacked by that wild boar? It was right around here. Man, that was scary. He was trying to make sausage out of us instead of the other way around."

Gianni, "I also remember you nearly hit me with a shot from that old rifle; the one your uncle brought back from the 1912 war in Libya."

"It was a good weapon."

"The key word being, "was".

The repartee was a small but pleasant relief from the previous harsh words and the overall tensions each held within.

They arrived at the rest stop and sat on a series of flat stones in front of the dilapidated hut and eagerly sipped water from German army canteens belonging to the two ex-partisans. They were at about 3,000 feet altitude, perspiring and shivering as they contemplated the descent.

The half-moon finally peeked through a few gathering clouds, gave some light and there was a degree of comfort knowing the shadows were friends.

Carla sat next to her lover and cuddled up to him. Gianni, in turn, put his arm around his *amore.*

They were so close, Gianni thought. So, close to the American lines he believed he could smell their field kitchens. He drew Carla to him, kissed her on the forehead, a thousand thoughts racing through his mind. Thinking of the ordeal ahead for Carla and his unborn child caused an unrecognizable angst, an emotion he never experienced. He shivered, not from the cold or his physical pain, but from fear and worry for his loved ones.

"I love you more than life itself, Gianni"

He patted her swollen stomach, "Now we truly are one. Our little bundle is our love; one person, one angel who is you and me. The baby is our oneness and must be loved beyond anything we have ever experienced before."

He drew her closer, his emotions afire, kissed her again, "The baby is everything; our today, our tomorrow, our life, our hereafter."

Carla sighed and submerged deeper into his arms.

He sat silently, returned to the moment and chastised himself. He was deeply torn; he wanted to be with Carla but knew he was a stumbling block to the group reaching safety.

He said nothing.

Mico, hoping Gianni would say a word about his ankle, also remained quiet.

After the short rest, they helped each other adjust their packs and began their decent, slipping and slithering down the mountain side. It must have rained earlier as the rocky path was a dicey downward challenge for everyone. Michelle led, followed by Mico holding Carla's hand as they descended; Gio trailed, following Gianni as he labored to remain upright.

Michelle slipped, his hand grabbing a bush to stop his slide, "Donkey shit! Mud and mule shit!"

He pulled himself into a sitting position, his right-hand glove was ripped and coated with mud.

"You alright?"

"Ýa. But, be careful. It is slippery here. I don't know if its mud or mule."

Despite the scare, everyone had to chuckle at the lad's response.

They recommenced the descent but Gianni, after tripping and slipping for ten more agonizing minutes, knew he couldn't continue. He felt as if he were at the gates of hell. Throbbing bolts of lightning streaked through his entire leg while his ankle was being attacked by hot needles.

With his stamina now being acutely tested, he began talking to himself, "Only a few more kilometers; only a few more hours and we'll find a bit of peace. Please Lord, help us."

"Stop your mumbling, you'll wake up the dead. Take my arm, I'll help you walk."

Gianni stopped. "No, Mico, let me be, I can't continue. I'm done. I'm back tracking to the hut; you just worry about the girls and Michelle. No way I can climb or slide on any more of these damn rocks." A pause, "Let alone the long hike across open territory when reach the low land."

Mico, without conviction, "We'll stop and rest a while; we'll find the Americans a bit later."

Gianni smiled, "Mico, what a formidable group you are leading into the front lines; a *bambino*, a pregnant woman, a crippled hero, and your sister with a rifle that belongs in a museum. I'm sorry I got you into this…you were right…Stupidity has its own reward."

A furious Michelle hissed into the conversation, "Bambino? I'm not a baby! Damn it! I'm not a baby!"

Gio interrupted and took charge, "Right, Michelle, you sure are not a baby and what is done is done. Let's stop with the "should haves". Look, there is no easy way out of this. We can't carry Gianni down the rest of the way, it is too steep. He can't stay here alone and Carla, as much as you would like to stay, you've got to get through with your treasured cargo."

She pushed her brother towards Carla, "Mico you've got to go on ahead with Carla and Michelle. Gianni and I will go back to the hut and we'll make do until Gianni can walk a bit. Give me whatever food you have. Then we'll join you in Cutigliano …."

A harsh, uncompromising, petulant voice interrupted her, "And what am I? Your diapered wannabe? As I said, I haven't been a *bambino* for quite a while and I'd wish you stop pampering me. I can handle myself and Gianni. I'm the one to stay behind. It's the only logical alternative."

Gia, "Michelle, I'm not pampering…"

Michelle, with force and determination, interrupted, "Mico, you are best able to get through to the American side and I am strong enough to help

Gianni. Despite what you think, I am the best choice to help Gianni until he is ready to go."

The lad was fuming, not noticing the smile on everyone's face, "Mico, you know I've been ready for the partisans for months but, because of my mother and grandmother, you've denied me the opportunity. It is time I contribute and you can't stop me."

Gianni, "Michelle, I love you but you go, too. I'll be ok…."

With determination, "I'm staying. Gio, give me that damn rifle. It's nearly one o'clock in the morning, if you don't get moving you'll hit the plain in broad daylight and…"

As the caterpillar turns into a beautiful butterfly, all were witnessing a metamorphous; a boy turning into a man right in front of their eyes. Gio thinking, "He has become a man before his time; one of these days he is going to make a fine husband for some lucky young lady …"

Mico, reverting to his Ivan personality, interrupted Gio's flight into the tomorrow, immediately interjected, "Good for you, Michelle. You have been ready for a long time and you are right on. And since you all agreed I am in charge, I give the orders! Michelle, take the cripple back up to the hut; you stay behind with Gianni."

"Mico, I think…"

In a very rough commanding manner, "Gianni shut up and you, dear sister, give Michelle the piece of junk you call a rifle, then help Carla to the path and follow me down. Let's get moving."

He handed Michelle both canteens, a chunk of the polenta and half of Beatrice's bread, "You two stay at the hut. Damn it, don't go anywhere! Once we get through, I'll come back for you."

Pointing at the lad, "Understand, Michelle? Did you hear me Gianni? I said stay at the hut until I return. *Capisce*?"

No one dared challenge the man. He was in war-mode.

Gio, nodded to her brother, gently tugged the sobbing Carla away from Gianni and pulled her towards the path. Mico gave the two men brief hugs and followed the women down the slippery slope. They were out of sight in an instant.

THE WALK TO FREEDOM

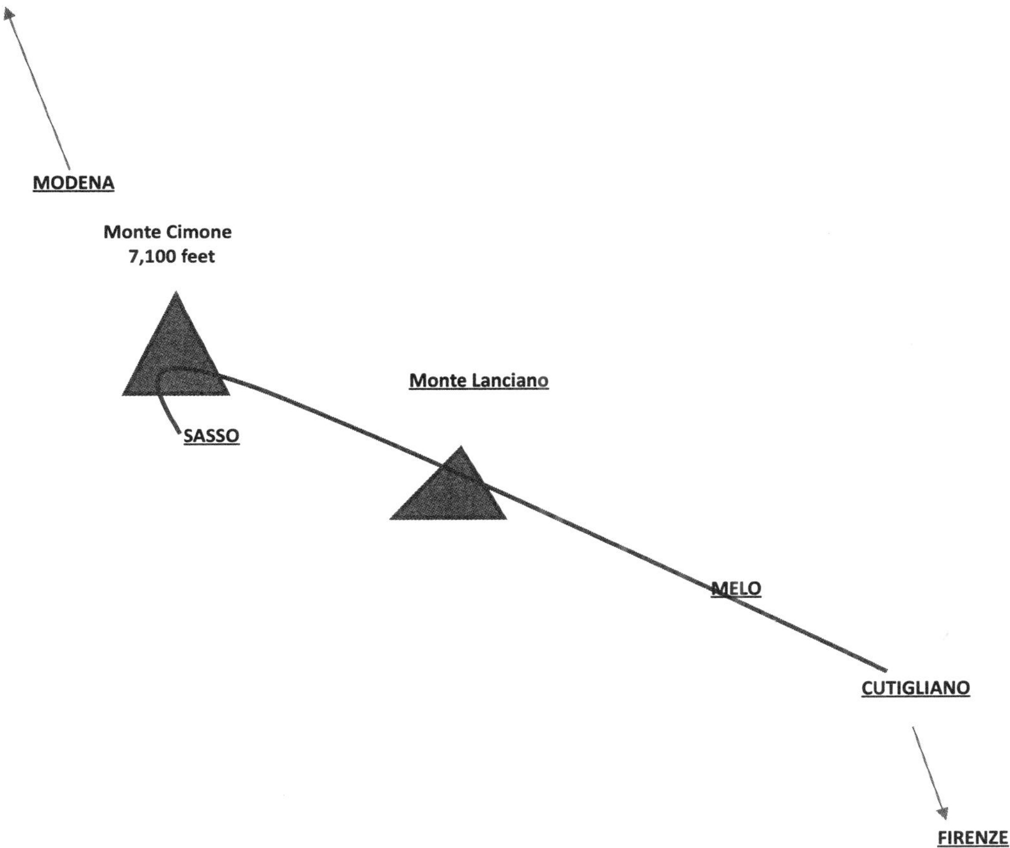

CHAPTER 10

THE EIGHT DIMENSION AND BEYOND

The first dimension is responsibility. He must protect his sister and a woman with child. The second is distance, followed by height, weather, Germans, partisans and the eight would be the Americans shooting at them for being on the wrong side of the line.

And then, the "beyond dimension": "How in the hell am I going to bring Gianni through?"

The answer eluded him.

The war had confronted Mico with many challenges over the years, but this time it was different. This time he was responsible for the lives of his family; responsible for people he loved for a lifetime. It was this new fear which attacked him as the trio slipped and slid on the cold, wet mountain side. A new anxiety instilling an unrelenting, continuous pull on his emotions. He looked back at the two women and felt grateful for the darkness. The hands of the war-tested ex-partisan were trembling.

After conquering the challenges of the mule paths, the three reached the plain as dawn was breaking. Carla was exhausted, continuing on spirit alone.

Gio looked as strong as ever, helping Carla and keeping her eyes and ears in a state of constant vigilance. Mico felt much pride and love for his sister, "I shouldn't worry about her" he thought. "She sometimes blurts out when silence would be better served, but she is a jewel" he smiled and added "… perhaps cut a bit on the rough side, nevertheless, a precious jewel." He looked at her and she responded by winking an eye. He smiled, thinking, "there is a real woman; I am sure one lucky man to have her in the trenches with me."

He returned the wink, felt encouraged, "My two ladies and me, we are going to be fine. We will get through."

Edging away from the mountain's coverage, the three went on complete alert for German patrols. They gazed through the mist and saw a flat expanse of land upon which the little town of Melo once stood. The town had been leveled by Allied and German exchanges and was now a sort of "no man's land" between the opposing military forces.

In the distance, they saw the skeletons of bombed-out buildings adding an eerie sadness to the smoky morning haze. The melancholy gloom caused additional discomfort, but the poor visibility was a welcomed friend; it would serve them well when they crossed the open field.

After walking for about ten minutes towards the town, they came upon two elderly ladies tilling a small plot of ground. They wore ragged blacks and browns, the taller one capped the ensemble with a dark grey *bombetta* (a man's round brimmed hat). Her soil mate held a pinch of snuff under here lower lip, the drool painting her chin in a chocolate brown matching the kerchief covering her head.

Studying the two beauties for a moment, Mico politely asked, "Good ladies, we are trying to get through to the American lines. Have you seen any German patrols?"

The women looked up, continued hacking at the mud.

"What is the best way to get to Cutigliano?"

The women looked at them somewhat suspiciously; the *bombetta*, without saying a word, pointed her rough, scrawny hand towards the south.

"Look, we are from Sasso. We have been walking all night; my cousin here is pregnant with child; please help us. Are there German patrols in the area?"

"Sasso, heh? That's why the silly accent", said the black coat wearing the brown kerchief.

She rested her chin on the hoe handle, "There hasn't been any shooting for a day or so but a German patrol comes through here every morning, came past about a half-hour ago. Probably be back around noon. The Americans won't come this way", she hesitated, "yet."

She wiped her chin with her sleeve, "I'd get out of here quickly. Follow that path and go around the south side of what was once our pretty little town." A giggle, "If you are lucky and get to the other side of town alive, start looking for a dirt road south."

"How long a walk to Cutigliano; to the American side?"

Mumbling, "Americans? Not yet … lot of people fleeing."

She pointed east. "If you use the road, a couple of hours. Of course, if you run into Germans you'll have a much longer trip." The old crone was enjoying herself.

She addressed her friend, "Cutigliano has become an Apennines resort; all sorts of strangers trying to pick up souvenirs of chocolate, American cigarettes and other goodies our liberators are using as currency for favors of all kinds."

The brown kerchief, "The price might be an American or German bullet shot up their behinds."

She cackled, "Then, they could say they have lead in their pants."

She turned to her partner for approval, "Right, Matilda?"

Matilda pulled her *bombetta* firmly down, turned from her little plot of ground, "Ya, that's funny, Elisa, but the real comedy would be if the hard heads catch us talking to these three idiots!"

She started hoeing again, barking, "Get the hell out of here; we don't need you to give the Germans an excuse to kill us! Get out of here!"

"Thank you, *amore*, may He bless you."

Through a gurgle of brownish saliva, "We accept your blessing, but a slice of bread would have been better."

Even Mico had to laugh.

The sun showed an orange face as it elbowed itself into a new day. On full alert for any movement, they slowly crossed the field. Within a half hour they arrived at the edge of the town, or what had been a town. The mist was lifting, providing them with a better view of the devastation; bomb craters and blackened trees. Dozens and dozens of scorched buildings, wetted from a recent rainfall, cast an aura of death and bereavement.

The small narrow streets were covered with garbage, broken timbers, ragged furniture. Dirty mattresses were piled everywhere as huge black flies, undisturbed by war, did their morning shopping. The stench was revolting, causing Carla to cover her mouth for fear of vomiting.

Mico sat down on a tree stump and called for a rest stop. Carla refused to stop and sharply rebuked Mico, "I don't need to rest. The smell is suffocating; the stench is making me sick, so let's get our asses out of this hellhole. I want to get to Cutigliano; stop patronizing me!"

Gio, "No wonder there are no people around." She giggled, "Not even the Sauerkrauts can stand the smell."

Gio, looked at the belligerent Carla, smiled, winked at Mico and said, "Let's get out of here."

They began the last leg of their journey to freedom.

They hiked a short distance, walked into a burnt shell of what had been a barn of some sort and were confronted by four rifles held by soldiers dressed in strange uniforms.

"Alto!"

A big man wearing a corporal's stripes and sporting a grandiose handlebar moustache, asked in broken Italian, "Who are you? Where do you think you are going?"

Mico was dumbfounded, Gio cringed. Carla spoke in German, "We are from the Village of Sasso; we are looking for a hospital for me and my baby."

In broken Italian, the huge man stepped closer to Carla, "I don't know what hell you are talking about. Speak Italian or, better yet, in Portuguese and, if you can do that, we'll surrender."

His three compatriots couldn't hold their laughter. The leader, with his mustache extending from cheek to cheek, barked "You three shut up." Then, with a mischievous smile, turned toward Carla, "Now, *signora* or *signorina*, or whatever you are, start talking. In Italian!"

Mico stepped forward, "You are neither German nor Italian so you must be part of the Allied forces. Are you Spanish?"

"Who in the hell are you to ask questions?", growled the mustache, rifle pointed at Mico, "Shut up and let the lovely lady speak."

Mico recoiled, seething underneath.

"My name is Carla Berti", nodding towards her companions, "and these two are brother and sister, Giovanna and Domenico Carboni."

Carla, totally fatigued but resilient as ever, "We are from the other side of the mountain, as I said, we are from the village of Sasso. We have walked all night trying to escape to the Allied lines. Will you let us through?"

"You are out of your minds, but you are lucky this day. We are part of the proud 1st Brazilian Division that has been risking the lives of its valiant men, like us, to rid your country of the pestilence."

He gave a loving stroke to his mustache, which had a faint red hue, turned and smiled at his buddies. The men appeared to come to some form of attention as their leader continued, "You have been saved by the four heroes of the Brazilian Pampas, proud citizens of the state of *Rio Grande du Sul!* Attackers of The Gothic Line and liberators of some fine Tuscan *red*!"

The huge gorilla then extended his hand to Mico, clasped it in a stranglehold and began shaking. Mico, a big man himself, lost his hand in the Brazilian's huge grip, "Welcome to hell! Give the ladies and their escort their first taste of what has already been liberated by Brazil!"

Mico, freed from the hand shake, turned to the ladies and raised his eyebrows in acknowledgement that the four Brazilians were dead drunk.

Carla took the bottle, handed it to Gio who, despite not having eaten since the cold polenta the night before, lifted the bottle in a salute towards the corporal, shouted "Viva Brazil", immediately guzzled a mouthful, and handed the bottle to Mico.

Seeing the red and realizing they were in friendly hands, a mollified Mico raised the bottle and saluted the four men, "If there is a God, may he bless you, the Pampas and all of Brazil." He tossed back his head and guzzled as if he were drinking water.

"Hey, enough celebration; I said a taste, not the entire damn bottle", as the mustache took the bottle away from Mico and offered it to Carla, "Here pretty little lady, have a bit of Tuscany."

Carla, feeling queasy, patted her stomach, "No thank you, it's too early in the day for my baby."

"Nonsense! A little of the *red* will give you and your baby added strength!"

The trooper stopped pressing Carla, turned to the others and gleefully shouted, "Here's to the new Italian; I hope his or her life is a bit easier than the mother's."

He raised the bottle towards Carla and emptied the contents onto the sea of wine already at high tide within him.

"What is your name?", cooed Gio.

The big man raised himself on his toes, straightened his back, clicked his heels and saluted Gio, "I am Corporal Bruno Nasciente. I was once a *Primiero Sargento* (1st Sergeant), but was promoted down to Corporal as an Easter present."

"What did you do? Why did they demote you?"

Private Felipe, a dark skinned frail little man, pogoing around like a pond frog, "He stole a Jeep, drove down to Pistoia, found a woman who owned a keg of new wine and didn't return to his duty for four days…"

"It was only three days…"

"No, it was four; they took away a stripe for each day you were testing the new wine and your old gears."

"Oh! Shut up. You can hardly read, so how in the hell do you think you can count? What do you know about it anyway?"

"Well, all I know is on Easter you were a *Primiero Sargento* carrying six big stripes on your uniform and by the end of the week you were a Cabo (corporal) wearing a uniform held together with only two stripes. You are fortunate you didn't face the firing squad, deserting ….."

The leader interrupted the little frog, gave him an Italian "up yours" arm salute and turned towards the others, "Luiz, give them some of the bread and cheese then take them to the American quarters. Felipe, Gustavo you stay on guard here with me. And, Luiz, straighten your uniform or you'll get shot as a run-away. Tell the new sergeant it's time to send us a relief party. I'm tired of sitting here with you three idiots guarding against German infiltrators who probably are no nearer than twenty kilometers up the mountain."

There was sound of nearby gun fire as Luis gave each a parcel of food. Nasciente, meanwhile, broke off a piece of cheese and pointed it at Gio, "The noise you hear comes from American artillery. I'm told the Germans, using slave labor, have dug over two thousand machine gun and mortar nests up there. It sure is going to be a hell of a dance when we start to..."

He stopped in mid-sentence as a barrage erupted from some nearby position, "The Americans are playing tic-tac-toe hoping one shell out of hundred will find the prey. They have been shelling the entire Apennine mountain range for days", he swallowed another mouthful of wine, "but after all the noise is finished it will be grunts like us who are going to pay the heavy price."

He looked at Gio, smiled, "But don't worry your pretty head about the German artillery; we are out of harm's way." He stuffed the cheese in his mouth, "well not really, but this is safe as it's going to be for the next few weeks."

Gio touched the Brazilian's sleeve as Mico asked, "You been here long? I didn't even realize you Brazilians were in Italy."

"Well, we arrived in September, lot was going on. We thought the German was on the run but, hand it to those bastards, they held. We tried to advance, but the ox-track and donkey roads were muddy and the German defensive positions made for suicidal conditions for we poor "grunts". We lost a lot of men in these mountains of yours. Monte Castello, Monte Belvedere, in particular. We had no real combat experience; we were green, but they sent us anyway. Lots of casualties," he stopped again, inhaled, "The Brazilian Expeditionary Force we are called; it was an expedition, alright. So damn cold, like the high Andes in August. A half dozen attacks before we ran those sons of whores; but finally, they ran."

"How did you end up here with the Americans?"

"As I said, we Brazilians were thrown into the battle of Monte Castello. Three months scrapping mud off our boots and pinching shrapnel out of our asses. Six times those bastards sent us up that *frikin* hill! Believe me, I earned my stripes. Six *friken* times!"

A sardonic chuckle, "We lost a lot of youngsters whose only combat experience was in Rio walking the beautiful *Playa de Copacabana.* Young men who, five months earlier, strolled sunny beaches fighting over the pretty girls, were sloshing, sliding on some damn Italian mountain at the cost of frozen toes, frozen fingers and their very lives. Instead of investing their youth chasing a pretty smile or the swish of a colorful shirt, they risked their lives following the orders of some idiot with stars on his lapel..." The sentence was left unfinished.

"So, how did you get away?"

"Got hit, no big problem. I had a small wound in my side and my good *Capitano* thought his favorite sergeant deserved a vacation, so he ordered me to drive a Major back to Division Headquarters in Porretta. I'm sure you know the town, right?"

The Italians nodded.

"I knew the mountains around Porretta were still heavily infested with Germans but forget that; forget the intense cold and I'm in an open-air jeep, forget the rain and mud. I was elated to get the hell out of the real front lines."

The ex-sergeant, now a corporal, was at his best; the audience secure as the wallet hidden inside his uniform. His huge right hand scratched at his arm pit, "If I was an eagle it would have been a twenty-minute trip but driving around those mountain roads took me all day. Lucky some *kraut-head* didn't use us for target practice. Damn officer hardly said a word the entire trip. I didn't think I stank that bad," he slapped Mico on the shoulder, "Har, har, maybe fear had him making *cacca* in his pants. Anyway, we made it without incident."

The *red,* having sharpened the Brazilian's wit and totally unhinged his tongue, continued, "I think all military officers have cotton brains," he hesitated, "well, maybe not the Germans", a giggle, "they probably have steel wool."

Hearing no reaction, he took another sip out of the bottle and continued, "Anyway, I hung around Porretta for a couple of days, then was ordered to drive the same Major to Cutigliano where I found these three idiots living a life of ease, running errands for the Americans and doing guard duty. I was assigned to lead the contingent and await new orders."

He sat down on an empty ammunition case, "I've talked enough, what about you? Please don't tell me you are not Fascists. It seems no one in this country was Fascist. Where in the world could they have gone? I'm sure there must be a few unburned black shirts."

Mico laughed, "I was with the partisans to the northwest, near Pavolo. Because of the vicious cold we really did not do much damage to the enemy. In retrospect, we may have done more harm than good…"

The big man stopped, stroked his moustache and dolefully interrupted, "The winter weather was horrendous, plans to advance, thank our good fortune, were cancelled. With the arrival of the bitter cold and snow, the cannons finally stopped firing and, except for a few enemy raids, there was no fighting down here. We have been in a war of attrition since Christmas but with the big guns now firing more frequently, looks like we are going to be re-asked to join the party."

He chuckled, "Maybe they won't invite Brazilians this time."

Luis interrupted, "You are such a comedian, Nasciente. I think the *red* has numbed your already dulled brain. Nobody, especially your favorite *Capitano*, has forgotten us. You damn well know our asses will be climbing up to heaven before we finish the wine we liberated", he squinted, "and if you keep it up, they won't wait for the Germans to do the honors; they'll put you against the wall for being drunk while on guard duty."

Nasciente responded loudly in Portuguese and from the little man's reaction, death would be a welcome alternative if Luis said another word. The little soldier retreated and the big man continued, "This is Pecorino; made right here in Cutigliano by a fearless ol' girl who lost two of her sheep to the Germans. She wailed and cried until the hard heads, showing Teutonic mercy, agreed she could shear her treasures of their wool before they feasted on their triumphant conquest."

The corporal chuckled, "They didn't know she had three other sheep and a cow hidden in a hut high above the town. The Germans weren't about to go into those partisan infested hills and, as a result, she and her three sheep, cornered the Pecorino market in Cutigliano."

He cut a small piece of the cheese and, using the knife as a serving utensil, offered the delicacy to Gio and advised, "Better to hide here with these three idiots, pray no Germans are looking for early mushrooms and hope everyone has forgotten about us."

Mico, "No I want to get the ladies to the Americans and I must return to …"

The Brazilian ignored Mico, turned towards Gio, stroked his moustache and asked, "And you *Bella* in the boots, what markets have you cornered?"

Gio smiled at the big man, "I haven't the slightest idea what you are talking about."

"Corner the market means you own something of value no one else has. You have it all and, therefore, can command whatever price you want."

Still smiling, "Corporal Nasciente, what I own, I own and I have it all, as you say. But, it is not for sale and if it were, the payment, I assure you, would not be measured in liras, dollars or francs…."

Private Luis interrupted the repartee, "Let's go, you three, it's time to get you off our hands and, more importantly, it's time to re-supply my brave *companeros* with the nectar befitting heroes."

Gio, turned her attention from the Brazilian Romeo and asked Luis about his jacket's shoulder flap carrying the word "BRAZIL" arched over the caricature of a hissing snake. "What is that insignia on your sleeve, Luis?"

"It is The Smoking Snake, the proud symbol of the Brazilian 5th Army. The snake will protect us", then, turning to Nasciente, "that is, if we ever get started…"

Corporal Bruno Naciente, once again looking at Gio, "As the *Americani* say, Ok! Ok! Get the hell out of here!"

He patted Gio on the backside, "Luis, go ahead and surrender these three ex-Fascist to the Americans. And find them a place to sleep before they both fall over."

Luis immediately broke off a piece of cheese, stuffed it into his mouth and walked towards the framework of what had been the back door of the building.

Mico, not moving, turned to the leader, "Corporal, we left two men back up the mountain. My cousin, who is hurt and being attended to by his young nephew. I promised to go back for them once the ladies were safe, with your permission, can I rest up here for a bit and then…."

Nasciente interrupted, "Are you crazy? As I said, the Germans are pulling back, but they aren't dead yet. Dumb luck got you across the field. In broad daylight, no less."

"There was a covering fog."

"What you really were was a bit foggy between the ears. German patrols are still around; I can smell them! Our men are having a helluva tough time advancing and now you want to push your luck and go back alone. I know the Tuscan *red* makes people happy but I didn't know one swallow would turn brave into stupid!"

He stroked his mustache again, "…also, I hear a few of your fellow partisans are not being too discreet as to who they are attacking…"

"Corporal", given the same situation, you wouldn't leave your *companeros* behind; you'd go to them."

Nasciente opened another bottle of wine, Mico wondering how many bottles these idiots had stolen. There was a long pause as the Corporal thought about the situation, then forcefully blurted, "You are right, *Italiano*; Brazilians would save them all."

He stopped, took a nip of the red, "except for Private Felipe who has no respect for anyone."

The ex-Sargent wiped his mouth with his sleeve, "Private Felipe, give your *pistole* to this crackpot-soon-to-be-dead hero."

"I'm not giving up my *pistole* to anybody; you and your new Italian friend may be nuts, but not Felipe Del Santo; this little *bambino* stays with me!"

"You know, you have been on my nerves for a Brazilian year now; give him that damn pistol or you'll be reported missing in action!"

The corporal, bottle in his right hand, started walking towards Felipe Del Santo, "Give me the gun or I'll feed you wine through a new crack in your skull."

Felipe cringed, shuffled towards his corporal and meekly handed over the gun, mumbling as he hopped away.

Nasciente shook his head and addressed Mico, "This is an American made Colt M1917; the Americans used them in the first war, now they are hand-me-downs, good only for their allies. They tell me it still works, but I wouldn't trust it any more than I trust Private Filipe, who is now going to give you some bullets; and his canteen. Right, private?"

Another sip of wine, "They trained us so well before sending us across the sea to your stinkin' mountains," he snickered, "even Filipe knows that to kill the enemy, the American made Colt M1917 requires ammunition."

Nasciente gave the pistol to Mico and Felipe handed over a dozen bullets and a canteen filled with water, Filipe snidely commenting, "I filled the canteen with water or, Corporal dear, would you I rather give this soon-to-be-dead hero some of our hard-earned bounty of wine?"

Naciente's retort was in Portugese, but everyone understood where Felipe would find his canteen if he said another word. The big man turned to Mico, "You can lay down behind the kitchen wall if you want to rest at bit."

Mico thanked the Brazilian, turned and hugged the two women. There were no outward emotional reactions. The three strong-willed escapees fully understood that, at times, situations arrive which necessitate actions based upon love of family and friends, rather than good judgment. They had to split; Mico had to return to the mountain.

After thanking the Brazilians, Carla followed Luis out the back door. Gio walked her brother to the kitchen area, hugged him and whispered, "I love you; we will see you in a few days." She then strode towards the door, turned and threw her brother a kiss, wondering if she would ever see him again. Turning towards her "hosts", a quaint smile, "Thank you Bruno Nasciente, I hope we meet again. I hope we see you soon."

"I will look for you all over Italy", stroking his moustache, then, once again, patting Gio on the shoulder, "You will be my treasure, my Mona Lisa."

"Your what?"

"A work of art any man would be willing die for."

Gio burst out laughing, "You are so full of it."

"Wine?"

"Yes, that too! You are also a liar and a thief."

"You are right on all counts. But, I am also poor."

"So?"

"It is less sinful for a poor man to lie and steal."

"Really? Did you read that in your Brazilian bible?"

Bruno's voice became gentle, docile, "I believe if one is hungry and steals food, there is no sin unless he has taken from someone who also feels the pain of hunger. Sin occurs when someone steals to add to their surplus. And the sin becomes monstrous and horrific if he or she steals from someone who is poorer."

"So, did you make sure the wine you stole was taken from someone rich?"

"Certainly! They had several barrels and we did not have a drop."

Gio's mouth opened, she did not know if she should laugh, argue or agree. She hesitated a moment, looked at the pleased smile on the big oaf's face, decided silence was the best alternative. She quickly turned away and followed Carla and Luis into the opposite clearing.

Bruno never noticed she was wearing boots.

CHAPTER 11

ANOTHER LONG TRIP

Mico felt someone kicking at his feet, "Time to get up hero, you've been snoring all night; you drowned out the rumble of the artillery."

Nasciente went to a back room, returned and gave Mico several tins of American rations, "Here, take these. Wouldn't feed these to pigs, but they are better than starving to death."

"What can I say, my friend? My eternal thanks."

He stuffed the tins and the weapon into his pockets, embraced each of the soldiers and started the dangerous morning walk towards the foothills.

The morning mist, good protection earlier, had lifted. The brief appearance of an afternoon sun benefit the hunter more than the prey. So, for extra cover, he decided to go through what had been the center of the town. Skirting it, as they had earlier, he would be more in the open; more dangerous. He had to go through the town.

The stench was worse than it was earlier. Death had donned its afternoon bouquet.

The bile rose, he held his nose and walked faster. To no avail. He vomited! The wine, the cheese and, now inhaling the acrid aroma of a town devastated by foreigners were too much for his stomach! He wiped his mouth with his coat sleeve.

Movement to his right! He froze. Looked again, "Rats! Filthy rats all over the place! This is too much! Germans or no Germans, I 've got to get the hell out of here." He covered his mouth, made a quick turn and jogged towards the open field.

After a very nervous thirty minutes, Mico reached the skeleton of a burnt farm building, went inside. The wooden floor cracked as he stepped into the gloom and was greeted by the familiar odor of old sheep dung. He kicked at a filthy straw mat, seeing no lice nor other "critters", he sat and rested for a moment. He nodded off.

He bolted awake. How long had he slept? Not very long; a few minutes at best. He chastised himself, "Can't risk doing that again."

He stood, walked towards the door and looked back at what had been the town of Melo. Wisps of smoke continued to cast an eerie glow on the little town leveled by American cannons. The stench, now a good distance away, would remain etched into his memory.

An unworried crow flew toward the town and swooped down to peck at a morsel, "Tell me, bird, how many beautiful dreams were obliterated over there? How many nightmares?"

The unflappable bird continued casually pecking away, still unconcerned.

At full alert, he slowly crossed the field and reached a path leading upward. Despite his weariness and uncomfortable damp clothing, he felt an uplift in spirit. He was now close to "his" mountain and forest, where the air was fresh and the terrain offered him much needed protection. He figured he was several hundred meters from where they had exited earlier. He smiled thinking of his conversation with the two old hags working their garden plot.

A sad smile, "Two poor souls trying to eke out a living at the gates of hell. What a world."

He entered the foothills and started climbing. He pushed the negative thoughts from his mind and reflected upon the "Brazilian Experience". He chuckled to himself as he recalled Gio's shameless boldness. The kid-sister was no "femme fatal", but she sure knew how to handle members of the opposite sex. She was a tiger, and a damn smart one, at that!

He sensed a deep appreciation for Corporal Bruno Nasciente's help and understanding. The man may have been from a far-away place, and the moustache was a bit much, but he and the Brazilian were, nevertheless, kindred spirits.

In his younger days Mico, like Nasciente, enjoyed the company of pretty girls, a bit of *the red.* In that "other life" he was a young, jovial rascal worrying only about the next *festa,* the next girlfriend. But the war had interrupted the party and shortened his salad days; his good times could now be seen only in the rear-view mirror.

As he continued his climb, bitterness replaced nostalgia; an acrid bile replaced the savory sweetness of youthful memories. He didn't realize he was talking in a loud acrimonious voice, "Mussolini served me plates of death and retribution. War became my main course. Isn't it about time someone served dessert? When will I taste my mother's sweet *biscotti* and *zuccherini*? How many wars? How many innocent lives? How much longer can this go on?"

He continued trudging up the slope, thoughts changing as he chewed on the foul American GI rations. A melancholic nostalgia overcame him as he thought of his little family back in France; his bride Suzi and his precious little girl, Beatrice. He had not seen them for more than two years. Were they alive? Did the hard heads discover Suzi was a Jew? Mico had seen, first hand, the Italian Fascist's change in attitude towards the Jews, even those Jews who had supported Mussolini from the beginning. He knew anti-Semitic propaganda was ignored by most Italians but as the war drew closer, Fascist hooligans repeated the smut, tormenting Jewish shopkeepers, in particular. They found courage and importance strutting about in their military uniform and stealing from the rich and poor, alike.

But, overall, Italy was not Vichy France where he knew Jews, by the thousands, had been vilified, arrested and sent to the camps. He stifled a tear knowing, to his everlasting regret, he had left his family in France and now they faced an evil worse than war, itself. But, he thought his decision to help was an obligation that had to be paid. And, once committed, you obey, even if it means leaving one's family and friends. After all, you became a soldier, not a politician.

He shivered and asked the wind, "Did my wife and father-in-law escape? Did they consider my little girl a Jew?" His mind filled with bad possibilities and agonizing thoughts. He felt so helpless. His stomach tightened realizing, once again, he had to fight off these worries for now.

But, the juices were boiling. He needed to cry. He could not. Instead he returned to the present and hurried his pace. He kicked at a branch lying broken on the path, "One mission at a time; one goal at a time. France is a world away."

After walking uphill for another hour or so, Mico sat down and drank from the canteen. It seemed he had been walking for days. Despite the short rest with the Brazilians, he felt exhausted. He was fortunate in not having encountered anyone, but his battle experience thought him one couldn't afford to become lax; one never knew where danger lurked.

Danger aside, he needed to rest a bit longer. The hard climb to the higher elevations lay ahead. The mountain path climbed over ridges and wet, gray rocks. The sky contributed its slate gray to the tableau all contributing to the melancholy of the early Apennine spring. Mico, to avoid a bit of depression, sat on a huge bolder and re-directed his thoughts to those long gone, "better days."

He recalled happy times when he and Gianni, emboldened and fortified with a few bottles of a good *red*, chased rabbit, wild boar and pheasant. "Ah! Those were the days. We walked in daylight or under a full moon along the *Cimone* mountain crest as if we were the masters of the world. How often we awaited night fall and, from our heavenly location, watched the peaceful valley lights flicker to life. Remember Gianni? You said they were little earth bound stars creating places one could only find in fairy tales or in a six-year old's story book."

Mico sighed, "And now, our little towns are tired and sick. They have shriveled into the protection of blackouts, closed doors and saying prayers that one's family will be fortunate enough to survive another day under a siege from multiple enemies."

He reflected on his days with the partisans and the many times he risked his life as part of a positive force to free Italy from the evil ones. He mumbled to himself, "Cutigliano may be a safe-haven, but this war isn't over yet; men are still dying and the hard heads are still in Sasso. The entire continent has been liberated but we are still sitting under the German boot."

"I wonder how my partisan friends are finding the pickings. That craven, spineless Vaccaccia and our esteemed leader Capitano Tulio probably are raiding the American stores now that the hard heads are heading north. Wonder if I'll ever see them again. It would be an interesting reunion."

Mico giggled at the thought.

He rose, took a second sip from the canteen and restarted his climb, "I've got to push those idiots to the part of the brain that helps one forget. There is still work to do. Peace hasn't yet arrived and I guess I'm still a partisan… so is Gianni and so is Michelle."

Speaking aloud to the trees, he continued the litany, "But, you know, our problem is a tricky one. There is no easy answer. Exactly who is my enemy? The German? The disappearing Fascist? Or, how about our old partisan band of friends?"

He kicked at a small pebble, "Good questions, Mico; good questions."

CHAPTER 12

IT'S OVER—MAYBE

With some difficulty, Michelle had half-carried his uncle back up the incline and now the two were, once again, seated on two of the huge boulders in front of the refuge. Both were perspiring profusely from the difficult climb. Michelle unbuttoned his heavy winter coat and rested his back against the stone.

"Button up! Do you want to catch pneumonia?"

"Is she pretty?"

"Who?"

"Newmonia."

"Very funny, but if you get sick it won't be so hilarious for either of us. Now, button up!"

The lad, a smile on his face, sat up and re-buttoned the coat, "Do you want some water, *Zio*?"

"No, I'm set for now, Michelle. Let's just lay back and rest, the next few days are going to be brutal for us."

Gianni lifted his ankle, grimaced and tried to find a comfortable position on the hard ledge. A breeze caressed a few leaves still clustered on a bare beech tree to his left. The moon peeking through the clouds spoke of hope, but reality was a swollen ankle and the dire predicament the two men faced. Poetic observations would need to wait for better times.

Gianni wanted to go into the hut and lie down on the wooden plank inside, but before he could rise Michelle asked, "What happened to Lorenzo? Is the devil dead? Did you kill that Fascist bastard?"

"I didn't kill him. He was, as they say, a bit disheveled, but alive when I left the partisans. Mico told me Renzo was still alive when he left camp."

"I don't think I would find any sort of fulfillment in killing anyone, but I'd join the partisans to help drive the Germans and their black shirted allies out of Italy. If that means killing someone, I think I could do it. What I don't understand is how a man who says he has religious beliefs can torture, maim and murder in the name of his "cause". Worse, how can someone kill, with great satisfaction, an acquaintance, a neighbor or a relative? Why do men find satisfaction in this brutality, Uncle Gianni? Why are they willing to risk their lives to feed this devil within them?"

Gianni was awed with the depth of the questions from his young nephew. He smiled at the lad, tenderly tapped him on the shoulder and said, "I don't know. Sometimes politics and religion are twins, Michelle. They can stir the juices and bring out the worst in man. People think they are correct, their quest is the valiant one; they believe "theirs" is the only path to whatever the goal. If a stranger disagrees, the stranger becomes an adversary; however, if someone close, a friend or a relative disagrees, they become more than adversary; they become front line enemy. The bitterness is always greater in one's own house."

Gianni shuffled his legs, wincing as he moved the sore foot, "Lorenzo believed Fascism and Mussolini were the answers to Italy's problems. "Il Duce" and his cohorts made laws forbidding everything and then enforced them selectively against their enemies. Much of the world either ignored him or hailed him as a great leader. Most of Italy sang his praises; even those who would soon send their sons to be killed in places far from the gentle skies."

Gianni's voice grew louder, his "*Grugno*" coming to the surface, "Thousands killed to the tune of a song of glory written and sung by a liar, the real enemy living right in one's own house. And the crowds believed!"

Anger boiled his innards as he spit out the venom which had been eating away for so long, "The young shouted their praises to the new Caesar; they couldn't wait to die for him and his promises. And the scum, like Lorenzo, were ever ready to feed these new patriots to the Ethiopians, the Albanians, the Russians, the French, the Greeks and, lastly to the Allies."

Michelle remained quiet, reflecting on his uncle's outburst. "My father lost his life and is now buried in a forgotten far-away Russian field all because of another man's bluster and lies. You were right; the Italian Fascists killed my father, not the Germans, not the Russians. I'll never forgive or forget the damn Black Shirts."

The moon disappeared as a mist began to softly surround the two men. After a few moments, Michelle asked, "What is the difference between adversary and enemy?"

Gianni, returning from some far-away place, hesitated and then in a low, calm voice, "Well, I guess they mean the same but to my mind, an adversary is a challenger; a rival who wants to defeat you but does so in a civil, gentlemanly way. He tries to follow the rules of the contest and has respect for your effort to defeat him."

"...and the one we consider as the enemy?"

"The enemy, to me, is a person or a people who hate; a foe who not only wants to defeat you, he wants to kill; a nemesis who will use whatever means available to subject you to his rules, his way of life."

The juices were beginning to simmer again, "the enemy will cheat, torture, enslave or kill to achieve their objectives." He hesitated a moment, "And, as I said, the vilest of these is the one who lives under your own roof; the beast who knows you well."

"Do you mean Lorenzo or Mussolini?"

He smiled, "Aha! There, you go! The answer is both, I guess."

Gianni moved his leg, the pain excruciating. "As I said a few moments ago, Mussolini, while pretending to be a friend, conspired to harm the nation. He murdered and jailed his enemies. It was the black shirt or prison. There was no "loyal opposition"; it was a complete dictatorship. He ruined us and most certainly was the "enemy within" the nation."

He continued, "Lorenzo was Sasso's "enemy within". He saw the road to Fascism as a way to achieve stature in the community. He knew zilch about politics, cared nothing about a greater Italy or the enemies threatening the motherland. He was in it for his own self-serving interests and would stop at nothing to better himself." He hesitated, "Including his not attempting to stop the hardheads from sending you and me to the camps up north."

Wistfully he turned to his young nephew, "Lorenzo, my half-brother", another hesitation, then, patting the lad's shoulder, softly said, "Making him our enemy within."

Gianni looked at his handsome nephew. The deep blue eyes of many present and past clan members. A high forehead covered with jet-black hair that was sure to disappear by the time he turned fifty. A smart charmer who brought smiles to the old grouches in town. He surely was a Carboni! A thought raced through his mind, "He is so much like me he could be my son…"

"What about the partisan movement?"

A hesitation, "Well there are partisans and there are partisans. Some are nothing but brigands, raiding their own people, stealing from their own and killing Germans without regard to the consequences their actions created for our villagers. They are not Italians; they are the enemy of our people, thereby making them the scum of the earth, in my opinion."

He looked at Michelle and saw a perplexing look of disbelief, "I think the majority are freedom fighters. True patriots fighting for a free Italy. Men and women taking great risks to damage the enemy and help the Allies send the Germans back to their Deutschland. And, better yet, send the Black Shirts to hell!"

"What about Mico and the rest of your band? Yours was a Communist group, you had your own political agenda, right?"

Gianni having avoided the question previously, decided to bluntly answer the lad, "Right you are, Michelle. The Communists and other partisan groups originally joined in a holy crusade to rid Italy of our northern friend, turned enemy. No question we helped the allied cause but often at the price of additional hardship and death to innocent Italians."

"In recent months, the partisans have been fighting each other," Gianni sighed, "and the situation will get worse. The Communist partisan movement plays its song to the beat of the baton held by their maestros in Moscow. In time, they'll make the same kind of music as the Fascist, albeit wearing red shirts instead of black ones." He hesitated and in a low half-snarl continued, "More than a few partisans are as much a threat to Italy's future as were the Fascists and the Germans."

"Really?"

"Partisans, like the coward we called "Vaccaccia", steal from our own people and when asked to fight, find excuses to be out of harm's way. To call them despicable is a compliment. Vaccaccia was a coward who was in it for the loot while hiding with us for fear of the Germans."

"Why didn't you force him out of your group?"

"Ask cousin Mico, or Ivan as he was called then, when you next see him."

"What about the leader you both talked about; Captain Tulio?"

"He is a committed political animal; a Communist to the core. Nothing came ahead of the party. He was valiant in combat, smart as Lenin, himself. He never wavered, used whatever tools at hand, including people like Vaccaccia, to defeat the enemy and to punish those who didn't obey his command."

"Like you?"

There was no sound. No air. The breeze disappeared. No movement. In the stillness the darkness of the forest pressed down, the blacks and browns contributing to the melancholy; each branch slowly adding a sad, wet ominous color to another day's end; the shades of death, itself.

"Like me."

"And like Mico?"

Gianni hesitated, picked up another stick and began to draw another circle, "Yes, in the end, like Mico." He touched his nephew's shoulder, "Politics have a way of eroding happiness and contentment and serve as a fertile feeding ground for greed, chicanery and broken promises. Beware the politician, Michelle; especially if he or she is wearing an expensive perfume."

The wet mist clung to Gianni's clothing, sending a shiver streaking through his body. The stones glistened and Gianni thought they were smiling, eagerly awaiting the opportunity to cause additional pain to his ankle. He thought about Carla and their baby, turned his head away from Michelle as tears glistened and joined the mist dampening his cheeks. It was another melancholy moment filled with sorrow, want and loneliness. He thought of his unborn child again and asked the stones, "Would it ever end? Would his child be brought into the world to live through yet another debacle, another savior/politician who would want to fight another war for a meaningless word called, peace?"

He returned to the present, "You wanted to join the partisans to fight the enemy, but thank the Lord you didn't. I don't think you could have savaged another human being in the manner now in vogue. I couldn't kill Lorenzo; I could not make a man dig his own grave and bludgeoning him before the execution. War is war, it is said. But savagery is savagery; brutality is brutality, war or no war."

Michelle remained quiet as full night arrived. He gazed at his uncle, thought the ankle must be giving Gianni great pain. For the first time during this escapade, beads of doubt trickled into his thoughts, "Let's go inside the hut, you can lie down and rest the ankle."

Once inside, Gianni immediately laid down on a crudely fashioned wooden plank which served as a table and a bed. Michelle, sitting on a small metal box, shivered and reached into his knapsack for the last of the cold polenta. He gave a chunk to his uncle, ate his share in one swallow and resumed the conversation, "Zio, do you think my father will ever come home or do you think he is dead?"

The debacle at Stalingrad happened two years before and there never had been a word as to his brother-in-law's circumstances. He was either dead or a prisoner of the Russians.

Gianni hesitated, asking himself how to answer the boy. He stifled a short laugh remembering his nephew no longer was the little boy trying to play the ocarina; he was now a combatant trying to escape the war. He deserved a true opinion, not a vague answer best left to one too weak or too young to face reality.

"I don't know Michelle", Gianni responded softly, "we have not heard anything except for the "missing in action notice" from the military. Evidently, no one knows." Gianni hesitated as his old friend, *"Grugno",* tugged at his stomach. He finished eating the polenta then gently put his hand on his nephew's shoulder, "I suggest you not live on false hopes. If he is alive, we would have heard from someone by now. I'm afraid he is dead, Michelle." Gianni, rocking back and forth in an attempt to stand, did not mention the Russian prisoner of war possibility; he reasoned that would be a death sentence, anyway.

After a few moments of silence, the boy uttered a comment way beyond his years, "We all die sooner or later. My father's time came sooner; I just pray he died quickly."

He picked up the old rifle and continued, "I think we are heading for some special place, a place where we will be welcomed because we helped those in need, we genuinely and sincerely rue our errors and have asked for

His forgiveness." He caressed the rifle, "But, I can't believe those who sent my father to die in that far-off place will be forgiven." He looked at Gianni and scowled, "just because they ask for forgiveness at the last minute."

Gianni rubbed his eyes, turned away from the boy saying, "Who knows? Who knows? Let's talk about it later. Go to sleep."

Gianni had spent everything he had. His ankle throbbed. He wondered at what point he would reach complete exhaustion; what his limitations were. He had met two similar situations in the past but this time it was different; this time it wasn't a matter of putting a fellow warrior at risk; this time he had put his sister's son, his own flesh, his own blood in harm's way. He ended his contemplation with a prayer; a silent, fervent plea his young nephew would not pay some horrific price for remaining behind.

CHAPTER 13

THE AMERICANI

Private Luis led Carla and Gio through a tract of charred chestnut woods; "black sentinels to the gates of a different hell", mused Carla. They turned onto a rutted dirt alley, came around a bombed-out shell of a house and entered the town square. They saw and heard the roar of motors and dozens of men barking at each other in English.

The town was a bustling, energetic cornucopia of trucks, soldiers, many carrying the American 5th Army patch, ordinance units, pyramids of munitions and medical tents. At the periphery, a slow steady caravan of equipment and troops was preparing for the move towards the German's awaiting them at the higher altitudes.

In the center of the town, an incongruous air of festivity pervaded. Men sat smoking, carrying on conversations and quite a few drinking "liberated" red wine. Occasional spurts of fire from the Germans scattered along the mountain-top could be heard. Fortunately, the enemy's salvos were kept at a minimum as the Americans answered with blasts from dozens of their huge 88s positioned along the perimeters. The infrequent exchanges and the movements north, reminded everyone they were still in harm's way.

The Allies, as they drove up the boot, had picked up hundreds upon hundreds of Italian runaways. The escapees worked in their kitchens, in ordinance tents and attended to dozens of front line menial needs. For the escapees, it was paradise. They were given food, shelter and no longer needed to worry about Germans or the Fascist Republicans. The war was over for them and although Cutigliano wasn't quite paradise, they knew they had escaped a real hell. An elated Gio and an exhausted Carla were now members of this most fortunate collection of survivors.

The Brazilian Luis walked towards a tent with an exploding bomb insignia on its front flap. He tried to explain it was an American ordinance tent and something about Italians, but the women misunderstood the broken Italian/Portuguese account and entered the tent with ominous feelings.

Luis guided them to an American officer sitting at a metal table reading a newspaper; his back to dozens and dozens of motors, axles, various auto parts and barrels overflowing with motor accessories. Luis introduced Lt. Mitchell to the ladies, bowed to the lieutenant, said his goodbyes and rapidly exited the tent.

"Buon giorno, signorine" welcome to *paradiso* where Italians are becoming more numerous than the spark plugs I have in those barrels."

The two women understood the greeting, but otherwise did not have the slightest idea of what else was said. Mitchell put down his newspaper, "*Le signorine speaka Inglese?*"

"*No. no. Siamo Italiani.*"

"No shit! You've got to be kidding me. I thought you were Austrian", the man snickered knowing the women didn't understand a word. He continued, "Hundreds of you in town, all claiming to be ex-Fascists."

"No! No! *Non siamo Fascisti*, siamo……"

Lt. Mitchell did not let Carla finish, in an English accented broken dialect yelled out, "Cesare, *ven qui*"

A young man, dressed in green grease-stained dungarees, emerged from behind a barrel and approached the officer. Cesare nodded as the officer, addressing no one in particular said, "If this influx of escapees continues, the town of Cutigliano will soon be a resort town. I'm beginning to feel more like a hotelier than a soldier."

He looked at the ladies and smiled, "OK, we can use some help. Cesare, take them to the main hospital; I'm told they've just brought in another truckload of wounded. Maybe these ladies can help clean up or whatever; they've got to earn their keep if they want us to feed them."

The officer sighed, "Then give them the rest of the routine, show them where they can get some food and a place to stay. "*Capish?*" He pointed towards the front flap, "Go! Get the hell out of here. They can clean up and rest later. And bring me back some cigarettes; this time remember I want Lucky Strikes, not those damn Chesterfields!"

Neither woman understood a word said by the Lieutenant, but they sure knew they had been dismissed. They bowed, backed away from the officer repeating, "*grazie, grazie*". Without another word, Mitchell picked up his paper and waved them towards the tent's exit flap.

The young man, no more than seventeen years old, pulled a pack of cigarettes from his blouse, lit it and blew a beautiful white smoke ring into the air, "I'm Cesare Romeo from Naples; Avelino, actually."

He admired his disappearing work of smoke and returned his pack of Chesterfields into his pocket without offering the ladies a cigarette and said, "You are mighty fortunate to be here. Yes, very lucky."

As they crossed the piazza, the two women were greeted with remarks and smiles from an assortment of military personnel. Several Italian *carabinieri* standing in a doorway were particularly obnoxious. The *carabinieri* were the King's guard and had been the first to jump to the allied cause when, in the summer of 1943, the Italian Marshall Badoglio sued for peace with the allies. They strutted about with a certain haughtiness, prompting Carla to say, "You'd think they are the ones who are winning the war."

Gio agreed and was tempted to make a derogatory remark, thought better of it, replied, "These animals, ogling and flattering two women wrapped in dirty wet coats, mud on their boots and needing two hours soaking in a tub are real heroes, aren't they? You wonder why the Americans took them in."

Cesare, lifted and pointed his longest finger at the Italians and in a very loud and clear voice said, "Don't let those dim-wits bother you. They are braver whistling at women than stalking the enemy."

The soldiers, with great delight, howled less than gentlemanly responses.

Gio answered with one word, "Idiots!"

Cesare stopped for a moment at the town's World War I monument; a rearing warrior steed sans rider. He said a sword-carrying general once straddled the horse. The general was nowhere to be seen. Carla commented that the monument was a symbol of a different war; albeit one that finished with the same results as the current one.

Gio added, "Ya! And a new general will find a new horse to ride. How long did you say you have been with the Americans?"

"I've come all the way up the boot with them, right after they landed at Anzio," he proudly crowed, "I was there in the beginning and now I'm here with them at the end. So far, I am still in one piece."

The ladies looked at each other; Gio raised her eyebrows and cast a skeptical wink towards Carla. Neither knew anything about Anzio or the war's progress up the boot, but they sure knew their young guide had been at the far rear of the advance.

"I am Giovanna Carboni and", Gio thinking it might not be a good idea to mention the Grandi name, "this is Carla Berti. We are from the little village of Sasso, up near Abetone, where I imagine the worst of it is going on right now."

"Lot of payback being doled out by the partisans up there; they'll soon be fighting each other rather than the Germans and the Fascists", Cesare wryly remarked.

Carla asked, "What do you do for the Americans?"

"They call me a grease monkey."

Gio, "What does that mean?"

Cesare chuckled, "It means "*una scimmia unto*."

Both women frowned, "Saviors or not, that's a shameful term."

"Not really. They call each other in the same way. The more they insult someone, the more they like them. And, ladies, insults or not, be thankful you are here with the Americans; you are going to eat a lot more than your services will be worth."

Gio, "What do you mean, "Our services?"

Again, Cesare chuckled, "No, no! That's not what I mean. You will need to help; either in the field kitchens or at the hospital tents." The young man, with a sense of authority, "The Germans will be throwing everything at them as they retreat north. Casualties already coming down from the up-mountain battles; and this is just the beginning of the advance."

Gio, "We are very tired; we haven't slept and Carla, as you can see, is with baby…"

Cesare interrupted, "I can see that, but orders are orders; hospital first then a place to sleep. I usually show you newcomers the kitchens and the field laundry area but I'll skip that part of the tour for now. Help is needed everywhere, but at this moment you probably are most needed by the doctors, nurses and medics, so Lt. Mitchell wants you to see the hospital first."

Gio started to respond but Carla softly said "I'm okay Gio; let's get it over with."

"You are about to fall over…"

Carla, "Hush up."

Gio shook her head and told Gigi to slow down. The man did not respond and, instead, appeared to quicken his step.

Gio, in an aside to Carla, "One more Italian idiot!"

Carla chuckling, "You mean grease monkey."

"Were you a mechanic down in Naples?" Gio asked.

Laughingly, "Mechanic? I was a fruit picker for a wealthy family from Rome. You know, oranges, lemons." A giggle, "Until I joined up with the Americans I had ridden in a car no more than a couple dozen times in my life."

"How did you ever manage to become a mechanic?"

"Well, at first, my job was to clean spark plugs and run around as a "looking for", that is, stealing spare parts from other units. I am good at acquiring things my captain needs."

Carla, "What is a spark plug?"

"In Italian, it is called a *candela* (candle); I guess because it helps ignite the motor."

He stopped, "Do either of you have any hospital experience?"

Gio giggling, "Well, if a fruit picker can be a mechanic, I can be a doctor. I have delivered dozens and dozens of lambs … "

Cesare's mood and tone of the conversation shifted. The young fruit picker quickly responding, "Have your fun ladies with me now, because it won't be so funny when you step through that door. I deal with grease and broken vehicle parts; the people working inside this tent deal with blood and broken body parts."

Gio, speaking in a subdued rapid fire manner, "I'm sorry. No, neither of us has any hospital experience. We are tired and worried. Carla is four months pregnant with child. The father and his young nephew are stuck behind enemy lines. My brother has gone back for them. Both men fought with the partisans; believe me, we are more than willing to help the Americans."

The "mechanic", seemingly mollified, changed the subject, and pointed out one of the town's two hotels, "This is *Albergo Bel Aria.* I'm told that before the war it was a very popular watering hole for the business and commercial people living in and around *Firenze*. It now serves as a soldier's barracks; Lt. Mitchell allows me to use one of the rooms as my own. It's better than the spark plug shed."

They arrived at the "hospital"; a large cross lay atilt on its roof; an inscription etched into a piece of concrete slab over the door reading, "St. Maria–1902 ..." , crowned the entrance way. The other half of the slab lay on the ground to the left, face down in homage to the destruction leveled against its mate.

Cesare threw a *"buon giorno"* towards several Italian civilians wearing U.S. Army fatigues and commented, "This was the school annex; thank the Lord they hit at night when the school was empty. The wounded are brought here for preliminary treatment then shipped south depending on their condition. There hasn't been much to do the past weeks, but, as I said, lately things are beginning to stir and the medics aren't getting much rest."

They entered a large hall fronting additional rooms towards the rear. Men and women wearing red-cross bands were attending to a dozen or so wounded men. The pungent aroma of medicine, blood, body odor and dust permeated the area. A hazy ray of sunshine attempted to lift the spirits of the occupants sitting or lying on their cots. There were no cries of pain, but every so often, low moans would break the eerie silence.

The two women would become very familiar with these surroundings in short order.

CHAPTER 14

SEEMS LIKE OLD TIMES

A dusting of snow crept through the shepherd hut's door as the new morning shivered its introduction to a new day. Michelle, trembling, reached into his pocket, brought out a small hard piece of bread, carefully broke in half and gave a share to his uncle, "I grabbed this when we left the house; a dozen times I have been tempted to eat it, but it will taste better for the waiting."

A morsel dropped to the floor, Michelle licked his index finger, stabbed the crumb and put it in his mouth, "Dessert. Now, if we could brew ourselves a nice *cappuccino*, we'd be set for the day."

Gianni laughed, carefully ate the tidbit, looked at his ankle and fully realized his flight to freedom was over. He was about to speak when Michelle stood to help Gianni to his feet, grunted, "Come on, Zio, let's get started, we have a long way to go."

"Mico said to wait."

"Mico said ... Mico said ... He's down there having his morning coffee and we are here with no food, a swollen ankle and a potential snow storm in the making…"

Gianni managed a smile.

Why are you smiling? You should be crying for Lord's sake!"

"A smile is a great weapon, Michelle".

"Ya, a great weapon alright. It's like a pig who thinks he is being fattened for its own benefit. Little does he know the bigger the grin, the sooner he is *prosciutto*."

Gianni's smile broadened; before attempting the first step of the day, he thought of last night's conversation, put his arm around young man's shoulder and for the first time, truly understood his nephew no longer was a boy playing at a game. He had become a man, a good person; someone he would want in the trenches; a man who would meet the challenges ahead.

"Given the way my ankle looks, I think you should return to Sasso, enter at night, and hide at *La Rimessa*; I'll wait for Mico and ..."

"Are you crazy? I'm not going anywhere without you. The situation has changed from yesterday. We can't wait for Mico; the daylight will make it easier for us; we've got to try going down towards the Americans ..."

Remaining silent about the possibility of walking into German patrols, "But ..."

"Uncle Gianni, shut up! No buts or ifs. You are hurting, so I am now in command!", the new senior officer declared with a smile. Gianni raised his right arm, palm forward, mimicking the Fascist salute saying, "Yes my Duce, it is as you say."

The light snow had turned into a gloomy, heavy mist as Michelle half-carried his uncle down the muddy, slippery terrain. Fifteen minutes later, Gianni suggested they stop for a rest. Sitting on the ground, their backs against a couple of beech trees. Gianni, eyes closed, commented that, thanks to the cold, the muddy terrain and intermittent rain, they would have a better chance at avoiding German patrols.

Michelle noticed one of his uncle's boot laces was missing and thought, "Obviously, the foot is so swollen he couldn't fit..."

Before he could finish his thought, Michelle lied, "Yes, we are fortunate and before long we will be safely behind the American lines."

Gianni, eyes closed, smiled, "Yep, just a few more hours."

A few moments later they heard a crunching sound to their left, Michelle reached for the rifle but a muddied black boot locked the piece to the ground.

In heavily accented Italian, "Get up you!" The boot slammed into Michelle's leg, "I said get up!"

Michelle stood, immediately recognized the uniform and insignia of a *Jager Division* officer, a special force dealing with mountain terrain combat; some of its men had been stationed in Sasso for a brief period.

Michelle, "We are from Sasso...."

"Shut up! You smell like a partisan piece of shit!"

In a staccato, machine gun pace Gianni interupted, "No! No! We are from Sasso! We boarded some of your comrades, members of the 114th. My mother, Beatrice Carboni, housed and cooked for you for nearly two years."

The officer, ignoring Gianni's plea, jabbed Michelle, "And who are you, piglet?"

Michelle knew his comments would hurt Gianni, answered, "I'm his nephew, Michelle Pasqua and you should know his brother is Lorenzo Grandi, head of the Fascist Party here in the Frignano. His wife is Carla Berti; German officers have lived in her house all last year. Some officers still sleep there."

The man lowered his rifle, "Where, then, are these two great friends of the German soldier going?"

Gianni lied, "We are desperate for food; we were hunting wild boars, I twisted my ankle and we are trying to get back to Sasso."

The soldier, giving Michelle a push, the lad stumbling to the ground, said in perfect Italian, "Let me see the rifle."

Steely gray eyes shot lightning bolts at Michelle as the officer grasped the old rifle, then turned to the rest of the squad, said something in German, causing the men to laugh. He sneered at the Italians, "Not even a *Jager* (hunter) like me could kill a wren with this antique, let alone a *cinghiale* (wild boar). For now, my Italian allies, this piece of junk is your salvation; even the least of your partisan friends would refuse to admit this relic is a weapon."

He slammed the old piece against the tree, breaking the barrel from the wooden stock, "Get up great friends of your German defenders. Get on your feet! We will head for Sasso so you can introduce us to all those good German friends you know down there."

A derisive chuckle, "We'll let the *Kommandant* determine if you are full of shit or spaghetti! Frankly, right now, you sure don't smell like a good ragout."

He spoke to his troopers again; their laughter indicated he must have made an accurate translation of his comment to the two Italians.

They headed back. No one, including Gianni, knew Michelle had his Lugar holstered in the backside of his trouser belt.

The long walk was an excruciating struggle for Gianni. His ankle was swollen to the size and color of a ripe eggplant; each step tormented him, the pain sheer torture. He continued walking oblivious to the exhaustion, barely aware of the direction they were heading.

The Germans, making a game of the situation, constantly prodded Michelle with their weapons, as he half carried his uncle toward Sasso. About an hour later it began raining again, two degrees lower it would have been falling as snow. Michelle slipped in the mud, fell and took Gianni down with him. The Germans were furious. Gianni smiled and started to right himself. With the Germans jostling and yelling, Michelle righted himself and pulled to his feet.

One of the soldiers, a thin skeleton with a stiletto nose not even a mother could love, jabbed Michelle quite violently, once again, causing him to stumble towards the ground. He extended both arms to lessen the impact of the fall and, to his dismay and Gianni's horror, the hidden Luger fell from his belt.

"Stiletto Nose," in German, "A pistol!! He's hiding one of our Lugers! You no good piece of crap!"

A kick to the boy's side. In Italian, "You son of a bitch!" Another kick. The sergeant stepped in screaming, "Get up! Both of you! I'm going to have you both hung in Sasso's town square!"

The two looked at one another other in silence. Limp smiles as the rain fell harder; holy water for two dead men walking.

CHAPTER 15

DEAD ONE KING—THEY'LL FIND ANOTHER

Mico made good progress and arrived at the shepherd hut at sundown. He rushed into the shelter fully expecting to find Gianni and Michelle.

"Empty!" He dashed outside and called out several times. No answer!

He was stunned! His first reaction, absolute fury, "Those two dimwits must have left for Cutigliano and I missed them on their descent." He hesitated a moment, ran back into the hut thinking, "Maybe they left a note…"

He kicked the table, "Nothing! Nothing!"

"Stupidi! Stupidi!" he screamed at the ceiling; it took great restraint not to punch the wall. He calmed, took a sip of water from his canteen and sat on a bench located at the back of the hut.

"There is no way I could have missed them if they proceeded towards the Allied lines. Gianni's swollen foot would have forced them to use the path; it is the only way they could make their way down."

He was beside himself, "So, either they are in partisan hands or the Germans captured them." He hesitated, "or they are trying to make their way back to Sasso. If they are, and if the Germans are still in or around Sasso, the two will be asking for a quick trip north … at best. If the Americans have taken the town, squads of partisans, including my old comrades will be there. Those bastards would surely salivate deliberating the proper punishment for Gianni's insubordination."

He mulled the possibilities, "Who knows when they left? If they left at day-break, hobbling or not, they could be near Sasso right now. There is no way I can help them if they are down there."

He took a deep breath, "And, if I search up here, where in the hell am I going to look? I'll end up who knows where. And how long can I go on without food?"

"Further, what the hell can I do, Germans or no Germans?" He kicked the bench, an uncontrolled sob, a sigh and finally admitted his worst fear, "There is also the distinct possibility they are no longer alive. Right?"

He laid down where Gianni had slept the night before. He tried to calm down. He was so tired. So frustrated Gianni and Michelle had not waited. He gazed at the ceiling to reconsider his options, closed his eyes and, instead, floated into reflections of his time with the partisans.

He thought about some of many other difficult decisions he had to make. He felt a tremor remembering his battle field decisions where his men's lives depended on the correct option. Many, many times he made decisions without much information. A leader took those risks when action was called for. A leader could not opt to forego deciding, for that would be a decision. You must plan. And you do. Over and over, again and again you make decisions and thus, people die. Your men die. Innocents die. And another bit of you dies. Over and over, again and again, a small part of what you were dies.

You also obey commands from a higher voice. It is your duty to obey. And you obey. Sometimes knowing it is a despicable order that will result in the death or maiming of innocents and your own men. But you obey and for a lifetime the stains remain within you.

A sigh, a sip of water, he arose, walked to a nearby tree and sat. He was positive the surrounding rocks and trees were staring at him and asking why he wasn't taking any action.

He responded, "I can't do anything until morning and even then, where do I start? Damn idiots, why couldn't they have waited?"

Ignoring his surroundings and the cold, he laid back, cradled his head in his arms and looked upward at a sky promising darkness and more rain, "Got to wait 'til morning; can't do anything for those two now."

After a short while, he rose and went back into the hut to sleep. But, try as he might, sleep did not arrive. Instead, he started philosophizing again, "Peace. Ah! Peace. What will it be like? Flowers will grow again; gardens will flourish. We'll walk down to the river, unafraid. Children will sleep in their beds with windows open, unafraid of bombings, night raids and the glowing reds and yellows launched from far off cannon fire.

Little boys will throw rocks at birds or try skip-skipping them across the river and we will listen to old men talking as they sun themselves on one of the piazza benches. They will be speaking, in our dialect, about the state of world's affairs; each with a firm conviction theirs' is the correct point of view. Except for a few, the men will be disinclined to discuss their war-time experiences; even if their scars are there for all the world to see."

Sleep continued to elude him; he turned over, "Bystanders will see the war memorial standing tall in the center of the piazza; the replica of a once famous general, holding a sword and leading the charge. However, they likely won't notice the listing of new names; husbands, fathers, sons who lost their lives fighting the enemy, now an ally. New names etched into a stone of short term memories."

He sat up, "And practically no attention will be given to the plaque listing names from the First World War. The memorial to those poor bastards who lost their lives in a war against our recent ally who was then a brutal enemy."

He sighed, thought about Michelle, "And the young will enthusiastically talk about their visions for the future. In a babble of words, they will be telling the world how to correct my generation's errors. They will talk about how the old made things bad and, once we are gone, great and better things will be accomplished."

The thought sent shivers through his body, "But didn't we say the same things? Too many went hungry; we were going to eradicate hunger, instead, matters did not improve; in fact, they worsened in many areas. For, even in little, lonely Sasso, we had the same youthful enthusiasm and ideals. But the interceders had different intentions and the old refrains, with new slogans, were repeated. Our generation replaced horse and saber, barbed wire and trenches with sophisticated machines and weapons resulting in a larger and more devastating war. A world war that turned our generation's peace efforts into a pathetic joke."

He stared into the darkness, "I wonder what deception will be played on the next generation? Will they recognize and condemn the new maestros? Or, like us, will they argue with one another even as their lives are being torn apart right in front of their eyes?"

His last thought before finally asleep, "Hopefully, they will do better than we did."

A gust of wind spanked Mico's face, awaking him from a deep sleep; for a moment he had no idea as to time or place. He bounced to his feet, rushed out the door and surveyed his surroundings, "Damn door blew open, lucky I didn't freeze to death."

He was startled at the movement of a huge hare jumping from behind one of the boulders. Mico reached for his gun as the hare sat, stared at the big man and scratched its nose. A chuckle, "He's thumbing his nose at me!" The long-eared creature, sensing danger, ran a half circle to a small ledge, stopped and again pawed his nose.

"That *s.o.b.* knows I can't shoot; the sound would invite hunters of a different kind. Who are you rabbit? One of my long-gone relatives in their second life? Or are you a spy for all your edible cousins still living in this hell?"

The hare thumbed his nose again, jumped behind the ledge and disappeared. "Maybe it's waiting for peace, too. If so, rabbit, you are mistaken. Peace will bring hunters of a different kind to our mountain and you and I will be prime targets."

The sun, deciding it would hurl its warmth in another direction, hid behind a grey shroud and left Mico shivering once again, "Enough of hares and hopes, it's time to move."

After eating another foul-smelling American ration, he considered his options, "The two girls are safe in Cutigliano; Michelle and Gianni certainly didn't try limping through enemy territory towards the American lines. Their only option was risking a return to Sasso."

He kicked a stone, "...and that's my only alternative, too."

He turned to pick up his cap, noticed a shiny object laying under a tree a short distance away. He walked towards the tree and saw his sister's old rifle lying on the ground.

Broken into two pieces!

An empty German Knackebrot (150 gr.) field ration box!

A touch of panic! Heartbeat thumping! The worst had happened. Gianni and Michelle were in German hands.

Or they were dead.

CHAPTER 16

AUF WEIDERSEHEN! ARRIVEDERCI! AND GOOD-BYE!

Down in Sasso, Mother Spring was announcing her arrival with her annual symphony, a driving Apennine rainstorm. She picked up her cache somewhere in the Mediterranean, carried the accumulation up and over the Apennine wall, rested for a while behind a dark curtain, and then began spewing a deluge as it began its decent. The wind, a cagey accomplice, arrived on cue from the north, pelting the poor innocents with slanted blown sheets of needles; drenching them to their shivering, frost bitten skins. The performances, which could last days, were not easily forgotten as the holes in the frozen terrain served as excellent receptacles for newly created mud-baths.

Sasso did not have a jail so, upon arrival, Gianni and Michelle were quartered in the town's one room post office building. The lashing rain, playing a staccato rat-a-tat-tat against the barred window pane, served as a perfect lullaby for the two men, as each fell into a deep sleep.

Gianni dreamed he was being kissed; he felt soft, cold hands stroking his cheek. He saw Mico, Gio and Michelle cheerfully beaming as he embraced his Carla. An American soldier approached, said something in English and shook him forcefully. He opened his eyes and stared into the scrubby face of a young blond man wearing the uniform of German infantry; his first thought was to ask if he was experiencing a dream or a nightmare.

A rifle barrel poked him in the ribs, "Get up! Wake up!" It was reality and reality was a living nightmare!

Gianni grimaced, sat up and, upon seeing the bluish-maroon colors of his swollen foot, confirmed he wasn't dreaming. The pain was real; the beginning of another nightmare. His world had not righted itself; he was, once again, in the hands of the enemy.

"Where is my nephew?"

Another sharp poke in Gianni's rib cage, "Not your business! Shut your mouth! We will be asking the questions, you partisan scum."

An officer entered, smiled and lobbed a Lugar towards Gianni, "Recognize this?"

Gianni's heart was about to burst.

"Bring him in!"

Needle Nose shoved Michelle through the door, hands tied, he fell to the floor. The lad had a swollen black eye and dried blood on his face.

"You bastards!"

A slap across Gianni's face.

Needle nose, "Your young friend is going to face more than a slap on the face; he is going to feel the mighty hand of true German justice!" The two Germans marched out of the room, Needle Nose departing with an all-knowing wicked smile, slammed the door and was gone.

Yesterday had been horrific but, sadly, Gianni knew today or tomorrow would be worse. A dreadful emotion overwhelmed him; a thunder bolt of panic stabbed his senses knowing he was going to be responsible for the death or the death camps for his sister's only child.

Gianni looked down at his young nephew, silently thought, "Luger or no Luger, this time we pay the price. If they don't shoot us today, it's the concentration camps tomorrow. Easy. Careful what you say. He is still a boy."

Tears blurred his vision as he heard, "I'm sorry about the Luger, Gianni."

Gianni quickly recovered. "It is what it is Michelle. If there wasn't a Luger, they would have found some other excuse."

He hobbled to help Michelle, "I'm OK Uncle Gianni. I have the skin and stubbornness of a mule. When whipped, I just get more stubborn."

Knowing the boy had to be thinking about a death sentence, he tried to console the lad, "The war is about over and "Needle Nose" isn't in charge; the Nazi's need laborers, so prepare for a long trip to Germany."

He stared at the boy's bruised body. Yesterday's maroons now had a touch of yellow, a new addition to yesterday's rainbow of black, blue streaks and brilliant fresh reds.

"How badly you hurt, Michelle?"

"Sticks and stones may break my bones but …" a short laugh, "Your ankle?"

"Ripe! What happened to you?"

"We were both asleep. They yanked me out of bed and took me to the main reception area."

"I didn't hear a thing."

Through a swollen lip, "Ya, you were snoring pretty good. Anyway, they wanted to know about the Luger. Every time I gave an answer they thanked me with a punch or a kick! Where did I get it? Slap! You killed one of our soldiers! A punch and a kick! You stole it from one of our brave men! Kick! That damn Needle Nose was there enjoying my party."

With a bit of difficulty, he shifted his body, "This morning an officer came in, stopped the festivities and ordered me back here. In one piece but with improvements."

The two men looked at each other; Gianni grappling with the urge to cry. They both smiled; understanding smiles of respect and love for each other. No other words were spoken. Nothing else needed to be said. Each lost in his own thoughts as they awaited their fate.

A short while later, a soldier dressed in the wet uniform of the Italian Fascist Republican army, brusquely entered the room, gave Michelle a shove and, without a word, motioned them towards the door. The man never looked them in the face.

As they stepped into a light rain, two German privates immediately grabbed them by the elbows, marched them through the mud towards a waiting truck and, with great difficulty, rammed the two injured men unto the vehicle. Six other haggard souls greeted the newcomers.

With his ankle continuing to pound for attention, Gianni looked at the poor petrified slob sitting across. The man's lips quivered, fear etched into his expression. Gianni would have liked to extend words of encouragement, but all he could offer was a rueful, sardonic smile.

One of the men, "P.P." (Pietro from Pavolo), sitting at the back, was assuring the others, "No way they are going to kill us; they need our backs for the ongoing glory of their 3rd Reich, we are on our way to Germany. Yep, we are going north..."

He was interrupted by a grizzly old man wrapped in a filthy blue blanket, "I wouldn't be too happy about that "P.P.", a shot in the head might be a better alternative."

Another voice, "Both of you, shut up!" The men became silent as the rattle of the motor confirmed the prisoner's inevitable dark future.

With their being moved to the truck, Gianni became confident they were being shipped to the camps; if it weren't for Hitler's need for laborers, the hard heads, now in full retreat, would have solved the prisoner problem with eight bullets and a goodbye.

The prisoners watched long lines of German transports, including motorcycles with little cabs attached to their sides, scooting ahead of the heavier vehicles. Each cyclist was accompanied by a second man sitting in the cab holding a carbine at the ready position. Armored cars, reconnaissance cars, jeep-like cars, troop transports and assortments of big weaponry continued chugging through Sasso's mud. All of them were heading towards Modena, the railroad center and major gateway to the highways towards Austria.

For the past week, they had been retreating from Italy to be re-deployed to the homeland so their leader, Adolph Hitler, could continue to fritter away additional Wehrmacht lives. In April 1945, Hitler's best were no longer singing *Deutschland Uber Alles*; instead, in quiet and somber moods, they hurled blasphemies towards their recent allies and the "crappy Italian muck" impeding their withdrawal.

Gianni assumed their convoy was low priority and would be among the last to go. The delay might provide an opportunity to free Michelle. He was finished but perhaps he could start a row of some kind and Michelle could escape.

"Maybe I could ..."

Suddenly sporadic gunfire was heard. It was coming from the south and it was quite close. The guards tensed, unshouldered their weapons; troops shuffled at a faster pace, traffic controllers started yelling at the drivers, "Faster, faster! Get your fat asses moving or you'll leave them here in "La Bel' Italia!" Above the roar of hundreds of motors Gianni could hear the urgent pleas, *"Schnell! Schnell!"*

A few moments later the world exploded! Incoming shells sprayed the mountain side above the piazza; huge boulders, dirt and stones began rolling towards the trucks and the buildings.

The Americans were close! Again, cries of *"Schnell"* echoed against the sound of vehicles roaring through an unusual combination; a haze of dust and a quagmire of mud.

It seemed an eternity but the shelling lasted only a few minutes. The guards came out from under the trucks, some laughing, some rather sober. Those imprisoned aboard the prisoner transports thanked their maker. Once again, one's fate determined by the gods' roll of the dice. Gianni and Michelle included.

Huge boulders now blocked parts of the road; some having rolled and crashed into a few vehicles and into several houses fronting the road. The prisoners were taken off the trucks and were added to the cadre clearing the road. Gianni, with Michelle's help, feigned effort; in the noise, confusion and in the fear of additional bombardments, no one noticed.

"Michelle, I'm going to make as if I am going to escape, when I do..." Gianni whispered.

"No! No! Don't be so damn stupid…"

"I can…"

A snarl, "I'm not running! I hurt everywhere and I'm not leaving you!"

"It's your only chance."

A guard nudged Michelle with his rifle, *"Arbeit! Halt die schnauze!"*

Michelle and Gianni stopped their conversation and, with much effort, began rolling a large boulder as the guard walked away, "You run Gianni, I run. That way we both need not worry about the camps."

Gianni heaved the boulder, another lightning bolt up his leg, "OK Michelle. OK."

In a matter of minutes the road was cleared, the captives returned to their trucks and the German exodus resumed. Gianni patted Michelle but words escaped him – there was nothing left to say.

An hour or more passed and the prisoners continued to wait. The heavy armor had moved on and it appeared only supply equipment and the prisoner trucks were all that remained.

Requests for water were ignored, making the wait excruciating. The prisoners dozed, some hoping and praying the Americans would not begin firing again, others quietly seeking remembrances and memories of the good "used to be."

Gianni was wrapped in memories of Carla and their baby when he heard a woman's voice.

Pleading! Begging! It sounded like his mother's voice. Was he dreaming? Was he fading into some sort of a coma?

Michelle, leaning out of the truck, screamed, "It's Nonna and my mother!"

The women were trying to approach the truck but were being held back by two guards. The grief-stricken Nilde, wailing for her son, unnerved everyone, German's included. Beatrice, wearing a widow's black dress protected by an everyday kitchen apron, groveled on the ground, her rough hands held in a prayerful pose. She pled with one of the German soldier who merely smiled and tried to push her away.

A German officer approached the truck, ordered the guard to stop pushing the poor soul at his feet, "Signora Beatrice, how are you?"

She recognized the young Lieutenant who, a few days before, was the uninvited guest at the family's Easter meal when he shared Beatrice's horse meat dinner and a bit of her liquor.

The officer dismissed the guards, helped Beatrice to her feet and pointed towards the truck, "Ah, what have we there? I'm told there are captured partisans on their way to help the Deutschland." A mischievous smile, "My list here includes two very familiar partisan names."

"No! Again, No! My Lieutenant!" she noticed he was now a captain, without hesitation she continued, "Excuse me, Capitan, I see you have been promoted."

The young warrior, smiling at the woman's courage, "Thank you."

"My son and nephew were trying to hide from the war and, as you can see..."

"Incredible! Inconceivable! How in the hell did you get so close to these trucks?"

"We heard prisoners..."

A smile, "Never mind." In a quiet voice and in perfect Italian, the officer interrupted the desperate Beatrice, "Keep quiet. Get away from here! Now!"

The women didn't move.

Briskly, with a touch of anger, "I said get the hell out of here!"

A smile, quietly,"I'll handle your two heroes. Leave it to me."

Beatrice, with tears of thanks cascading down her cheeks, turned to the blond Adonis and, prayerlike, whispered, "*Danke. Danke.* I'll never forget you." She smiled at Gianni and Michelle, took Nilde's hand and walked away from the truck.

The officer ordered the guard to let Gianni and Michelle dismount. He drew his Lugar, turned to Gianni and Michelle, pushed them back into the post office cell, and quietly said, "Just stay where you are; don't move from this room."

Looking at Gianni's ankle he added, "You wouldn't get very far, anyway. Just sit tight and remember, not all of us are animals."

In a nearly inaudible voice, "The last vehicles will be pulling out as soon as I give the order; the Allies are less than a kilometer or two away and coming up quickly. So, I repeat, don't go out until we are gone."

"With those black eyes, you look like a prize fighter who didn't win the prize. So, I will give you one. He reached into his overcoat, withdrew and handed a Lugar to Michelle, "You are a fortunate and blessed young man and you can thank your grandmother for my indulgence. You should be standing against a wall and eating dirt at this very moment."

Michelle was astounded, recovered, took the weapon, thanked the officer and, through a very swollen mouth, quipped, "Is it loaded?"

Gianni choked as the Captain shook his head as he walked towards the door; turned and in a stern voice, "I repeat, stay inside until we are gone."

Once outside, the officer walked towards Beatrice and, over the roar of the last trucks, shouted in a loud, coarse manner, "I ordered you to return to your homes. Now get the hell out of here or you'll be on the trucks!"

The officer removed his glasses, put his hand on Beatrice's shoulder and in a near whisper said, "You can see your men as soon as we leave."

Beatrice about to collapse, reached for the officer, "Captain I…."

"You know you could have left me a swallow of your schnapps."

He drew back, smiled, clicked his heels, saluted again, saying, "*Auf Weidersehen*, my friends, *Auf Weidersehen*."

Ordering the guards to mount the back of the truck, the officer walked through the mud, looked back at Beatrice one last time, entered the cab, sat next to the driver, leaned out the window and waved.

A friend who was the enemy was gone.

CHAPTER 17

THE WARRIOR PHILOSOPHER

After a fitful night's sleep and a worrisome down-hill struggle, Mico managed to reach the Sasso outskirts without incident. He then hid in the burnt shell of the house from which they had started their journey two days before. He was wet, cold, hungry and deeply troubled. He had heard sporadic gun fire and hoped it was a positive action and not another partisan raid on his poor little town.

The rain and mud probably slowed the American advance so he decided to wait until dark, then go to his mother's house and see if she or Beatrice had any news about Gianni and Michelle.

He lay down on the hard floor, scratched at his new beard, wondering if the shepherd's hut also had been a haven for scoundrels known as *pidocchio* (lice). The odor of smoke permeated the dark room; shattered glass decorated the floor and the staircase leading to the bed rooms which no longer existed.

Mico recalled German troops had set fire to the old house in a retaliation of some sort. He had been with the partisans and was sure his group had hit back in some way, but couldn't remember how they retaliated.

"I must have a warped mind; I can't remember how we hit back." he scratched himself again, "War is truly a farce. One big joke. Somebody kills somebody; then somebody's friend kills the first somebody and the battle escalates. Then, in a relatively short time, when the war is over – is it ever over? - the enemy of the first somebody killed, has become a friend; whereupon, the two new friends go after the old friend! And then, the absolute irony: a few short years pass and the historians, often writing lies, magnify or diminish the truth to enhance their particular point of view."

A stomach seeking attention wasn't listening to Mico, it cried out for food. He patted his belly, "Ya, old friend, I hear you. Just awhile longer. Hold on, we are almost home."

Trying not to think about food, he recommenced his one-man debate concerning his war time actions. "I don't know how many men I killed. Did I kill for my comrades in arms? My duty as a soldier to obey? Perhaps. My political commitment? No, certainly not that. To do my duty to help rid the plague that befell my Italy?"

A sardonic, scornful laugh, "What in the hell am I talking about? There is no sense to it all, no justification; it was simply kill or Mico gets killed. Not for country, not for our leaders, not for future generations. I killed because I didn't want my own ass shot off! Admit it, "It was your ass you were protecting."

Then in a quiet, pensive manner, he looked at the skin creases forming the letter "M" in each palm; his mother and wife and their suffering came to mind once again. A sigh, "My family and my country. There are the most important reasons for me to have killed another human being." A huge weight of guilt overcame him as he whispered, "They must be the true reasons for my actions! They must be!"

A flutter of wind brought him back to the present. He peeked out the window. The light had disappeared; he must have been day-dreaming or napping. There were no stars. A light rain. A breeze had carried a light mist from the broken window, seeking and finding his coat and trousers. He was wet and cold.

He thought about his family again. The beautiful and warm days on the French Riviera – palm trees guarding the old cobbled streets, flowers everywhere. He sighed, fantasizing he could see his little girl running towards him, followed by his wife Suzi, laughing, calling his name. A great sense of satisfaction enveloped him as he found, for a moment, happiness inside rather than the tormented reality of the moment.

Somewhere a dog was barking at the full moon. The only problem being the moon was hidden behind dark clouds. Mico shivered, "The beast must be reacting to the magnets in the heavens, those mysterious powers causing ocean tides to ebb and flow while, nurturing the insanity of human kind."

Moving away from the window, he laid down under the staircase. His stomach growling again, he whispered to the wall, "It won't be long now; it won't be long…"

He fell asleep in mid-sentence.

The growl of heavy motors awakened him in immediate full alert mode. He hunched down at the broken window and saw the sun peeking through the pervasive rain clouds that had delivered additional misery to his search for Gianni and Michelle. He saw the huge movement of military vehicles steadily moving north, towards the provincial capital of Modena. The Germans, he surmised, were in full retreat, "This damn war is about over. Today? Surely tomorrow! No sense walking into the retreat. Man, I'm hungry; but better to starve than to walk into the war again."

So, despite the fear the enemy might want to investigate his hiding place, he decided to remain hidden. He assumed the forces of the once mighty Third Reich were no longer interested in conquering; they were concerned only with stepping on the gas pedal and getting out of Italy.

The procession of the retreating forces continued unabated for most of the day. Not daring to move out of house, he listened to the beautiful symphony of the German retreat; the rumble and meshing of gears as trucks, armored cars and troop transports chugged north.

Again, talking to his favorite wall, "There sure are a lot of hardheads in the world. Where did they all come from? They spread their poison in Russia; all over Europe! In Africa! Why Africa? And, with the blessings of our great Leader, they contaminated La Bella Italia. Go home you bastards! Get the hell out of Italy and stay away!"

With his aching stomach still vying for attention, he sat on the floor and began a prayer, "Lord, I don't bother you very often and I sure don't deserve to be heard, but I pray for my little family; I pray Gianni and Michelle are safe." He felt like giggling, "Yes, it's me, Domenico Carboni, who has shunned you for so long, pleading for the lives of those two. Please Lord, deliver them into good hands. Please Lord!"

The ex-partisan, looking at the sky with a bit of joviality, asked, "Will He listen, would He respond to prayers from a Communist? Would He answer the prayers of a true sinner?"

He felt a new and strange emotion and the need to offer more prayers. He again thought about his family in France, his sister Gio, his mother, Carla and her baby, "Lord, protect them all. Please Lord, protect them."

The mighty partisan warrior didn't realize his head was bowed.

The day refused to pass and the challenge to remain quiet and hidden for such a long period was exasperating. His stomach was now aching, too weak to even growl but, ever the warrior, he controlled his fighting instincts, dismissed the pain and, once again, nodded off.

He was awakened by the sound of several short explosions. Risking discovery, he exited the house. Across the river, he could see smoke rising from what had to be the piazza area.

"The Americans are shelling Sasso!" he gasped, "Good Lord, they are bombarding the town!"

There was one more explosion, then absolute quiet.

Once again, caught in a most difficult, excruciating situation, he went back into his hiding place to consider his next move.

It didn't take long for his military side to win the battle over his heart. There was no action he could take that would be of benefit anyone – bombs or no bombs—he had to wait until dark before moving. To go now would be a foolish risk. He sat down, closed his eyes, patted his belly and nodded off as he awaited the sunset.

A faint melody stirred him; he awoke and went to the window and screamed, "The bells! They are ringing in Sasso!" An array of flaming emotions streaked through his body, "They are gone! The hardheads are gone!"

Tears of happiness streamed down his face, he did a polka step and continued shrieking at the walls. He could hear bells peeling from several churches located throughout the nearby hills. He peeked out the door, no one in sight. He stopped, tears now flooding his cheeks as he grasped the reality that the war was finally over! Suddenly he had an urge to run, he burst from the burnt house, sprinting like a madman towards the town, yelling to the sky, "It's over! Good Lord in heaven it is finally over. Peace at last!"

He crossed the bridge and headed toward his house, *Il Cassone*. The church bell continued its joyful song as he entered the town square. He saw dozens of familiar faces; ignoring the mud and debris, old men hugged one another; women, dressed in blacks and browns, hands clasped, pointed to the heavens; children, dressed in heavy, muddied clothing, held chocolate bars and screamed thanks to the American troops entering the town.

He was home free! He was home! He could hardly breathe for the excitement of the moment!

Mico stopped, absorbed the sight. More tears appeared as he felt a huge affection for the celebrating neighbors he had known since childhood. For a moment, these poor innocents ignored thoughts of desperation and, for some, the loss of loved ones. The Americans had created Christmas in April!

He declined a bit of the *red* offered by one of the celebrants and returned to the realty of the moment. He rapidly crossed the piazza, climbed Matinelli's path and, with his heart thumping at a rapid rate, rushed into his house.

Empty! No one answered his call! A familiar foreboding sent a frightening shiver throughout his body!

"Where are they? Good Lord, where are they?" He kicked off his muddy boots, opened a cupboard, found a slab of cheese, which he devoured in a micro-second. He then raced up to his bedroom and quickly changed into dry clothing and shoes. A much-needed bath would have to wait.

He ran out and rushed to *La Rimessa,* crashed open the door and saw one of the greatest sights of his life time. The war was now truly over!

Beatrice soaking Gianni's foot in a pail! Michelle, adorned with two black eyes, a puffy lip and a swollen nose, holding a glass of red in his hand! Nilde and his mother, Gina, sitting at the fire place!

Screams of joy!

Gina stood and raced into her son's arms repeating over and over, "Mico, my Mico, my Mico!"

The warrior Mico, the man with the partisan nom di Guerra "Ivan", a man who had stared into the face of death many, many times, failed to suppress an audible gasp, tightly hugged his mother and, once again, broke into tears.

Freed from his mother's grasp, he turned towards the others, a tearful smile, "Gio and Carla are fine; they are safe in American hands. I left them there so I could go on a search for these two idiots."

Michelle raised his glass "Long live the idiots. Especially those with German bruises tattooed all over their bodies!"

"You, Michelle, are *scemo (idiot) numero uno.* You should have waited… and saved yourself from German generosity."

Michelle glowed, again gave a toast, "To be insulted by a hero of the resistance is the highest of compliments."

Mico, nodding his approval of Michelle's sly insult asked, "What happened?"

"The *Wehrmacht* played "*futball"* and used my body as the field of play."

Michelle and Gianni quickly recounted their down-mountain experience, omitting a few of the sordid details out of respect for the ladies.

Mico recounted the "Brazilian Episode", then added, "With the roads still a risk and with Carla in a sensitive way, it's probably best to wait a few days before going down to Cutigliano."

Gianni interrupted, "I'm going down there tomorrow!"

Mico, "The hell you are! Look at your ankle; what will you be able to contribute if we encounter stragglers or whatever else is on the road, including mines the hard heads probably planted?"

Gianni scowled, started to object, but Mico, shaking his head, interrupted, "Further, what can you to do? Walk into the advancing troops? Don't you think they have a heavier job than making way for a love-sick broken down Italian?"

No one said a word.

"We wait a few days, commandeer a car of some sort and then we talk about going for Carla and Gio. And, as I said before, they are better off than we are; more food, some heat and the entire American 5th army protecting them."

Mico smiled, "Think man, think!"

Gianni remained silent; he knew his cousin was right, once again.

Scratching his beard, Mico turned towards the huge fireplace, "Aunt Beatrice, instead of wasting your time on your poor baby's foot, could you give me something to eat before I starve to death?"

"Only if you wash and shave off that damn beard!"

CHAPTER 18

NEL' VINO, VERITÀ

The news of Sasso's liberation reached Cutigliano the next day. Carla wanted to leave immediately but, upon the advice of both Gigi and the American officer, the ladies decided to wait until confirmation of safe passage could be assured. Gigi told them the officer had indicated he would try to have someone check on their family, adding, "But, don't count on any news; you know there still is a war going on."

Both ladies could only raise their eyebrows in response.

Gio and Carla spent the next day familiarizing themselves with the hospital area, then plunged into their assignments; changing beds, disinfecting, washing, sanitizing and scrubbing everything from tables to the coarse wooden floors.

One day led to the next and with the heavy work load the week passed quickly. The *montenaro* will-to-work mentality immediately endeared them to both the American wounded and the medical staff. Their contributions were needed and the Americans showed their generosity, showering them with a variety of canned foods, cigarettes and much, much chocolate; the first they had tasted in nearly two years. Even Lieutenant Mitchell asked about the adequacy of the old hotel sleeping accommodations asking, "Have you made friends with the bed bugs, yet?"

They had no idea what he was talking about but understood the word "hotel" answering, *"Grazie, grazie. Hotel va bene; molto bene."*

"The American officer is cute."

"Now, now, Gio. Remember you are wearing boots and he is not your type, anyway."

"Í didn't know I had a type." A slight hesitation, "Exactly what is my type?"

A giggle, "How about the Brazilian? Seemed to me he was very interested."

"That big galoot! So full of it!" A hesitation, "Probably won't see him again, anyway."

Another giggle and a slap to Gio's behind, "You never know, Gio, you never know."

The two women were elated to contribute, but continually asked Gigi if there was any news of their family and/or permission to hook a ride with the troops going north. The responses were always the same, "No news but just a couple more days, a couple more days and it will be okay for you to leave. Patience ladies, the war isn't over yet" or "It is still too dangerous and, more importantly, tons of equipment and thousands of troops are clogging the rutted, muddy road leading to Sasso. We can't put you in harm's way, right?"

And so, they waited.

Gio, on one of the most beautiful days of the early spring, was at the outdoor fountain busily washing sheets, thinking about her family when an American Jeep skidded to a stop behind her. She was startled, and about to direct some choice language at the idiot driving the vehicle. The car was still moving as a big man, sporting a red beret tilted at a jaunty angle, jumped to the ground, smiling like a child sneaking a peek at a hidden gift a week before Christmas.

"It's me, Bruno Nasciente, your Brazilian savior! I've looked for you all day, and finally here you are!"

Gio's heart fluttered, put hands on hips and responded, "What the hell do you want?"

"I come to say *"ciao"* to my beautiful Italian friend."

"Ya, you came to say *"ciao"*, alright."

Undeterred, the big Brazilian glided his hand across his huge outlandish mustache, reached into the jeep and produced a bottle of wine and two treasures, a loaf of real bread and a small *prosciutto*. "For the attention of someone so beautiful, I have liberated from the vilest of Fascist houses these treasures which, like the Magi, I lay at your feet in homage."

"You are so full of crap..."

"Ah, you are so shrewd, but I cannot be dissuaded. Come with me, we will drive towards Porretta, and in the middle of hell we will find a peaceful Eden. For a moment, we will forget the trials and travails of our generation and I'll…"

"You've been into the red again; where did you steal the Jeep?"

"Borrowed, my lady, borrowed. Borrowed from the rich."

Carla approached the couple, giggling a bit when she recognized Nasciente, "Corporal, what a pleasant surprise. Have you come to drive us back up the mountain?"

"Actually, I have thoughts of going in the opposite direction. I have asked your cousin to join me to celebrate the glory of this beautiful Sunday afternoon..."

"I'm not her cousin, it isn't Sunday and anyone looking for Eden in this hell-hole is more than a touch "coo-coo", interjected Gio. Without hesitation, she continued, "However, we have not tasted good bread and prosciutto for a century, so I'll accept your invitation provided Carla acts as *"la mia angela custode"* (my guardian angel).

The man was stumped; there was no stroking of the moustache as he replied, "Damn Italian women; you are so unfair." However, the big oaf regained his composure, laughed at the retort, bowed to the ladies, opened the side of the vehicle and said, "OK, jump in, we are off to Porretta."

Carla shook her head in disbelief, "Are you both crazy? I know the roads from Cutigliano to Porretta; they are like a web of winding snakes, twisting over rough mountain terrain. They are rutted, infested with partisan units and/or German strays and you want to go on a picnic! Jesus almighty you are a real Brazilian *cuckoo*!"

Carla turned to the south and pointed upwards towards a jagged landscape of gloomy gray slate intertwined with splotches of dull-white snow breathing their last gasps before their complete meltdown. They could see the dark remains of burned pine trees, denuded by American strafing of German gun positions a few months before, were ugly reminders of the carnage of those recent battles.

Carla continued, "Look to the southern slopes; those towards Lizzano. Not even the serene blue sky of this beautiful day can hide the harm man lays on man. How do you think those trees were turned into burnt skeletons?"

She kept staring at the burnt mountain side for a few moments, her composure changed, "We visited Lizzano once; a beautiful, quiet town. Its tranquil mountain faced the sun, welcoming us to partake in a good Tuscan meal", she hesitated, swallowed a tear. "There was an accordionist playing, tapping his foot to the beautiful sounds of old *"stornelli"* (folk songs) being sung by the local Caruso", a pause, "my husband actually was civil to me during those few days."

She stared at the southern mountains for a second, then, another abrupt mood change, "You want to know why the Apennines are no longer beautiful?"

Gio and Nasciente's remained silent. Not noticing the two were holding hands, Carla continued, "No? Well, I'll tell you anyway!"

"First, our great leaders promised we would own the world. Then, our northern friends talked us into killing ourselves in never heard-of places. Then, our leader burped and the entire *polenta* was turned into horse manure. Next, our former enemies arrived in our mountains, delivering death and destruction in their attempts to liberate us. Then, our former friends, who are now our enemies, answer in kind, thereby denuding what remained."

Carla, in an accusatory pose, challenged the couple, "So what do we have? We have nothing; actually, less than nothing and tomorrow some *sunnava-bitch* will take the nothing away, too!"

Gio knew Carla's diatribe was, in part, due to her bitter feelings towards her husband, Lorenzo, the Fascist consigliore. Looking towards the mountains and thinking of those long-ago days had provoked bitter memories of a marriage without love; a partnership that never existed.

Carla shivered and mumbled, "My Fascist husband is dead; he is where he belongs; in hell's highest, sizzling flames!" She paused, took a deep breath and looked away from the wasted mountainside, "I'm sorry, old memories aren't always pleasant."

Gio in a soft consoling tone, "Don't let the devil eat away at your good fortune. Lorenzo is dead. You have Gianni. And you are going to be the mother of his baby. Carla, we have survived the war and we have a nice future ahead of us. Don't let a ghost come between you and Gianni."

Carla remained quiet as Gio gave her a hug, "It would be foolish to do so and you are no fool."

Carla gave Gio a kiss on the cheek, turned and, with a huge smile, faced the two turtle doves, "Well, I don't know if I am a fool or not and I don't know about a bright future, but I do know you should not go on any *"peek-neek"*. Look at you two canaries holding hands not knowing you are already living in a cage. You think you are free to go picnicking? Do you think you'll find an accordion player down there? What the hell is the matter with you two? *Mamma mia*! Gio, you aren't going, hear me?"

Gio, having experienced Carla's quick mood changes for the first time, held her composure, hid her disappointment and patted her friend's tummy, "Active little angel in there Carla; calm down. You are right, no sense taking such risks at this point."

She gave a coy smile to the big man, "But, I have an idea; let's go to the hotel and have our picnic; it is a beautiful day but it still is too cold to eat *al fresco*, anyway."

Ex-Sergeant, now Corporal, Bruno Nasciente jumped to his feet, smiled, "I think that is…."

"You and me", a moment's hesitation, a mischievous smile, "and Carla, of course."

The big Brazilian's moustache sagged, shoulders stooped, palms up, "I am in your hands. Com' on, Carla, you can pour the wine."

The three hooked arms and walked down the middle of the street towards the "Bel Aria" hotel. The façade and front entrance of four story building, reminders of Bel Aria's better days, were silhouetted against the beautiful blue Apennine sky. Four white pillars standing at attention and two beautiful granite benches guarded four wide stone steps leading to the main entrance; truly, works of art.

A few years' prior, the hotel was a magnet for city folk wanting to breathe the fresh mountain air as they hiked the woods, hunted for porcini mushrooms and/or filled their ample stomachs with fine Tuscan cuisine and satiating their thirst with bottles and bottles of some of the best *"reds"* in the world.

But that was yesterday.

Although the hotel itself had not been bombed, the battle for the Apennines had aged the grand old lady. Paint was peeling and piles of debris covered the hotel's once beautiful grounds. American GIs had boarded up all the windows, including the stained-glass panels gracing the front door entrance.

Entering the hotel one saw dozens of unmade cots and beds strewn everywhere; the hallways, the foyer, even the kitchen had been turned into a makeshift dormitory.

Gio led them up a stairway and into a small bedroom furnished with a half-dozen ammunition boxes, a cot and an old mattress lying opposite two covered windows which, in better days, would have provided a view of the main square. A strobe of light emanating from one of the windows fought gallantly for their attention.

With true amazement, a flabbergasted Carla asked, "Gio, how in the hell do you know about this place?"

She threw her coat onto one of the boxes, "The fruit picker, turned grease monkey, alleges temporary ownership. He claims his lieutenant gave him squatting rights to one of the hotel rooms."

Nasciente nervously stroked his mustache as Carla blurted, "You mean you've been with what the hell is his name…?"

"Cesare Romeo."

Nasciente, "Romeo?"

"Yes, Romeo! And, no, I haven't been with him."

"But, he asked?"

"Yea, he asked! I said no, but told the young grease monkey I'd like to see his room someday."

"And I'm going to turn you into a lady? You've been here a few days and already you are dancing a tarantella with a Napolitano and about to do a Brazilian mamba with this big lug?"

"It's my boots."

"What boots? And who is this grease monkey?"

Carla, ignoring Nasciente, grabbed Gio's arm, convulsed in laughter. She hugged her friend saying "Gio, Gio, Gio, what in the hell am I going to do with you?"

Gio beaming, "Nasciente, you big klutz, clean off one of the boxes and get the food ready; I'm hungry."

Nasciente wasn't quite sure as to what had just taken place.

They chatted as they ate and, as Bruno chewed on a huge piece of cheese, Carla, a twinkle in her eye, asked, "Do you have a wife back in Brazil?"

A broad smile, "Wife? Me, a wife! Who would have me?"

He washed the cheese down with a big swallow of wine. "No. No wife. No family. Just me."

"What do you mean, no family?"

The big man took a package of cigarettes from his uniform jacket, offered a *Lucky Strike* to each girl. Carla declined but Gio took one, accepted a light from Bruno, inhaled and immediately started gagging and coughing. Bruno tenderly patted her on the back. She roughly took his hand away.

She wiped tears away, took a deep breath, "Never again! What in the hell did you give me?

"It's an American cigarette; it's more valuable than money."

"Well, next time give me the money and you know where you can blow the smoke from your *Lucky Strike* or whatever!"

He roared, smiled and said, "You are the tiger of the Apennines!"

"I'll give you a tiger alright. Now finish telling us about the "no family" story.

The smile disappeared, "My mother is gone. Never knew who my father was."

"Brothers? Sisters?"

Quietly, somberly "Not that I know of."

Gio, moved by his evident emotion and suspecting the big man was about to cry, patted him on the arm.

Carla, noticing the gesture with an amused smile, felt a new and strange attraction for Bruno; perhaps the boisterous stranger was nothing other than a big, loveable and lonely bear. A man whom life had treated unjustly. She looked at the couple and thought, "You know the old lady called *"Life"* plays a lot of tricks on us but, occasionally, she leaves a gift. Who knows, this might be one of those times. Perhaps he could be an ideal companion for my rough-edged friend..."

She stood, put on her coat, refused a second glass of wine, took a last swallow of the red and walked towards the door, "Nasciente, if you harm this jewel, I will personally rip …"

"I'll handle him Carla…"

"I am a gentleman, a …"

Laughingly, "You are a bull-shitter and one of the dangerous kinds, at that…"

"I assure you…"

"Gio, if you need me, just scream and I'll bring the entire 5th Army with me." She opened the door and said, "One more thing; you'd better put boxes against the door; I don't think this is what the grease monkey intended when he extended his invitation."

With a little wave, Carla shook her head and walked out the door.

The couple looked at one another, the wine working its magic on the Brazilian, tenderly touched Gio's hand, "May I kiss you?"

It would be her first real kiss and all she could say was, "Not with that moustache!"

"I'll cut it off right now!"

She turned, hungrily lunged into him; the moustache notwithstanding.

A week after Sasso was liberated, civilian traffic was permitted to travel the main road south. Gianni, foot not completely healed, accompanied by Mico and Michelle managed to hitch a ride with an American sergeant who was driving a huge two-ton truck to Cutigliano.

Michelle marveled at the painted white star on the door of the vehicle; "better than a swastika", he thought as he boarded. He sat next to the driver while the others rode in the back of the truck. Michelle was awe-struck as he had never ridden in such a huge machine and, of more interest, the truck was driven by a black American corporal. Michelle had seen black American soldiers – they were the first to enter Sasso—but this was the first time he had seen a black man face to face.

"I won't bite you, boy", the G.I. uttered playfully, "Looks like someone gave you a one-two punch in the face. Here, have some sweet medicine. Make you feel better."

Michelle had no idea what had been said, but understood the gesture and marveled at the man's generosity, thinking, "A ride and chocolate! The Americans, as they say, are OK!"

The candy was devoured before the corporal put the truck into its fourth gear.

The American drove rapidly down the mountain side, hitting shell holes, taking curves with force and sliding in the mud to the edge of precipice after precipice. Michelle was holding on for dear life, absolutely enjoying the first thrill ride of his life. The more Michelle yelled, the faster the G.I. drove.

The situation in the back of the truck was not as entertaining. Gianni and Mico were bumped, jostled and knocked into each other. Gianni making a poor attempt at a wise remark, "We made it through the war and now we are going to go to heaven while on an American joy-ride."

"What makes you believe you are going to heaven?"

"We've already been in hell. No way they'll send us back there."

A laugh, "You think?"

Despite the discomfort, the two cousins were a happy pair. Gianni would soon see the love of his life. Mico, happy knowing he would soon return to France; to his wife and little girl.

CHAPTER 19

AN EMACIATED ILLUSION

A few weeks after the American troops had moved on, peace was declared and the little north-central Apennine towns began their "adjustment period". The adjustments would not be simple.

The two families had been joyously reconciled, spring plantings had begun and, despite the heavy ongoing hardships, life returned to a degree of pre-war normality. The big Brazilian, Bruno Nascente, was enthusiastically accepted as a family member; his devil-may-care attitude blended perfectly with Gio's dry wit. They were a happy couple and both Mico and Gina were ecstatic seeing their sister and daughter so happy. Further, the big man was a powerful, solid helping hand for the entire family living at the house called *Cassone*.

However, at *La Rimessa*, the situation was not as pretty.

Nilde and her mother began bickering once more. Beatrice continued her drinking and Nilde's laments about her loss of husband were never ending.

Beatrice's sister, Gina, visited often and attempted to calm the pair; to no avail. The two women were de-clawed caged tigers; one drank and the other spewed venom. It was not an easy place to visit, but family is family and Gina had a responsibility to help as best as possible.

On a beautiful early May morning Gina, without knocking, stepped into the old house and immediately was enveloped by the ever-present aura of adversity and loss. It was ten o'clock in the morning and Beatrice was already in "*the red*".

"Where in the hell is she finding the wine?" was Gina's unspoken question.

"Good morning ladies. How are we on this beautiful morning?"

No response.

"*Ehy*, I baked a torte last night; Nilde put on some orzo and we'll sweeten our taste buds."

No response. Gina continued her attempts at conversation. The actions of her sister and niece were quite insulting; Beatrice staring at Gina without saying a word; Nilde scuffled around the kitchen pretending to be busy.

Gina continued for a few moments, but since neither responded, she stood and said she would return later. Beatrice grunted a snide *"va al inferno anca te" (you go to hell too).* Gina smiled, knew it was *"the red"* talking and let it pass.

At the sound of a knock on the door, Gina pulled her shawl over her shoulders, tapped Beatrice on the shoulder and opened the door.

A ghost dressed in ragged black rags, hunched forward. The man had a desolate, yet gentle, expression; his eyes glistened as he leaned against the threshold with his left hand.

Gina groused, "What do you want? We have no food. *Via!* Get away from our door..."

"Gina, don't you recognize me?"

She scornfully looked at the figure standing before her; a putrid, unkempt miserable skeleton but a moment out of his grave. The man began to talk again and his voice delivered a blow to hidden sorrows as she heard him whisper, "I'm Emilio Pasqua, Nilde's husband."

Gina gasped and struggled for breath as she screamed, "Nilde! Nilde! Oh, Lord in heaven, it's Emilio! It's Emilio back from the dead!"

Nilde shrieked, rose, took a step and collapsed, falling into the old couch.

Beatrice sobered immediately, walked towards Emilio and embraced the ragged skeleton, took his hand and led him to the couch. He sat down and silently stroked Nilde's hair; she responded and fell onto her husband's shoulders saying, "Emilio, Emilio" over and over. The man's frail hands shook with emotion, tears streaking his dusty face. Sobbing, as he embraced his wife, "I'm back, Nilde; I'm back."

He asked Gina for a glass of water and asked, "Where is my Michelle?"

"He is fine. He's out chasing the little *signorine*", Gina replied.

Emilio smiled.

"Do you want to eat?"

"Not now, later. "I'm so tired. I need to lie down."

Nilde and Gina helped the frail skeleton to his feet and led him towards stairs, "I'm sorry to be such a bother..."

Nilde, arm around her husband's waist, heart and mind floating on a cloud of jubilation, kept repeating her husband's name as he changed into an old night gown. He dropped into his bed and fell asleep hearing Nilde whispering, "Emilio, Emilio, hush up! The war is over and miracle of miracles you are alive!"

The next morning, after a long night's sleep, cleaned and dressed in fresh clothing, Emilio slowly came down the stairs. Michelle leapt from his chair and hugged his father; his Papa, risen to life from a graveyard called Stalingrad.

Beatrice and Nilde, transfixed at the sight, hugged and cried. Through their tears the two could see their world was righting itself. Miracles could happen!

While Emilio was eating a light breakfast, Beatrice, Nilde, Gina and Michelle gave a brief update on the other family members.

"And Gianni, where is he?"

Nilde, "Gianni is fine; everyone is fine. We've come through this. Zio died last year; it was a blessing; otherwise everyone ..."

Michelle interrupted, "Papa', we will bring you up to date later; tell us about yourself; we were sure you were killed somewhere in Russia." **(2)**

With a wide smile for his inquisitive son, Emilio slowly began recounting his odyssey. "I really can't describe the experiences of the last three years; maybe after I've been home for a while I can..."

Emilio stopped, stifled a sob, feebly looked at his son and wondered if he should continue. No one moved.

He looked down at his frail hands and, with head bowed as if he were to recite a prayer, he began, "After I left home, they sent us east; in late summer, we were in the Ukraine then we moved on to the Soviet city of Stalingrad, where we met our doom. A week or so before Christmas of '42, the Russians attacked in force and we were all in retreat; it was a debacle. Our grenades didn't explode, our machine guns froze..."

Emilio stopped, folded his hands. "Those of us that were still alive, retreated. Seven of us broke from the main group and began walking. We crazily reasoned there was no better alternative.

It was bitter cold as we staggered west for days and days. We scavenged food from frozen fields, houses and…" Emilio again looked at his son, sighed and continued, "four in the group starved, fell and froze to death in the first ten days; Giuseppe Conti from Rio was one of those; two of us tried to carry him but, after a few meters, we knew it was an impossible effort."

Emilio, in a low plaintive voice continued, "Giuseppe lay on the frozen ground," Emilio stopped again, "the lice were already beginning their feast."

Emilio took Nilde's hand, "There was nothing we could do to help; we were so weak we couldn't even dig a hole in the frozen ground. Lord, it was awful."

The emaciated Emilio looked at his wife, hands trembling, whispered, "We stumbled away knowing we all were going to suffer the same fate; we knew we were dead men already delivered to the darkest corner of hell."

Another long silence; Nilde laid her head on her husband's shoulder, "Let's continue this another day, I think ..."

Emilio, giving Nilde a small hug, interrupted, "Our first miracle arrived the day after Giuseppe's death", a sigh, "four trucks filled with soldiers thundered past. We waved, but all four passed by; we were devastated. Then, the last truck braked and we heard, "Get on! Quick, get on, you are wasting fuel" We ran best we could and were pulled onto the truck by a ragged, filthy group of Italian *Alpini* mountain soldiers.

The truck rumbled off as we repeated, "Thank you! Thank you for stopping; you've saved our lives." He paused, lost in some far-off place. Michelle watched his father for a few moments, touched his father's shoulder, "Papa…"

Emilio smiled, returned from the netherworld, "I remember a heavy Tuscan accented voice responding, "Your *Alpini* uniform is the reason we stopped; someday you can tell your grandchildren Il Duce provided you a uniform that saved your life."

Michelle, in attempt to interject a bit of humor, blurted out, "Viva Il Duce!"

Emilio smiled weakly, "Very good, Michelle."

Nilde, "Maybe you should rest now."

Beatrice, "Yes, we can continue another time. For now, let's worry about today; we can talk about yesterday tomorrow."

Hearing his mother-in-law's use of words amused Emilio; it was part of being home.

Before the big war, the months of May and June painted the mountains with cherry blossoms, brilliant blue skies and green hills. In the spring of 1945 the blue sky re-appeared, but the scars of war were evident throughout the valleys. The acrid odor of burnt wood still clung to the bare, yellow-brown hills and there would be no cherries to gather. After twenty years of Fascism and its wars in Spain, Ethiopia, Albania and six years of World War II, the Italian family wondered if true peace had arrived.

In time, the hills would be green again. The evergreen and the mountain flowers would spring anew and transform the scarred landscape. But, for the people living in the Sasso hills, the healing would take longer, much longer. To some, never to be healed scars were etched into their memory banks; for others, healed but not forgotten. For nearly all, the peace would bring challenges of a different kind.The Carboni clan members toiled long hours. Gardens were planted, a few baby chicks, lambs and kids were born. A peaceful rhythm appeared to be slowly returning as each family member worked their way back to a degree of normalcy.

Emilio, recovered physically, continued to have nightmares, bouts of depression and frequent long periods of silence. His best medicine was his son Michelle who kept conversations going, taking his father on mushroom and berry hunts and relating his own "war experiences."

The two had been hunting for porcini mushrooms and were resting below the area where he and Gianni had been captured just two months before. Michelle, relating the events of that day, noticed his father was no longer listening.

"Papa, what are you thinking about?"

"War. I'm thinking about war."

"The war is over. We are at peace."

In an uncharacteristic bristling voice, "What peace? Wait a while and man will be at it again. The devil is already pouring petrol on the smoldering ashes of the last few years. We are in hell, Michelle. We haven't died but we are in hell and the only escape is to die. People have rushed to prove this through the centuries and will continue to act the same evermore."

Michelle sat transfixed, not replying or reacting to his father's forceful comments.

"When I first returned home, I told you about my return from Russia." He stopped, appeared to be on the brink of crying, sighed and continued, "I did not believe there existed a hell worse than the walk home from Russia."

The man stopped, his frail hands shaking as he turned towards the valley. He hesitated and faced his son, "but it did get worse. There was another hell; believe it or not, a hell crueler than the first."

His lips were now also quivering, "Our truck ran out of petrol somewhere in the Ukraine; there were eleven of us. Over the next two months we walked west. We raided farm houses, stole food, ate objects without names and hid from allies and enemy. But we persevered and after months of walking, hiding and sheer determination to live, all of us made it to Italy. We were home!"

After a long, long pause, Emilio wistfully turned towards the town below and with quivering lips whispered, "But we weren't home. We were in Italy, but we weren't home."

Complete silence; a light breeze caressed the two men; Michelle remained silent and waited for his father to return from another place.

"I was only three hundred kilometers from home; I had recovered, so after all that time at the front, the long walk home, one would think I deserved to be furloughed." He looked at his son, "Instead, they kept us in Trieste and prepared us for the next disaster."

A sneer, "In September our great Caesar became a puppet on a string and suddenly we were the enemy. We were immediately transferred to a nearby vile camp and within a month I was sent north to a place called Buchenwald."

He abruptly stopped talking. Silence. Emilio was lost in a far-away place. He started to cry.

Michelle stood, walked over and sat down and hugged his father.

The subject would need to be re-opened at another time.

PART TWO

REVENGE AND PEACE

An incongruous paradox, nonetheless true:
Peace arrived but the war lingered

CHAPTER 20

REVENGE: THE DEVIL'S FIRST-BORN

Millions and millions of voices from the east, west, north and south sang the notes of a peaceful new beginning. The killings and inhuman acts of brutality were no longer part of their daily bread. Once again "hope" became the mantra, the hymn of reconciliation poured forth, as the common folk sang of "Cheers and good tidings, peace has arrived; better days lay ahead."

The theme resonated world-wide, but, not everywhere. In Europe, authority was weak at best, rules did not exist and vengeance was being served hot and cold. Historians have documented the horrendous acts of retribution continuing for years after the war ended; situations where neighbors assailed each other as political suspicions or personal affronts were bolstered with exaggerations and lies. Among the bombed-out ruins of many European cities, people were killed for their clothing, gangs murdered and stole at will. Women were raped and/or offered their services for a morsel of food. Yes, peace had arrived but a different kind of war continued.

The situation in Italy, though not as calamitous as in Germany and countries to the east, nevertheless can be justifiably described as a quagmire, an imbroglio. There was little food and other necessities non-existent. In the cities, the black market ran rampant; theft was a thriving business. American left-overs, stolen military equipment and provisions such as cigarettes, chocolate and other military provisions were the strong currency. Despite its great sacrifices and losses, the country continued to spin its way into an insensible whirlpool of labor strife, political instability and partisan ideology which augmented the desires for *"La Vendetta"*.

Diabolical acts of pay back were taken; scores were settled in the name of politics, sometimes without proof the individual had been political. Battles arose between Communists, Christian Democrats and a litany of various political blocs. Deaths were not infrequent. Women accused of bedding a Fascist or a German soldier had their heads shaven and paraded through the streets nude. Families were attacked because a relative had been a Fascist sympathizer or a member of Mussolini's Republican army.

These acts of retaliation and retribution were taking place throughout the boot, but were predominant in the Central and Northern provinces where, during the last month of the war, thousands were murdered by their own "*paisani*".

Thousands! In one month!

About six weeks after the American troops left the area, Sasso experienced its first bitter taste of the new peace.

A very pregnant Carla and Gianni, wanting to live nearer to the town, were temporarily living in the Grandi house. Gianni, quite unhappily, had deferred to Carla's wishes and had agreed to postpone moving to her house until after the baby arrived. Also, since mid-1943 the house, having hosted German officers, including SS and Gestapo members, was in shambles. It would require a great deal of work before it could be habitable. It was uncomfortable, but for these reasons, Gianni could stomach living in his half-brother's house for a short period.

Michelle came running into the house red-faced and perspiring, "They found a body in the back of Dina's bar. The war is over, the Germans are gone, Mussolini is dead and this stupid bastard was walking around wearing the pants of the Republican uniform!"

"Watch your language!"

"Well, how stupid can you be wearing Mussolini's army uniform, especially with all the Communist sympathizers here in Sasso?"

"Who found the body?"

"I'm not sure. I heard a commotion, went over to see what was happening. When I got there, Dina, Luigi One-Leg and Franco the shoemaker were standing over the body. Then a crowd gathered. There was a lot of blood." The lad smiled and quipped, "I guess the "Springtime of Peace" is turning into "The Summer of Revenge."

Gianni, "Not funny my boy. Now get home so your mother and grandmother will know you are ok."

Going out the door, "Remember Gianni, I'm not a boy!"

"Right."

A week after the murder, three men, later identified as "ex-partisans", raided the Grandi house. The bandits stole houseware, china and bedding. Surprisingly, they also knew where to find a box of silverware that had spent a three-year hibernation hiding behind a cellar wall. The thieves drove a Jeep, probably stolen or "purchased" from some profit-minded American supply sergeant, was so loaded with loot one had to wonder where the passengers would sit. The interior of the house was greatly damaged and a white swastika was crudely smeared on the front door.

Gianni and Carla arrived as the men were making their escape. Carla screamed and ran towards one of the culprits, "What the hell are you doing? Stop it! Stop it!"

The leader, a bearded young man carrying an automatic rifle and wearing ammunition belts crossing his chest, pointed the weapon at Carla, "You Fascist whore; your beloved Lorenzo had to tell us where and how to collect payment for your collaboration; what we have taken today is a small down payment; we will be looking for additional payments from you!"

A raging Gianni charged the man, landed a punch to the man's forehead, knocking him to the ground. It was the last thing he remembered. When he awoke, Carla was sobbing as she daubed his head with a wet rag. Mico, Michelle, Gina, the Brazilian and a sobbing Beatrice were all staring down at him.

Gianni, lashes of lightning zinging through his head, sat up and mumbled, "I think one of those bastards was Vaccaccia, that coward from our partisan group."

Mico, bristling with anger, maintained outward calm, "We'll worry about that "*merda*" later, come on Nasciente give me a hand, let's get him home."

Two nights later Dina's local bar was burnt to the ground; a scribbled crude verse was nailed to the door of the Village hall:

BEWARE U FACSISTS

She served the Black Shirt
So popular in the day
For their leader, a lifted skirt
What more need we say?

Dina was nothing more than a poor woman trying to make a living, and how many times and for whomever she lifted her skirt had little or nothing to do with politics. She was devastated and, unlike Gianni, had no one to come to her assistance. Her clients, the loud wine-drinking Romeos and bar-room philosophers were nowhere to be found. She was alone and without her little bar Dina, overnight, had become a complete outcast.

The following Sunday, a beautiful spring day, Gianni, feeling much better, accepted a glass of wine from Mico and began talking of settling scores.

"I'll find Vaccaccia and kill that squealing pig. I've fought too many battles and am tired of war and revenge, but I can't stomach Vaccaccia calling Carla a whore and then ruining the house."

He gulped a swallow of wine, "I'm going to find that bastard. It will take a bit of time, but I'll find him. You can bet your sweet ass, I'll find him!"

Before Mico could reply, Gianni asked, "What the hell do you make of the Lorenzo "down payment" comment? Do you think Lorenzo is still alive? Maybe they didn't kill him after all."

"Maybe you misunderstood. You were furious and …"

"Oh! I heard what I heard!" Gianni snarled. "Some of those partisan friends of yours would sell their own mothers for a dry pair of socks. I'll find those..."

Mico interrupted, "Calm down. Calm down." He put his hand on his cousin's shoulder, "I'm sure Lorenzo is dead. If not, when and if he shows up in Sasso, we will be more than ready to make his death permanent. Right?"

Gianni shrugged his shoulders as Mico continued, "My dear cousin, after the tragedies of the past few years it's time we smile a little; think about Carla, your baby, the family. Laugh a little, Gianni. Let's not go hunting for new problems and new tears. They will arrive without an invite."

He finished his wine, patted his friend on the back and strolled away.

CHAPTER 21

EVERYONE LOVES A PARTY

Mico also faced a challenge. To help his mother and sister he had delayed his departure for France. He anxiously searched for transportation and fortunately, a few days after his chat with Gianni, stumbled upon a free lift offered by a U.S. Army captain heading to the city of Modena. He packed a small cardboard suitcase, quickly said his goodbyes to the family, boarded the jeep and headed west. The partisan hero was finally returning to his little family. To his little girl and to his wife and to the peace he so well deserved.

The first segment of the road had been the same he and Gianni had taken a lifetime ago; two young men seeking their fortune in that foreign land, *L'America*. Back then there were confused feelings of exhilaration and apprehension as they went into the unknown. Now, as he walked *"il camino di speranza"* (the road of hope) to his wife and child, there was a different excitement, an exhilaration yet, tension beyond description.

Early the second day out, a speeding car whizzed past, nearly hitting Mico. A few meters later the driver slammed on the brakes and slid to a stop. Mico ran toward the vehicle, a U.S. Army officers' car flying a small standard on the front bumper. The standard, which normally would have flown white stars designating the rank of the officer, flew a red bandana.

The back door swung open and a huge hand pulled Mico into a cesspool of smoke, empty cans of spam, trash of all kinds and several empty wine bottles.

"Where you heading, comrade?"

The man's breath gagged Mico, "I'm on my way to Nice. Thanks for stopping; I'm really grateful."

Mico wasn't too sure he was being honest.

"You are in luck; we are off to Alessandria to visit Roberto's Mamma. He was due home over a month ago," A laugh, "But we delayed. We just couldn't leave the party of a lifetime."

He tapped the driver's shoulder, "Let's go, mamma's boy, we are wasting time."

The auto roared off, jolting a third passenger lying next to the driver, asked, "Where are we?

We near home yet?"

"Go back to sleep, Caruso, we've a long way to go."

"Caruso?"

"I don't know what the hell his name is. He likes to sing, so we gave him Caruso as his "*nom de guerre.*"

"You were partisans?"

"Damn right. We were part of Valerio's group."

Mico recoiled from the grappa laden stench as the man poked his index finger into Mico's chest, "Why in the hell do you think we are wearing red kerchiefs?"

Mico remained silent.

"My name is Mario; I'm from Turin. What about you? You French?"

Mio backed away, "Turin? I thought your accent was from the Lombard area."

No response.

"My name is Carboni. Domenico Carboni."

He looked the man straight on, "I'm from Modena. A *montenaro* from the mountains to the south. Back home they call me Mico."

"Lot of good comrades down there."

Mico, a bit uncomfortable, "Ya. Lots."

The driver took a sharp swerve left, off the tree lined road, jostling both big men into each other, "Damn it Roberto, slow down! The Germans and the Fascist didn't get me but this drunk is going to end up skewering me with one of these cypress trees! Slow down!"

Roberto answered singing a raspy rendition of the first stanzas of "La Donna e' Mobile"; it was obvious as to why he had not been given Caruso's name.

"So, you are on your way to France. None of my business, but why Nice?"

"Wife and daughter near there."

A slight scowl, "At first, I thought you were one of those Fascist Republicans running away from their just rewards."

Mico, temper rising, "Thanks for the ride, but the war is over."

"Calm down. Calm down. I'm just teasing you, *Modenese*."

The conversation stopped, their attention diverted as the car zig-zagged from one side of the road to the other. "Damn it, Roberto! One more time, I'm driving and you'll be walking to Alessandria!"

After a few minutes, "I was a partisan. Red bandana around my neck, hammer and sickle and all that."

Mario broke into a wide grin, "Comrade! I knew it the moment I saw you!"

"I left my unit before the war ended."

"You left? Before it was over?"

Quietly, "After Mussolini fell, we did a lot of good things. The Germans felt our sting, many times." A hesitation, "But, in the last months of the war, my group turned into a bad lot; anarchist for their own benefit." Quietly, "they hurt many good people."

Both men remained silent as a light rain fall started to darken the road. My *nom D'guerre* was Ivan; under Tulio's command. We roamed the mountains north of Lucca; we covered an area along the main road between Modena and Tuscany."

Quietly, "We did some damage but as the war ended, it seemed to me our group was more concerned with survival and less moved by patriotic aims."

Mico turned and faced the big man. He took notice of a long scar winding through a rough face that probably hadn't been washed in days. Bushie black eyebrows draped over deep- set brown eyes gave the veteran partisan the look of a Barbary Coast pirate.

They rode in silence as the rain began falling in earnest. Mico had the amusing thought that the rain made the outside of the car cleaner than the inside. There was no doubt about the odor being better.

They had been quiet for quite a spell when Mario poked the driver's shoulder, "Careful Roberto, we are getting close."

He then leaned over and shook the seat in front of him, "Wake up Caruso. Meet one of our comrades."

Caruso barely moved.

He turned toward Mico and picked up the conversation, "We didn't quit. Lost a lot of good men. We proudly wore our red neckerchiefs. We still wear them with ..."

A long hesitation, eyes piercing, defiant, "We were there when they killed Mussolini."

Mico, incredulous, his first thought was that he truly had hitched a ride with a squad of loonies. He smiled at the big man but remained silent.

Irritated, "You don't believe me?"

Defensively, "Why shouldn't I believe you? But you've got to admit I should be surprised."

The eyes! Piercing. Challenging. Mario continued staring.

"Our great leader and his entourage of Fascist pigs tried to escape to Switzerland. Can you believe our great Duce, the man who promised us the world, was hiding at the back of an armored car disguised as a German soldier?"

"You saw him?"

Speaking rapidly with enthusiasm, "Not then. I saw him later. We were near Dongo guarding the road leading north. We heard about it a few hours after the capture. It was raining white rice. Cold."

"Dongo?"

"Yeah. Up north of Como. Another group of partisans chased a bunch of those bastards. Some of them running and hiding like scared rabbits. But the Duce and a crowd of others were nabbed and brought to the Dongo town hall."

"Didn't you read or hear about what happened?"

"Oh, bits and pieces; I saw some photographs; I really didn't ..."

A raised eyebrow, "A few hours later, we tried to take control of the prisoners but the other partisan group wouldn't hand them over. Our leader, Colonel Valerio, a crazy bastard whose real name was Walter Audisio, was livid. I was sure we were going to have a fire fight right there. I'm sure you have heard of him by now. The newspapers and the radio were full of stories about us."

No response.

An arrogant smile, "I wished they had started something. We were well hidden and had new equipment – new sub-machine guns."

"Anyway, they swore at each other but Valerio stomped up the steps, raging mad and, with pistol in hand, marched into the town hall. We found out later Valerio's order came from our highest command, "You shoot Mussolini before the Americans arrive or we'll shoot you! And as you know only too well, we all obey orders."

Again a raised eyebrow, "Right, Comrade?"

"The Americans?"

"Yea. They were close and wanted Il Duce taken alive. Valerio was sure the other partisan group was in league with the Americans." A giggle, "They probably wanted to give the Devil a fair trial."

Mico, "So, then ..."

"I don't know what happened next, except that Mussolini and his lady friend were gone."

"What about the others?"

"We never saw them until Valerio returned a few hours later."

"Valerio walked across the piazza strutting like a peacock. He ordered several of our men, including our beloved Caruso, to put their guns at the ready. They then marched up the steps into the town hall. Caruso tell our guest about the roll call."

Heavy eyebrows, a coal-black beard and a shoulder length shaggy head of hair peeked over the seat; bloodshot eyes slowly focusing on Mico, "Where did this guy come from?"

"Never mind where he came from, tell our comrade here what happened when you were with Valerio in the Dongo town hall."

In a slow drawn out manner, "Well, we went inside the building, about six of us and Valerio."

Mico pulled back, the man's breath was repulsive.

Caruso continued, "Valerio pulled out a piece of paper and read off the names of individuals being held in custody by the other group. There was a squabble, Valerio had us raise our guns – our new machine guns. They were such shiny beauties and … "

"Never mind the guns. Tell him what happened next?"

"Valerio, along with one of the guards, went to the rear of the building and came back with a dozen prisoners."

Caruso scratched his beard, "All of them Fascist to the core."

An agitated, Mario interrupted, "OK. OK. Then what happened?"

"Valerio had us march the prisoners out to the piazza. A priest was called for."

Caruso continued, "A lot of pleas. They prayed and then, boom-boom, we shot them."

"You killed a dozen..."

A giggle, "More. One guy started running for the lake – found out later he was a big cheese - had killed a lot of our people. Wonder if he knew how to swim? Didn't matter."

Mico, "No trial? In cold blood?"

Mario, "Those birds have been on trial for a long time. They got what they served others. The best part of this came the next day. Did you hear what happened in Milan?"

"You mean the hangings? Were you there?

"Kinda."

"Kinda?"

"The Dongo town hall wall was splattered with holes and blood! Bodies on the ground! What a sight! Then, after the executions, we started drinking."

Mario's voice was rising, a gleam in his eyes, "Lots of vino and grappa. Lots! As I said, It was a celebration! For us the war was over!"

Mario, now wearing a big smile, lowered his voice, "We heard Mussolini's body was being brought to Milan for display. We wanted to be in on the party. Right boys?"

A couple of nods from the front seat. The rain cascading.

"The party?"

"And what a party! We've been partying ever since. Right boys?"

We slept a bit then "borrowed" this car and sped down to Milan. Do you know what else happened?"

"They hung the Duce's body by its feet."

A huge grin, like a child revealing a secret, "Oh, it was better than that! By the time we arrived, a few bodies were lying on the ground. Mussolini, his girlfriend and some of the bodies of those we had killed in Dongo were hanging by their heels from the crossbeam of a bombed-out gas station in Piazzale Loreto – the same place where the Germans had shot fifteen of our men last year."

A pause," But it gets better."

Mario came closer, his bad breath causing Mico to recoil, "Then some guy comes running towards the swaying bodies and clobbers Il Duce's head. People started to walk and dance around the rafter. It became a carnival. The crowd pressed into the bodies, hacking spitting and trampling some of the corpses lying on the ground. One woman walked up to Mussolini and pumped four or five shots into the body; one for each son she had lost in the war. Another woman spread her skirt, dropped her panties and urinated on one of the bodies. That was really funny."

Mico's stomach was churning, he felt a bit of nausea seeing the gleam in the big man's eyes. He had experienced many cruel acts and had witnessed evil in many forms, but never had he seen such enjoyment over the mutilation of dead bodies. He had to get out of the car as he was about to explode. "We are at the outskirts of Alexandria; the rain has stopped; I think I'll get off here and avoid the city. Thanks for..."

"Then they dragged the Fascist Secretary Starace, some name like that. The Secretary gave the salute to Il Duce's body and then he was shot right in front of the crowd!"

A slap on Mico's back, a huge laugh, "It was his last curtain call!"

Mico grabbed the driver's shoulder, "Enough! Stop the car!"

Roberto hit the brakes, the car sliding to a stop. Mario, startled, "What the…?"

Mico opened the door and jumped onto the pavement, "Thanks for the ride ..."

The car started to move away, Mario's goodbye undiscernible, but Mico distinctly heard a variation of a word that describes part of the fleshy part of the human body that one sits on.

Mico waved goodbye but only one word came to mind, "Idiots!"

As he walked the wet pavement he reflected he had lived through the emotional highs and lows of a brutal war. He had lived with and fought against heroes and cowards; humans at their worst and at their best. And after riding for hours with the ghouls from Dongo, he was sure he now had experienced every possible decadent human emotion.

Now it was time to find the good in people, time to forget war and brutality. It was time to be born again.

CHAPTER 22

THE ROAD TO NIRVANA

As Mico neared the French border, the thought of seeing his wife and child created a glow of tenderness, love and thankfulness. Old wounds seemed to dissipate, replaced by a suffocating joy which gurgled within. He looked upward to thank Him; then, looked down, smiled at his well-worn boots, quickened his step and spoke to the stones beneath him, "Can't over-do this prayer thing; one prayer request per year is the limit for me, right?"

No one answered his question but, in his way, Mico had just thanked someone for the gift of family; the entire Carboni clan and his dear ones in Antibes.

He walked a few steps, smirked, "there you go again, a Communist saying another prayer. I'd better be careful or I'll start going to church." He thought he had made a joke.

He was sitting on the edge of a flat-bed 4-cylinder truck taking him the short distance from Ventimiglia across the border towards the city of Menton, France, sitting majestically on the eastern edge of the *Cote' du A'zur*.

A mile or so from the border, he jumped from the truck, thanked the driver for the lift. The skies had cleared and a beautiful warm early evening glow greeted him; he was tempted to continue, but he was dirty, tired and there was no way of knowing how long it would take to arrive home. Better to be refreshed and rested, right? After two years, what difference another day? He was nearly home; one more ride, another twenty-five or thirty miles and he would be in Antibes. His silent prayer, "I'll soon see my bride Suzi and my little Beatrice; I'll finally be home."

As he headed towards an old hotel, a flock of running and laughing children crossed his path. A chubby little girl, dressed in a faded yellow sweater and black shorts trailed the group. She looked at Mico, stumbled and fell, bruising her knee. She wept for a moment, rubbed her knee, jumped up and continued the chase after her playmates. Mico, pleased she wasn't hurt, turned towards the hotel entrance thinking that could have been his little Beatrice taking the fall. The idea something evil might have happened to his dear ones entered his mind. He shrugged, quickly dismissed the thought and entered the hotel.

The next morning, after a resplendent late breakfast of coffee with heavy cream, fresh bread, sweet butter and jam, he thanked the inn keeper and said his goodbyes. He headed for the central part of the city where he was greeted by an air of festivity. People in Sunday dress, church bells ringing, a sizeable crowd entering the church.

His first thought, "It isn't Sunday, is it? No, unless I've lost track it's Wednesday; must be some big wedding."

He was tempted to follow the crowd, but considered his filthy clothing and thought, "I'm in rags and I'm carrying this small suitcase, tied with a rope, no-less; they'll be expecting me to sit at the doors looking for a hand out."

As he passed the church he approached an elderly fruit peddler and asked, "Who is getting married?"

Gruffly, "Married? Nobody is."

"What's all the commotion, it's not Sunday."

"We are celebrating the Assumption and end of the war, stupid! Even if you spoke perfect French, which you don't, I'd know you are another one of those Italians who shit in their britches as soon as they hear gun-fire. We endured your attacks on our motherland, you people helping the Nazi boot pounders and their *police secrete* and now, when we finally drive them out, the likes of you arrives, asking questions like a *vacancier* going to the *mer*!"

Stunned, temper exploding, Mico dropped the suitcase, bristling, replied in his very adequate French, "And you, hero of France, at least I fought them, but you, you son-of-bitch, succumbed to the Germans without a shot. You *"Vichyite"* collaborators, kneeled in front of their *gamm`ee* (swastika); you helped them send thousands of escapees to their camps! You, you..."

Mico, eyes popping, face flushed, his gnarled hands trembling, could not finish the sentence.

The two men stared at each other, the older man reaching into his jacket. Mico regained his senses, controlled his volcanic temper, walked away from the cart with a parting, "I hope you go straight to hell!"

He shook his head, thinking, "…just finished a war and this ol' guy, who probably has experienced two wars, is ready to start a new one. Maybe there is a hell; a hell we humans create and re-create ad infinitum; a hell we keep fashioning without the help of some horned deity; maybe we are living in hell right now. Maybe this earth, among the millions of planets out there, is hell. Maybe we have been sent here because of our sins in a prior life. The bigger the sin, the worse our earthly condition. How else could it be that we never learn and we continue the atrocities millennium after millennium? How can such a high intellect be so stupid, me included? Arguing with that fool makes me as big an idiot as he is."

Mico, the good Communist, was not aware the people of the French Riviera had been liberated on August 19,1944 and this date, Wednesday August 15th, 1945, marked the first peacetime celebration of the Assumption of the Virgin Mary. A day filled with hope and laughter, unknowns for the past five years. "Le *bosch*" had been defeated and sent home, there were some problems, but they would be solved; for now, it was a day of celebration.

There had been stumbling blocks on the pathway to peace. France capitulated to the Germans in June 1940. A puppet government was established, given various "legal names" but referred to as "Vichy France" (its capital located in a city of that name) and led by France's famous WW1 hero, Marshall Petain. The Allies landed on France's southern shores on August 15th, 1944, "The other D-Day". The Vichy entity existed no more and, from the ashes, France took its first baby steps in the long, long journey towards recovery.

As was the case in Italy, peace came at additional costs. Reprisals, including executions without trials, against German collaborators and political opponents, caused added difficulties for the average citizen.

Mico didn't remember the holy day, but was aware of these problems; however, his special concern and nightmare was the plight of the Jewish community in the south of the country; particularly the fate of his wife, daughter, father-in-law and, to a lesser degree, his friends in *"Et Eclaireurs Israelites de France (EIF)"*. **(3)**

In the early days of the German takeover Mico, joined the *EIF* and was sent on frequent secret trips into Italy as a liaison currier between French and Italian Socialist and Communist groups.

Because of his familiarity with the area Mico was given orders to return to Modena to enlist run-aways into a Communist cell already formed near Sasso. That was the last time he saw his family - late summer of 1943.

He had received a few short letters from France, including two from his wife; the last of these dated January 5th, 1944. He had heard the Italians in the Nice area had protected Jews and the *EIF* and other brave souls found hiding places for a significant number of escapees. But, because of his own experiences, he knew, war or no war, anti-Semitism still existed and he didn't expect he would now find much help locating his family. He probably would be on his own; especially if he did not find them in Antibes.

He again became aware of the peaceful, calming knoll from the mountains above, he mumbled, "Listen to that bell, my friend, listen to the promise of peace, generosity and the absence of malice. Forget your philosophizing and the old goat back there. Move on, Mico. Better days lie ahead."

The fading sound reminded him of the day, just a short time ago, when his cousin, Gianni, bravely walked away from the order to kill his own blood, his Fascist brother, Lorenzo. Mico recalled the confused state of his own mind that eventful day he struggled and questioned his own loyalty to the partisan cause and obedience to a battlefield order versus the love and respect of one's own family. The knoll of that bell was not the sound of peace but rather one of liberation; a salute to his cousin, a good man who gambled his life because he refused to kill another human being; albeit a fiend well deserving the sentence. Risking his life to die knowing he could not kill his own or to live a life free of everlasting guilt.

As he continued walking towards the west a few clouds appeared, briefly hiding the sun's sweet smile. The bell-knoll had faded into the before, but he kept thinking of that eventful day, realizing the bell of liberty also had sounded for him. He had been involved in multiple acts of savagery during the war, but by disobeying the order to kill Gianni, he had returned to the human race. He, too, could not kill his own. He sensed a great nostalgic and gratifying feeling as he exited his own confessional. Hopefully, memories of the atrocious acts of war in which he participated now could be stowed away and locked in the depths of his soul's inner sanctums.

Whatever might happen in the future, he could handle. The worst was over; he believed he had finally been liberated. He quickened his pace and was soon at the western end of the city limits. He paused at a black and white sign indicating distances to the west, Nice-21K, Cannes- 44K and between them in small black letters, "Antibes -35 K".

There was yet a way to go.

CHAPTER 23

PEACE IN HELL

He had walked four or five kilometers when a three-wheel motorcycle of some sort roared past him and skidded to a halt. A small man, black helmet strapped under his chin and dressed in the military uniform of a French enlisted man waved to him. Mico ran for the bike and jumped into the side car.

The little man wiped his dusty goggles, asked in French, "Where?"

"Antibes."

In Italian, "Can't do that. I'll take you as far as Nice."

"Are you Italian?"

The little man turned the handle, set his goggles and gunned the motor. The bike quivered, front wheel rising off the ground, Mico, holding on for dear life, barely heard over the roar,

"No, I just drive like one."

The ride was petrifying. The Frenchman drove like a maniac; rounding curves and hitting pot holes at a constant speed. Uphill, downhill, dust, rocks made no difference. They were in the city in short order. Mico, shaken to the bone, thanked the stranger, quickly dismounted, elated Nice was the little man's destination.

Between horse drawn carts, military rides, the "Dongo Express", motorcycle and walking, he had managed the 325 miles to Nice in three days…or was it four? He wasn't sure, but it didn't matter. He was close.

He walked the fifteen kilometers from Nice to Antibes; it was five o'clock in the evening by the time he arrived. Famished, yet wanting to get to his father-in-law's house, he kept heading west.

High above the city he saw Antibe's famous Fort-Carre' shimmering in the late afternoon sun; he remembered that Napoleon had been imprisoned there for a short while. He offered a silent "Thank you Signorina Cialli, at least I retained one fact from your history lessons."

He walked past the old Church of the Immaculate Conception, thought about entering but dismissed the idea immediately. He questioned why the idea entered his mind in the first place.

Antibes sparkled in the late afternoon sun, a cool breeze sent ripples to the rocky shore where a vacationer could see Antibe's famous *Chateau Grimaldi* castle. Mico had no interest.

He came upon a sign pointing towards *The Villa Eilenroc Gardens*; an Eden where, despite the war, pines, cypress, olive trees and varieties of luxuriant vegetation were laid out in an intoxicating array of unparalleled beauty. Mico, again showing no interest in any sightseeing, quickened his pace.

But in the distance, ah! There at the tip of the peninsula he saw the magnificent face of the *Hotel du Cap-Eden Roc*, perhaps the most glamorous, storied hotel in the entire world. "The" place for the world's richest, the ruling class.

Mico viewed it differently. He stopped, transfixed; thought about the innocents who had been subjected to actions of the hotel's recent residents. His stomach churned for he envisaged corruption, not beauty. He spat on the ground, saying loudly, "It was just yesterday, my people were starving while the Nazis and their Fascists sympathizers slept, ate and fornicated on embroidered, hand stitched *"Eden-Roc"* sheets. How many did your esteemed guests condemn to slavery and death? How many? Tell me, how many?"

The faces of those he tried to help during his time with the Jewish Scouts flashed through his mind and, sadly, the blur of the multitude he could not help, screamed from within. Tears streaked down his cheeks, his body quivered. He felt ineptitude, guilt and frustration. Emotions, beyond anything he had ever experienced in battle.

So many good men, women and children gone; oh, so many!

He continued walking, stopped, shoulders sagging, turned and faced the hotel and yelled, "Here's to you Eden-Roc!" The man's left hand pounded his upper right arm. The massive structure had received a derisive, but classic, extravagant Italian salute.

He laughed at his foolishness but, somehow, he felt better.

He found the chalet owned by his former employers, the wealthy Samuel family. Mico's father-in-law's house was located at the back, near the gardens. The big house's shutters were closed, the white of an old paint job showing through a more recent green. Two of the concrete steps leading to the massive front door were crumbling, appearing to having been intentionally damaged. The other three steps were in excellent condition. He considered knocking on the door, thought better of it, and walked around the house towards the rear gardens.

The sun was beginning its decent into a deep purple, shadows echoing against the little house welcoming him. He rushed to the door and knocked. He knocked again, his spirit soaring. "Someone must be living here" again talking to himself, "shutters are open and somebody has started a garden."

He called out, "Hello! Hello!"

"Who is there?" came a gurgling reply. The voice was familiar, but Mico was unable to discern its owner.

"Mico Carboni, Suzi David's husband. I worked here for a short while. I took my father-in-law's place here."

The door was opened by a gnarled runt of a man wearing a black waistcoat, baggy wool pants tied with a rope at the waist. He wore what appeared to be wooden beach sandals. A smile, no more of a scowl, "Ah, Mr. Carboni. Perhaps you don't remember me, I'm Josef Tovier, before the war I worked at the old *Lesarde* mansion, down towards the point."

A huge grin exhibiting a few browned teeth, "I knew your father-in-law well. Please come in."

The old man smelled of the evening sea and five night's perspiration. Mico thought, "Guess they don't have toilette paper over here, either."

He managed to overcome the distinct aromas and asked, "My people, my wife and child, where are they? Do you know if they are still in Antibes?"

The man sat down on an old divan and pointed to a chair; a chair Mico recognized as belonging to his father-in-law. The chill returned.

Mico could sense an ominous evasiveness, "I really don't know. The Samuel family abandoned the big house in late '43, I think your family left here shortly thereafter."

"What do you mean by you think they left?"

Mico, ready to explode, watched as the old geezer hesitated, reached for his pipe and began to fill the bowl, "Some bad things happened in our part of the country, the resistance reared its head, Frenchmen were fighting Frenchmen again; collaboration with the Nazi increased and people were sent away to camps near Paris and to the camps already here in Vichy France."

Mico was about to vomit, "What people? When?"

"Gypsies, homosexuals, those kinds of people…"

Explosion!!

His voice choked the words, "Those kinds of people? Those kinds of people! What about the escapees, what about the Jews, what about my family? What happened to them?"

A slight hesitation, a seemingly dispassionate reply, "One day they were here, the next day they were gone."

Mico, although positive the man knew more, calmed the gurgling volcano as an idea jingled through his mind, "What the hell good would it do to pop this guy?", he grinned at the old man thinking, "Too bad I didn't smash the peddler this afternoon; I could have had two "pops" in one day."

The absurd levity of his play on words helped him regain his composure, "How is it you are living in our house? Who gave you the keys? Who granted permission?"

"Well, a few the houses were left unoccupied, so those without damage have been taken over by those of us who had no place to live. I came here, the door was open and I kinda moved in."

It had been a long, difficult day and he wasn't going to accomplish much more by questioning the man; questions could wait until tomorrow.

"Well, Josef Tovier, that is your name, right?"

"Yes sir."

Suddenly such respect, reflected Mico, "You can stay here for now; I'll sleep in the back bedroom, I assume the beds are still here."

"The beds were not stolen but there are no sheets, no pillows. I brought my own possessions over. Nearly everything had been taken away."

He was about to say Mr. Tovier might have had something to do with the "taken away" part, but instead said, "You mean stolen."

The man again slouched, raised his hands palms up and responded with an indifferent shrug.

Mico ignored the gesture, “Do you have anything to eat?”

Some bread from yesterday, a small piece of *calendos* (camembert), you are welcome to it.”

“...and, you must have a bit of *pinard* hidden, right?”

A quick “danger-ahead” snap of the head.

“Don’t fret, I’ll pay you for the wine.”

The old man relaxed and smiled for a second time.

CHAPTER 24

MON CHE'RI, MADAM BEBE'

A full week passed but Mico found no one with information about his little family. He called on homes of neighbors and local stores. He visited a half dozen churches and synagogues along the coastline, including two trips back to Nice. Questions regarding the disappearance of his family were greeted with shrugs, teary eyes, resignation, hostility and indifference.

Each reply evoked unbelievable emotional responses and by the end of the week he was exhausted, frustrated and, once again, angry at the entire world. He was a man possessed by the dark side and, worse, he began to doubt he would ever find the light as each negative response punctured his heart and bruised his soul.

Staying with the old grump was a grating and exasperating misery and the belief Mr. Tovier knew more than he let on, disturbed Mico greatly. He was running low on money and realized the hunt for information might need to be delayed. Perhaps he had better return home and find alternate ways to continue the quest.

"Tovier, I'm going back to Italy for a while and when I get back here I expect you to be living elsewhere."

The old man looked up, a quizzical look on his face, and did not reply.

"I'll be back soon. Do you understand what I said?"

"It's not your house."

Explosion! "Not my house, not my house.... why you *sunnavabitch*, I'll break your neck...."

The old man retreated into the big chair, looked at the floor and quietly said, "Why don't you visit Madame Bebe' at the "Baby Doll" down on Rue Rouge? She may know something."

His heart jumped a beat, he forgot about the house, "Who is she? Why didn't you tell me about her before?"

"Madame is", a hesitation, "an entertainer of a sort". Continuing, head down, "One must be careful these days with the ongoing charges of collaboration with the enemy, reprisals, the shaving of women's heads because of their taste for German sweets, black market risks and so forth..."

Mico, beside himself, rose to his feet, responded with a sardonic, "Thanks much!", and ran out of the house.

Ten minutes later he entered "Madame Bebe's. Dark drapes, covered the walls, yellow lights shimmered against a huge mirror, a crack splitting it into two triangles. A low soft voice came from a radio or phonograph. He recognized the voice of *"La Mome"* (The Little Sparrow), Edith Piaf, singing her pre-war smash hit, *L'Accordeoniste*. He looked around the room as the frail singer's plaintive voice reminded him of lost love and lost hope.

From behind one of the drapes came the festive growl of a tiger making love, "Welcome to the Baby Doll, *m'sieur*, I am Madam Bebe' and since I am the madam, you must be the doll. Ha! Ha!"

"Will it be coffee or something stronger?" Her Italian was perfect; the Tuscan accent, pleasant to his ear.

Common language aside, the veteran of many battles automatically went into a defensive mode. He looked towards the drape and saw this magnificent giant of a woman bursting out from a yellow and red *peignoir* (kimono); the light reflected blue eye shadow, red lips the color of fresh blood and a crevasse that would have been a haven for the entire French army. The sight was so overwhelming he didn't notice the burnt red hair and the pounds of jewelry she wore.

"Ya, she is an entertainer of sorts, alright", reflected Mico. He gently shook the lady's extended hand, and as he had done so many times during the past week, nervously explained the reason for his visit. He repeated the names of his family and asked if she could provide any information.

To Mico's frustration, Madame Bebe' did not answer the question. She released his hand and sat down on a plush, gold lined red sofa. She sank into it with great delight and patted the pillow to her right, "Please rest yourself next to me."

The big man remained standing.

"I came here from Tuscany, Prato to be exact, just a couple of months before Mussolini attacked France."

"Prato?" that's fairly close to my home", interjected Mico.

Madam Bebe' continued as if she had not heard, "I bought this little paradise and offered entertainment, libations and good times to Italians, Frenchmen and, yes, Germans. One had to live, you know. I was not political and remained pretty much ambivalent to the political changes here. And, yes, the Nazi's stationed along the *Riviera* were also huge fans of my offerings."

Mico remained silent as he dropped into the sofa.

"Over the years, I tried to maintain a "neutrality"; it was essential to my survival. Then, things began to change. The rise of the *Resistance*, collaborators spying on their own, the ongoing accelerated deportation of "foreigners" forced me to re-think my survival ideas."

She straightened one of her bracelets, "One morning, it must have been four or five o'clock, one of my girls awakened me, a man was standing next to her. At first I was angry for being awakened and finding one of her clients in my private bedroom."

Madame Bebe' hesitated, "He wasn't a client; he was a member of the *Resistance* on the run."

She took on a defiant tone, "I did not hesitate; we immediately brought him down to the cellars, where he remained for over three months."

Mico anxiously interrupted, "Do you know anything about my family?"

The woman's demeanor softened as she asked to have the names repeated.

His hand quivered, thinking, "Is it possible the moment of truth is to be revealed from this most unbelievable source?"

He obliged her.

She straightened in her chair, appeared to be struggling to maintain her composure. Touching his hand, "I knew who you were soon as you walked in. I was told you were asking questions."

The big man nodded, clasped his hands together. He was shaking.

Quietly, "One still needs to be very, very careful."

After an eternal hesitation, she looked into Mico's eyes, a tear ruining her mascara, "I knew them, Signore Carboni. They took them away."

An inhuman wail, Big Mico slumped gasping for breath; he fainted. Big, bad Mico had fainted!

Upon reawakening a few moments later, perfumed lilac invaded his nostrils. He felt the wet rag against his face, opened his eyes and stared into the crevasse. Piaf's voice was replaced by the loud scratching of needle against record.

"There, there..."

He collected himself, "I'm OK. My apologies…"

"Apologies? Hardly. There is no easy way. Do you want me to continue?"

He straightened, the voice from afar, resumed, "Over the next year or so, until the August liberation, we hid eleven different escapees. Two from the *Resistance* and the others were Jews, French and foreigners. Your family, including the baby, lived here for about six weeks, hidden in the cellar most of the time. You can imagine the strength of our girls, doing business, knowing they would be killed or sent away themselves if we were found out. Several friends, including Mr. Tovier, suspected we were hiding escapees, but despite the risk, no one reported us. We continue to hold our secrets; as in many other parts of Europe, including our Italia."

A second from falling into a complete state of shock, Mico barely heard her words.

He returned to the present upon hearing, "In early October or late September of '43, your father-in-law decided to leave. We all tried to convince them to wait, but they believed it was best to get your little girl out of here and into a safe house somewhere high above Nice."

She hesitated, gripped Mico's arm, "The next day we were informed of their arrest. We knew the culprits were a few Vichy collaborators, a few pigs from up north who called themselves *The French Legion of Fighters.* Mr. Carboni, we don't know what happened after the arrest but most of the Jews..."

She did not finish the sentence. With heartbeat racing and head exploding, he stood, offered his thanks, walked out the door and, without hesitation, began walking towards the Italian border.

He just left the world.

CHAPTER 25

PEACE— SUCH A WONDERFUL WORD

"They say the war is over. No Germans, no Fascist, no air raids, no big guns, no anthems, no casualty lists and no death notices. Now, if we could just find something to eat..."

The peace brought many political confrontations between Italy's political parties; many were violent. After such a brutal war and much suffering, communities experienced new post war fears. Anger and hatred rushed to the surface, lacking sense and direction. Payback for unforgotten insults and slights were remembered and dealt with in the form of personal vendettas. The anger was deep and violence was the palliative administered, even to one's own. Justice was rendered locally, quickly and without appeal to higher courts.

Like the gone Fascist, ex-partisans Communist now wielded the all too familiar truncheon against their opposition. Especially brutal, they hunted ex-Fascists, others who had served in Mussolini's Republican army and innocents who might have offended them in the past.

In many cities, where the hammer and sickle dominated, men suspected of having had Fascists leanings were beaten or killed; women who had offered their delights to the Germans had their head shaved and paraded through town. The "rich" were easy targets and were assailed with false or exaggerated remarks regarding their involvement with the Fascist or as having given assistance to the Germans.

The Communist were particularly strong in the recently liberated northern Italian cities and towns. Gianni knew of several cities in the Northern provinces that were forcefully taken over by the far left. In Como, for example, the Committee of National Liberation appointed a Signor Nulli as temporary mayor of the city, but upon arriving to assume office found the office occupied by a Signor Manni, a communist leader. After some rather ominous threats, Mr. Nulli lost his desire to be mayor. In Turin, the new mayor, a Communist who, two weeks before, escaped from a Verona prison, claimed and now held the mayoral seat.

In Sasso, the pretty Oliveri twins, accused by life-long neighbors of having taken on German lovers, had their hair shorn and paraded nude through town. Instead of a little understanding, others, like Beatrice and Carla, were singled out for having housed and fed Germans. Little thought was given to the fact that to live, one must do what one must do.

Martyrdom can be an overstated virtue.

After spending weeks traveling his "Via Dolorosa", Mico reached the walls surrounding the city of Lucca in late September. He was in a tormenting stupor, his mind and psyche so troubled he barely remembered the journey. The long hours sleeping in the open air, stealing fruit and vegetables from road side fields and the walking, riding jeeps, mule carts and an assortment of vehicles born of different mothers, had weakened the big man. He needed to rest.

He still had a few liras remaining and was considering a rented room for the night. He could clean up, eat a good meal and be better prepared for his return to Sasso. He started crossing the road leading to one of the city gates when an American Jeep came roaring through the gate, screeched to a stop nearly hitting the filthy carcass trying to walk like a man.

In broken Italian, "Watch where in the hell you are going!"

Mico looked up, sad eyed, quietly said "Corporal, you were speeding."

A few bystanders were gathering around the jeep, someone honked a horn, as the smiling GI asked, "Since you recognized my high rank, "Can I give you a ride? Where are you headed?"

Mico, understanding the man's attempt at Italian, answered, "The cut-off towards Sasso."

"Gimmee your suitcase and hop aboard "*paisan*"; that's a short hop, right?"

The corporal assumed the grunted reply was an affirmation.

A moment later the corporal continued his attempt at conversation, "Lots of fighting in this area just a bit ago, huh?"

A nod.

"You in *Italiano* army?"

"*Partigiano.*"

"Communist?"

A hesitation, a side glance, "*Si.*"

"No problem for me. I'm heading for New Jersey next week. Don't know much about politics except for those idiots put this corporal's ass at risk for nearly two crappy years."

He looked at Mico's well- worn dirty clothes, smiled and asked, "*Capeesh*?"

Mico nodded yes.

"My Italian ain't too good. Learned it from my Ma. She was born in Naples, speaks the dialect." He hit the steering wheel and laughed, "Hell, her Italian is worse than her English."

Mico opened a bit, "Your father is Italian, too?"

"Sicilian. Never spoke to us in Italian. Always English. He wanted everyone to know he was an American. Never gave a crap about *La Bella Italia.* Came to the States when he was fifteen and never looked back."

He looked at Mico, "Understand what I'm saying?"

He bristled, wanted to tell the man there once was a *Bella Italia* and, someday soon..." He was too tired to argue and, instead said, "Si." A smile, "Yes."

"You know these mountains?"

Mico wanted to stop the conversation but, owing a debt of gratitude to the chattering American, pointed in the direction of *Mt. Cimone*, "Born and raised up there, fought the Germans and Black Shirts all over the hills," a hesitation, "and probably will die there."

The American stopped talking and Mico looked out the window and saw thirsty trees; cypress and emaciated olive trees, looking upwards hoping, this time, the gathering clouds would deliver wet manna from heaven. He nodded off.

When he awoke, the busy City and its Serchia River were well behind them. He now was very familiar with the sights whizzing by; old familiar stone houses, with names very familiar to Mico, dotted very brown hills. He saw ruined barns and fences waiting to be repaired. Without emotion, he reflected he and his partisan group could have been enablers of the damage.

"How long have I been asleep? We didn't miss the cut-off to Sasso did we?"

"About a half hour. Sasso cut-off up ahead. You got *famiglia* up there?"

Mico, flinching at the word *famiglia*, answered, "The cut-off is about a kilometer up ahead; I'll jump off there. Can't thank you enough."

"Okee-doe-kee, *paisano*. It has been my pleasure. You know, us *dagos* got to stick together. "

Having heard the Americans use the derogatory term when referring to the partisans, Mico bristled, but kept his temper, saying "There's the sign pointing to Sasso. I'll jump off here."

Laughing, "*Buona fortuna*, Kilroy! Nice, knowing you."

Mico assumed it was an American way of saying *arrivederci.*

Somewhat refreshed, Mico walked up a narrow asphalt road from the main highway into the wooded slope. He intended to rent a room for the night at the back of "Pitini's Café/Bar". The bar was a very well-known watering hole for many of the locals wanting a "refresher" before beginning the long climb towards the hamlets at the higher altitudes. Mico and the entire Carboni clan had given Signor Pitini plenty of business over the years.

During the war, Pitini served everyone – Fascist, German, partisan – he was adept at warning the partisans of enemy presence while earning local Fascist and German officers' good will by providing them with the best available food and drink. Everyone in this partisan infested area knew of Pitini and his love of money. To no one's surprise, the man was playing and winning at a very dangerous game.

Mico shuffled upwards for a couple of hundred yards when he noticed a roadside shrine; a small concrete hut with a cross above the open entrance.

There were many of these simple structures throughout the mountains, but Mico never had given them much attention.

A small fountain, dribbling fresh water from a small stream, drew him towards the small chapel. He washed his hands and face while slurping mouthfuls of the refreshing cold water. He was coming back to life.

For some reason, the once ardent Communist then walked towards the opening of the little chapel. Not noticing the faded red plastic flowers guarding the entrance, the big man stooped, entered the shrine and knelt before a washed-out print of the Madonna. A faded gold tiara sat atop the forlorn face. A blue shawl covered a gray-white dress. Outstretched arms called to him.

He hardly looked at the print, but instead read the various scribbled prayer pleas laid on the small bare altar. He remained stoic, unmoved by the beseeching words of others.

He was in a prayerful posture for a few moments, his mind impassive; a complete blank. He turned and looked at the faded print again, awakened and began to weep; a whimper and then uncontrollable sobs.

"They killed my wife." He choked, "They killed my baby." It was not a prayer nor was it a plea. It was merely a statement of fact. He had lost everything that mattered. The French nightmare was reality and there was not a thing the hero warrior could do about it.

He was alone.

Nothing would ever be the same.

He stood, wiped his eyes with his sleeve and noticed a small plaque beneath the faded print. He read:

> Sinner, there are only two dates that matter to you.
> The date of your birth and the date of your death.
> The in-between days are merely an audition.

Mico thought he understood, looked at the print again, exited and headed upward toward the roadhouse. It began to sprinkle; each rain drop exposing the hungry dust-covered asphalt and teasing the thirsty over hanging trees. He brightened, lengthened his step and trudged upwards.

Signore Pitini, ignoring the big man's shabby appearance, greeted Mico as a long lost relative; even proffering the partisan hero a glass of last year's *red.* Given Pitini's avarice, the offer was a remarkable act of generosity and/or respect. Mico courteously declined.

He noticed several Communist propaganda posters hanging behind the bar; the usual "Let us Unite" message springing up all over this area of Italy. Evidently, Mr. Petini knew good politics were especially advantageous for his business.

Pitini handed Mico a key, "Your room is at the back, the last room; room number 5. Be careful, it's quite muddy." He took the key and walked toward the back of the café. Noticing the new wooden planks serving as a sidewalk over the mud, Mico thought Pitini was taking quite a risk providing such a nicety for his guests. Things had a predictable way of disappearing during these difficult times.

He walked past four rooms, each with paper-thin-doors and close-to-the-ground windows. The key was a heavy jail-cell size piece of metal chained to a slab of wood, upon which someone had painted a crude #5.

Slotting the key, a smile, "Pitini, you old bastard, don't worry, no one is going to walk away with this beauty; it's stronger than your doors."

He removed his wet shirt and shoes and sat down on the small bed. For a brief moment he looked out the dirty, eye-level window, thought about his family, laid back and fell asleep wondering if his lice would get along with the mattress's current occupants.

Three or four hours later he awoke, walked to a chipped enamel bowl sitting on a small table near a water faucet. He twisted the spigot, the faucet sputtered, refusing to free its treasure. Mico, with a forcible twist, won the battle as a steady stream fresh cold water flowed free. He splashed water on his face and chest, thinking, "This is a good place to start a new beginning, I've cried and moaned enough; got to face life again."

He splashed a good amount of water on his head and chest, shivering, he laughed loudly, "I baptize myself in the name..." He shivered, again, the joviality disappearing, looked up and addressed his wife and little girl," I will never forget you nor ever forgive those bastards that took you away."

He dried with a small hand towel, looked up again, erased a sneer with a burst of laughter, "Now there is a baptismal vow for you!"

Refreshed and now dressed in dry clothing, he picked up his room key and walked back and into Pitini's now very crowded, noisy bar.

The smoke-filled room, lit by the dull yellow light bulbs belonging to the last century, was alive with political wine-laced chatter. He heard shouts from men standing at the bar, holding their glasses high:

> "Those Catholic bastards kicked us out of the government!"
>
> "Viva il Socialismo! Viva ltalia!"
>
> "We march again!"
>
> "Raise your glasses to the Hammer and Sickle!"
>
> "Pitini, pour another for my Comrades."

The Communist believed they had been the "real partisans". They had been well organized and, with instructions and assistance from Moscow, the cohesiveness continued. Their political strength was not to be denied and the Communist party, particularly in this area of north-central Italy was particularly strong and its members aggressively confrontational. Pity any ex-Fascist or suspected sympathizer they encountered; these warriors considered revenge the fruit of winning the war.

Mico had fought many a battle with men like these, but for him, that was then and today was today; he no longer held any political beliefs; he had left most of that far behind.

Paying little attention to these self-proclaimed patriots, he walked to an empty table, sat and scanned the room. In one corner, under the critical eyes of two kibitzers, four men sat at a heavy wooden table playing a game of *briscola*. Empty wine glasses evidencing that someone had lost at least one game.

At the far end of the crowded bar, three very inebriated woodsmen were arguing about some phase of the recent war. Mico nodded toward Signor Pitini as a short, stocky waitress began to noisily clear a few dishes from the table. She was the only female in the place.

Wiping her huge hands on an apron featuring souvenirs of a week's worth of entrees, "What the hell do you want?"

"Whatta you got?"

"Polenta."

"Polenta with?"

"With more polenta?"

"Any cheese?"

"Ya, but it will cost you extra."

"Bring on the polenta with two slices of cheese. Is the cheese Pecorino?"

"How in the hell do I know. Do I look like a *campagnola* (farm girl)?"

Mico laughed heartedly for the first time since his world had come to an end; even ready to tease the girl. Instead replied, "Bring whatever you have. I'm sure it will be fine."

He finished his meal and a second glass of Pitini's *red* and was about to return to his room when two of the men he had first noticed arguing at the bar, came up to him, "Pitini tells us you were a big-shot war hero."

Mico ignored the man, rose to his feet to pay his tab but was roughly pushed down, the chair nearly capsizing, "We know who you are and you are no damn hero."

The man poked his index finger into Mico's chest, "You are a deserter, a …"

A huge fist holding a heavy key crushed into the man's nose, knocking him to the floor, blood gushing from both nostrils. Mico rose, smiled at the second man, "Want some?"

A red faced Pitini came running, screaming, "Stop! Stop!" He grabbed Mico's arm, "They have been drinking; they don't know what they are saying!"

Several others crowded the table as Pitini pleaded, "Please, no more fighting! No more. Everyone have a drink on me!"

Mico stood, finished his glass of wine, left a few coins on the table for the waitress and turned toward the owner, "Once again, I must decline your generous offer of your *red*." He smiled, transferred the key to his other hand saying, "The polenta was delicious. I'll pay you tomorrow morning."

Feeling better than he had in weeks, the ex-partisan leader "Ivan", nee Mico, went back to his room where, not even bothering to undress, immediately fell asleep.

He is awakened by a bad dream. He was back in the mountains; a voice was calling to him "Hey Ivan, open up for your old comrades."

To the accompaniment of a rumbling cascade of thunder echoing down from the mountains above, he looked out into the darkness, "Who are you? Whatta you want? Get the hell out of here!"

Again, the somewhat familiar voice, "Come on Ivan have a glass with us. Just one for old times."

"It's me, Vaccaccia, your old partisan buddy coming to say hello. Heard you were in France. Visiting that little Jewish wife of yours, huh?"

No answer.

"Also, I heard you damn near broke my friend's nose last night. Sure good having you back, great hero."

Thoughts raced through Mico's mind, "Vaccaccia, the laziest guy in the entire group. Vaccaccia, the coward! The shirker who, in the last days of the war, wanted Gianni's head."

Knowing the man, Mico was sure this was to be the vendetta the weakling had promised in that prior life.

It was quiet for a few moments. He peeked out the window. It was raining; the raindrops playing a staccato introduction to the new day. There were others waiting; the weakling would not act alone. Worse, other than the heavy key fob, Mico was unarmed. It would be light in a short while; he decided, "better remain locked in the room and wait it out."

He sat on his bed, "Better not think of France." He turned, looked out the low window, "Think about the family up in Sasso; I'll be seeing them soon. They will be …"

A huge stone came crashing through the window hitting Mico's right shoulder and sending him to the floor. A dark shadow followed the rock and landed on Mico and hit him with a club. Another body leaped at him and delivered a kick to his shoulder; the pain excruciating!

Dazed, he tried to roll away. A sharp pain, screams; more pain followed by the gurgle of a soft stream coming to life at winter's retreat.

Then, through a babble of muted voices, he heard a familiar, forgiving voice softly calling to him, *"Mico, your audition has ended. Welcome home."*

Signore Pitini, ever the businessman, told the police Mico had a short tussle with a stranger; they seem to know each other. He reported that, after finishing a glass of *the red*, the big man left; Pitini assumed Mico was going to his room for the night.

That is all he knew; he heard nothing and saw nothing until the next morning when a couple of mushroom hunters knocked on his door and told him they saw a bloody body lying in the mud.

The *Polizia di Stato* reported that the body, marked with bruises and slashes, evidenced the great pain the man must have endured before succumbing. He had been clubbed, his throat slashed and, as further insult, the assailants had stuffed a huge key fob into his mouth.

The police concluded the report, "The former partisan leader, Domenico "Ivan" Carboni, had faced and met an ignominious, despicable death.

CHAPTER 26

THE REWARDS OF WAR—OCTOBER 1945

A cool wind hurried down the mountainside; one could hear a slight murmur as golden leaves were gently caressed and sadly snipped from the few remaining on the six trees standing guard outside the cemetery gate. The quiet of the moment, the chalk gray clouds and the somber brown of the hastily made wooden coffin, all contributed to a sense of overwhelming melancholy and sorrow.

After a youth of war and loss, the big man was gone.

A few men and several women, dressed in death's colors, stoically faced the wind. There was no priest present; Communists didn't need prayers. And though he had softened his biases, everyone in the area was sure Mico was still a Communist.

What they didn't know was that man's inner beliefs are not always worn as a waist-coat for, not too long ago, Mico had pleaded with his Maker for his family's safety. In fact, on several occasions the avowed Communist prayed for the very people now standing around his grave; on his knees, no less.

All of the survivors of the "The Cutigliano Escapade" were present. Gianni and Carla stood near his old friend's casket. Beatrice remained motionless between her grandson and her daughter; Mico's sister Gio, dry eyed, stood close to the big Brazilian while supporting her mother, Gina.

Carla had given birth to a beautiful little boy they named Pietro, in honor of Carla's deceased father, Pietro Berti. She and Gianni had moved back to

Casa Berti. She also owned the vacant Grandi property, making her dirt rich but lira poor. Beatrice, Nilde, Emilio and Michelle remained at "*La Rimessa*".

The improbable lovers, Gio and the Brazilian were living at the *Casone* with Gina. Bruno deserted the army and was now a fugitive from Brazilian law. It mattered little to him, as Brazil was far, far away and he was confident a resolution to the question lay in the distant future. Gina reluctantly accepted the situation and was a happy woman. Bruno became the "man of the house"; she reasoned he was a good man and would eventually agree, as the Brazilian would say, "to commit marriage."

Unaware of the catastrophe in France, the family assumed Mico had been trying to return home because of money problems or to arrange his little family's move to Sasso. They spoke of a band of rogues roaming the mountains in northern Tuscany and assumed Mico was murdered in a robbery attempt or because of a political argument.

However, remembering the anger and threats made by some in the old partisan group, Gianni believed someone in the old partisan group killed his friend. The longer he stood at the grave the angrier he became. Poison filled his veins, dark shadows deepened, "Whatever the reason, they killed you; then, to further insult you, your own supposed brothers in arms, spit on your body."

He continued gazing at the soon to be barren trees; a quiver his only movement. He felt a bit guilty as he was unable to shed a single tear even as the body was being lowered. His mind raced ahead of the wind, whirling in anger as he now dredged up memories of the first days after the liberation. Fury raised within as he evoked memories of the gang of thieves that burned Dina's little bar; the men who assaulted and clubbed him senseless and, most infuriating, the pig who called his Carla a whore.

He returned to the present as Gio threw the first handful of soil on the casket and said for all to hear, "I know, and your Maker knows, you always served to the best of your ability, you were always true to your cause, faithful to your friends and loving and caring towards our family", a short gasp, "Mico you are my brother and you will always be my hero."

The wind began to show the stronger side of its personality. Coats were pulled tighter as the mourners hastened their goodbyes and left the little cemetery. Only Gianni and Carla remained.

Gianni had lost an old friend; a man with whom he had argued, loved, fought with and fought against. He would never again experience the hug of a true confidant; a man he could trust with his innermost secrets and with his life. The world doesn't often endow the gift of a good friend and, when it does give, it often takes away, creating a never to be replaced loss.

Gianni Carboni felt the gurgle of a blood vendetta as Mico's body was being lowered into oblivion. "You survived the war dear friend, but the great new peace killed you."

He threw a flower into the dark hole and silently swore, "Vendetta and control is their anthem. Our vendetta is my promise to you. Mico, I'll never forget."

Then he mumbled, "Vaccaccia … Tulio … you sons of a bitches!"

It was not a prayer Carla wanted to hear.

CHAPTER 27

ALL SORTS OF IDEAS

Over the next year, living conditions in Sasso slowly improved. Gardens were planted, chickens, sheep and goats were raised thus providing basic necessities. However, the lack of simple everyday essentials fed a smoldering fire. Soap, toilet paper, coffee, sugar, etc. were part of a lengthy list of basics difficult to find and any family possessing these items were subjected to jealous innuendos and rumor mongering.

The Carboni clan had two strong supply lines for these basics.

The most important source was Beatrice's eldest daughter, Roberta, who had married and moved to New York before the war began. Wrapped in flour sack cloths, later used as towels and rough bed sheets, Roberta sent packages crammed with toilet paper, canned sardines, salt, corn meal, sugar, coffee, clothing and other essentials.

Packages also arrived from the Texas cousins who sent cartons of American cigarettes – always Lucky Strike and Pall Mall brands – and tobacco – valuable items that could be used as ready cash.

However, the *Americani's* acts of compassion, consideration and love for their far-away relatives created problems for the family.

The acts of kindness stirred jealousies and envy among some Sasso neighbors. The local postwoman, a die-hard Communist, bristled with anger as package after package arrived from *L'America* for "those Carboni who already have so much."

Spreading her vicious gossip as she delivered the mail, she reminded one and all, "Her first husband was Sasso's Fascist leader during the Mussolini years; or the Germans were welcomed and comforted in both Carla's and Beatrice's houses. The hag always neglected to mention Mico Carboni had been a Communist partisan trailblazer.

Fear of the new local Communist party leaders in town and avoiding the risk of being labeled themselves, most neighbors said little in defense, even those who were helped by Carboni family members.

Gianni, aware of these sentiments, itched to leave Sasso even though Carla was now considered wealthy by local standards. She had inherited her father's property and, with Lorenzo's death, now owned the Grandi property… thereby making her the largest land-owner in Sasso. But, as she would laughingly say to family members, "You can't eat rocks and dirt."

Gianni thought more and more about asking Carla to sell the property and move away, perhaps, to "*L'America*"; to New York, where his sister Roberta lived, or to Texas, where his Uncle's family lived. He hoped Carla would agree but wasn't too convinced the rest of the family would move. The challenge might be too great for some; particularly his mother and aunt.

The idea floated in and out of his mind, but as time passed, the embers of vengeance also continued to flicker and continued to dominate his thoughts. Revenge gnawed at his innards and continued to breathe life to his sense of guilt for having yet to fulfill his graveside promise to Mico.

His mind-set, Mico first! America could wait.

In September, on the feast of St. Mercedes, the patron saint of Sasso, Beatrice hosted a fine dinner for the entire family. Everyone had eaten their fill; the wine supply sufficiently punished. Gianni stood, raised yet another glass, "I salute Mico and this day by announcing to you ladies that Michelle, my "Brazilian amigo" and I are going on a hunting trip; we are going down to Lucca and…."

Carla, "The hell you are!"

Gianni ignored the interruption, "We are going back to the bar where Mico was killed, talk to the tavern owner again; I'm betting he knows more than he told the police. I'm going to find out who was responsible. If he doesn't know anything we are going to search for and find the roving vigilantes and ask…."

"How are you going to find…."

"They are led by some Italian Robin Hood called Julius the Great. He and his band are petrifying everyone in Tuscany; believe me, I am betting he will be easy to find."

"You are betting? You are betting your life and our family's future for Mico? Mico is dead. He won't return. It's over. Gianni, let him rest in peace. And if you win your so-called bet and find him, then what? Are you going to kill him? Beat him? Curse him? Then what?"

The festive aura immediately disappeared into an ominous silence. No one had ever heard Carla speak in such a manner towards her Gianni.

Nilde, in a low-voice sarcastic tone, "Michelle is not going on any so-called hunting trip!"

Gio and Beatrice remained quiet.

"It's a year Mico has been gone..."

Nilde, "I don't care if its ten years. You've got a child to worry about now; not some wine fed idea of vengeance for something that happened in a different lifetime!"

Gianni turned from his sister and addressed his wife, "Carla, I made a promise; a solemn oath to Mico..."

"You made the promise, not my son", Nilde interrupted, "you want to go and get yourself killed, go ahead; but you are not taking Michelle with you! You hear me Gianni?"

Michelle, "Aw, Ma, I'm not your little boy anymore..."

"You shut up; you are not going anywhere!"

Carla, cradling her new born baby boy, furious with Gianni, stood and without saying another word, left the table, sat in the old sofa chair, stared into the fire place, opened her blouse and began nursing the infant.

The big Brazilian stood, sipped a bit of wine, wiped an index finger across the jet-black moustache, "Michelle needn't be with us; Gianni and I can take care of our business and be back in a couple of days..."

Gio, who had been continually smiling, interrupted, "Let's see, as I understand the first part of the plan, you will arm yourselves, hunt the quarry in the mountains where you have no friends."

She stood, glass of *the red* in hand, and paced like a prosecuting attorney in a courtroom, "Then, you are going to ask some stranger to lead you to Mico's murderers. Right?"

She continued uninterrupted, "Now let me unfold the possibilities of such a truly imaginative plan. First, let's assume you sleuths succeed and you slay the dragon or dragons." She took a sip of *the red*, smiled broadly and pointed the glass at Gianni, "Do you really think their pals won't retaliate? Or, if the *polizia* enter the game, and they certainly will want to play, how about twenty years' jail-time for Gianni-boy and his side kick Sir Michelle?"

The smile disappeared as she then turned towards her Brazilian lover, "And we can be assured of a lovely decade in jail and then a trip back to Brazil for my mustached deserter. What lovely changes in our lives. Right?"

Bruno bowed his head and scratched his ankle, his moustache sagged as it seemed to have taken on weight.

Gio continued, "But let's examine the other possibilities. For example, you two are captured by the ex-partisans; Gianni, wouldn't that be a wonderful reunion? Then what, Gianni? Bruno? Then what?" Mockingly she added, "I wonder if you considered these possible scenarios."

She turned towards the ladies, "I must have missed something for I'm sure they considered many other possibilities. Right ladies?"

Furious as she had been, Carla stifled a giggle.

Gio, "Oh! Please. Please share with the family you are leaving behind, the wisdom and details of your wonderful plan. Especially the details and, of course, the logic used to lead you to such a brilliant, splendid conclusion."

Gio finished her wine, sat, folded her arms and awaited an answer. No one replied; the silence broken only by the contented cooing of the feeding infant.

After a few moments, Beatrice, took a sip of wine, bit into a cookie, "When did you three generals think this up?"

The three men stared at the stone floor as their aura of bravado melted into remorseful schoolboy frowns; there was no response to Beatrice's question.

Beatrice continued, "The *red* is an amazing, mysterious tonic; sometimes it turns frogs into tenors, klutzes into combatants, toothless wonders into Romeos and brilliant into stupid; and, Michelle, do you know the most amazing fact about the red?"

The young man didn't dare raise his eyes.

"No? Well, let me tell you. It is an absolute proven scientific fact the more sips of the grape, the smarter and braver one becomes. By the time a bottle is finished, one has attained a level of knowledge worthy of a doctorate; two bottles and he is king of the universe."

She tasted a bit more of her red, "Now, I figure you three have finished about a bottle apiece. Which means one of you thinks he is a Romeo; the second, a military force worthy of Italy's highest Medal of Honor and the last one has reached such a point we can call him a complete idiot."

Beatrice tipped her glass towards Gianni, "For now, I'll concentrate on the idiot!"

"Mico is gone; nothing you can do will bring him back. You are now a father, a husband, an uncle, a brother and, lastly, a son. She stared at her love child, tears forming, "Tell me, Gianni, does your blood boil so high you would take a risk that could affect each of your loved ones for the rest of their lives?"

It was so quiet one could hear the wind softly wooing the trees, then Gianni raised his head and, with deep emotion, quietly answered his mother, "He killed Mico; he burned down Dina's place; he stole from us and, lastly, he called my wife a whore. Only a coward would walk away from answering his actions."

"You can't be sure of all that and, furthermore..."

"I think …"

"Stop interrupting me; right now, I don't' care what you think." Beatrice stopped for a moment, turned and angrily faced her son, "Prison? Or walking around for the rest of your life worrying one of his friends is going to carry out his equalizing vendetta on you or a member of our family; your baby, for example?"

The room was so quiet one could hear the soft coos of the happy, well-fed little one; Gianni shuffled his feet as his mother continued, "Revenge breeds revenge and even if you succeed in your vendetta you will live the rest of your life with a curse that will never heal. And, you'll place the same stigma on Michelle, plus putting us all in danger."

A steely stare towards her precious son, "The war is over for us, Gianni; let it remain so."

She finished her glass of red, went over to Carla, picked up the baby, cradled him in her arms and walked into the kitchen.

Gianni went over to Carla, "Look, it's my …"

"It's your what? Your duty? Your moral obligation?" She stood, looked up at him, "I'll tell you what it really is Gianni; it's your last goodbye to me and the baby. You will never be able to atone for this", tears glistening, "for it proves your lust for revenge is greater than your love for family."

She turned, "I'm sorry but it's time for me and the baby to leave."

Gianni's *"Grugno"* was biting at his innards; he had more to say but all he could do was scowl and head towards home with his wife and child.

He had some re-thinking to do.

CHAPTER 28

SOMETIMES THE BOAR CATCHES THE HUNTER

Winter arrived. Brutal. Cold. A never-ending panorama of grey slate skies, shriveled trees and deep snow drifts continued to add to Sasso's misery. The first peace-time celebration of the birth of the Prince of Peace brought more snow, then on New Year's Eve a brutal whistling wind created huge snow drifts, keeping everyone indoors, adding to the isolation of most households.

Despite the weather, the Carboni clan gathered at *La Rimessa* for a New Year's Eve celebration. Much wine fueled the conversations while pasta dishes calmed appetites. Thanks to the goodies sent from America, desserts and real "grappa-improved" black coffee escalated the chatter and heightened the jovial holiday atmosphere.

Gianni stood near the huge fireplace, threw two small logs on the fire, turned towards his family and in a quiet, serious voice said, "I have a few words to say."

The chattering stopped, only the crackling of the logs as the flame ate into them could be heard. Gianni walked over to Carla, put one hand on her shoulder, "First, I wish the year 1946 a happy death and I raise my glass to *bambino* 1947; may the new year bring a lasting peace, good health and", grinning towards the Brazilian Nasciente and Gio, "a huge wedding celebration."

Once the laughter subsided he recommenced in a low serious manner, "Mico and I were re-united right here at La Rimessa, truly one of the most important days of my life. We had a problem when we left the partisans but, like good brothers, we solved it and bore no grudges. We knew evil and, together, we did some good."

He took a deep breath, "We were brothers in every sense of the word," he lowered his head, eyes glistening with sorrow, "I owe him my life and he will be part of me forever."

He hesitated, "You ladies were right; the vendetta idea was stupid and the possible costs certainly would not have compensated for Mico's loss." A small, sheepish smile, "Although It took me a while, I now realize a vendetta will not re-pay my debt to the Devil."

Carla touched his hand as he pressed her shoulder, "We were fortunate to have listened to your advice." He chuckled, "Or, perhaps, it is more correct to say we obeyed your orders."

Everyone laughed as Michelle, raising another glass of the red, took his mother's hand, gave her a kiss on the forehead and yelled, "Here's to our ladies!"

"Sit down! You are drunk!" His mother's voice was stern, but the smile on her face undermined the command.

Gianni finished his wine and continued, "There is one other item I'd like to talk to you about. As I have indicated to you, I've been thinking about leaving Italy and get away from this misery. We have Roberta and her husband in New York and Zio Gigi in Texas. I am sure we can all find work and an opportunity for a good future, unlike the turmoil knocking at our doors every day."

Immediately the mood changed. Carla's hissing "Geezus" was the only sound.

Unflustered, "Mamma, you could see Roberta again after all these years; a better future for you, Emilio and NIlde; especially for Michelle; the same for you Zia Gina."

He turned towards Gio, smiling, "and I am sure we can work out something for our Brazilian brother."

Gianni, raising his glass, "I'll write Roberta and ask for her thoughts; meanwhile, think about the idea."

Silence.

After a short pause, "If we don't like the place, we can always return here."

Michelle started singing his Italian version of Yankee Doodle Dandy.

Nilde once again rebuked her son, "I told you to shut up; you are drunk!" She pulled him by the sleeve and made him sit.

The others smiled but no one outwardly reacted to Gianni's comments until Emilio, who usually had little to say, broke the silence, "Italy has ruined my life; I won't let this country ruin my son's life. I won't stand in Michelle's way if he wants to go."

The quiet man's hands were shaking, "and Nilde, you too, deserve better." Nilde put her arm around Emilio, gave him a kiss on the forehead and, for once, said nothing.

Beatrice, sensing Carla's displeasure softly interjected, "Let's change the subject; I think the wine is talking right now. If you are serious, Gianni, I suggest you talk about the matter with your wife before you bring others into the discussion."

"I know, I know, but …."

Beatrice, "Gianni drop it! Now!"

Gianni looked at his mother, then his wife, saw the smirks, stopped talking, tipped his glass to his mother and swallowed the remaining red.

The uncomfortable quiet was disturbed when the Brazilian, who also had sampled plenty of the red, excused himself with an "I'll be right back", threw on his coat and stumbled out the door.

Ten minutes later he returned with a jar-full of home-made *grappa*. Without removing his coat, he poured himself a generous amount of the white fire, raised the cup and proudly shouted out, "Happy New Year! Here is to my new son!"

Gio, face turning red as the wine in her glass, nearly choked on her *pasta fritta*; Beatrice dropped a spoon while Gio's mother, Gina, screamed so loudly she awoke baby who added his wails to a scene of absolute joyful confusion; even Nasciente's moustache appeared to be smiling.

The women rushed to the expectant mother's side, showered kisses on her; Gio responded with a gracious, but subdued smile. Gianni noticed Gio's glowering stare towards her lover; and thought, "My Brazilian friend you are going to have hell to pay."

It appeared the innocent baby New Year 1947 wouldn't be in diapers for very long.

CHAPTER 29

TOILETTE PAPER, COFFEE AND GUESTS

The weeks passed. On April Fools' Day 1947 the residents of Sasso and the surrounding hamlets awakened to a winter wonderland. Several inches of pure white covered the landscape and the gods were sending more. Heavy flakes continued to fall obscuring the Apennine summits and aborting all gardening or cultivating ideas.

Around noon the postmistress, driving her blue-painted U.S. Army Jeep, delivered another box from *L'America* and addressed to Gianni from Miss Olimpia Martinelli, Mingus, Texas, USA.

The woman was particularly rude and left no doubt she was not pleased to be of service, snarling, "You and your Americans have everything but someday soon…"

"Thank you for delivering our package in this bad weather…"

A vicious, "Up yours Carboni; I hope you are happy sleeping with the Fascist Lorenzo's widow," a snarl, "you two make me sick." She dropped the box at the doorway, stepped into the Jeep, gunned the engine and roared away.

In other times the couple would have laughed at the woman's insult; however, on this morning there was no levity. Carla stared sardonically at Gianni and, without a word turned away from the door. Gianni, to no one in particular, "How would you like to wake up to that beauty every morning?" He picked up the package and went into house.

Carla looked at the return address, "Who in the hell is Olimpia Martinelli; one of your old Texas girl friends?"

"She is my cousin; my mother's cousin. I've told you about her."

"Why is she sending a package to you instead of your mother?"

Irritated, "Maybe it's an April Fool's joke?"

"Maybe. But, who is the joke on? You or me?"

There had been an uncomfortable peace between the two since Gianni's "let's all go to *l'America*" suggestion he introduced earlier. He attempted to discuss his "to America" idea several times, but Carla would merely walk away, exasperating her lover. After a few tries, he averted the subject; hoping matters would improve.

The distantness continued and, during the past ten days or so, she had been particularly sullen, overwrought, and taciturn. Conversations were short, words brusque and her temper, volcanic.

Carla and the baby were Gianni's life; he could not continue living this charade. Slowly, bitterness was building. He did not understand what was happening to their relationship; the situation was becoming unbearable, excruciating. More so, when Carla continually refused to respond to his requests for an explanation.

With that matter grinding away over the weeks and now with the foul weather, the hostile postmistress's words, Gianni exploded, "Carla stop it! What in the hell is the matter with you? In the time we've been together, we've never had bitter words; we've gone through hell together and now, when times are better, you put me through this garbage."

"You conveniently forget your great vendetta scheme."

Gianni bristled, but didn't respond.

She was dry-eyed but her eyes were puffed; he could see she had been crying.

"When you wrote to Texas, who did you contact?"

In a harsh tone, "My Uncle Gigi. But even if I had written to Olimpia and even if we were lovers, which we were not, what does that matter?"

He hesitated, but hot embers are not doused with a thimble of water, "As I recall, you jilted me for Lorenzo, that wonderful husband of yours, long before I found myself in Texas!"

Carla's eyes bulged, mouth agape. He never had used such a harsh tone nor exhibited such a temper towards her. She shrank into her chair, remained silent.

Gianni retreated a bit, but his temper continued trampling on his usual reserve, "Look, Carla, I love you; I always have. But I'm tired of this bullshit. I dropped the vendetta idea; you don't need to remind me it was a lousy idea; I know it was; I told you so. You never have shown jealousy of any kind and now", a hesitation, "what is it with this mood? There must be something more."

He reached out to her but she moved away toward the fireplace table, considered the fire and didn't respond.

Another hesitation but in a calmer tone, Gianni continued, "… and I got the message; you don't want to leave Italy. I hope you noticed I dropped the subject. You and the baby's happiness are what matter most. Haven't we had enough trouble these past years? Do we really need to invent new ones of our own making?"

He calmed a bit more, "Don't give me this silent treatment. Don't lay the guilt on me….it shatters me..."

An agonizing scream filled the room. The distraught woman turned, stood and ran towards Gianni and clutched him, "Gianni I'm sorry. I'm sorry. It's not you; it's not you."

She held him even closer, swaying, sobbing, "Gianni…"

"Damn it Carla, stop it! This crap has gone on too long!" He pulled back, looked at her, "What the hell is going on?"

She looked up him, lower lip quivering. She made a gesture he could not understand. It was as though she wanted to talk but couldn't find her voice.

Her silence stirred the fire again. In a harsh, punitive voice, "Damn it, Carla, what is this all about?"

The love of his life withdrew from him; she was shaking. Running the gamut of emotions, Gianni took her hand, caressed it, softened his voice "I'm sorry; take it a step at a time. Talk to me."

"Gianni", a long hesitation, she pushed strands of jet black hair from her face, tears now cascading down her cheeks, head down, a whisper, "Lorenzo is alive!"

"What?"

She looked up, stared at the love of her life, "Lorenzo is not dead!"

Stunned! Gianni's knees buckled. His half-brother, Carla's husband, alive?

He was screaming, words came spewing like lava from Mt. Etna, "What? How do you know? The partisans killed him! Who fed you this garbage? Lorenzo Grandi alive? Impossible!"

He grabbed her shoulders, "Look at me! Where did you hear this crap? What are you trying to do?"

A knock on the door as Gianni turned, trembling, his innards bursting with the poisons of jealousy and incredulity. The door opened and Beatrice strode in, a cheerful, "Hello, hello. Anybody home? It's me."

To the chagrin of the couple, Beatrice, now a new grandmother, had made it a habit of stopping in unannounced; her timing of the visits often annoyingly irksome. This moment, not an exception.

She stomped her boots, brushed snow from her coat started taking off her gloves," Brr! Is it the first day of April or is it Christmas?"

Neither Carla nor Gianni responded. The silence was ominous.

Beatrice had been aware of problems between the two, looked at the couple, an involuntary quiver of her left hand, "What the hell is the matter; Gianni, what has happened?"

Silence.

"Damn it, what the hell is the matter between you two lovebirds? Carla, you have been crying."

Gianni hugged himself, looked up at his mother and whispered, "Carla tells me Lorenzo is alive."

An eternity, then "Who said so? How do you know?"

Carla, "I saw him. He came to the house."

Another lightning bolt jarred Gianni. Fuming, he leaped out of the chair, "He came here? You saw him and you didn't say a word to me?"

Beatrice, "Gianni calm down; calm down."

Fueled by hidden jealousies from deep within, a second volcanic emission erupted into a river of lava flow, "Calm down my ass! Start talking Carla and it better be the best story you've ever told."

His world had stopped. He was a dead man breathing.

Carla began sobbing as Beatrice interjected, "Go get a glass of water."

Gianni didn't move.

"Damn it Gianni, go get the water. Stop jumping to conclusions without a safety net. This is Carla; not one of the scalped Oliveri twins."

Gianni went to the kitchen and returned with the water. Carla sipped a bit from the glass then, continuing in a low, subdued voice, "This is what he told me." A hesitation. "Remember the ex-partisan raid on the house?"

Nods.

"Gianni, you were right, that was the ex-partisan Vaccaccia, you saw."

"So?"

"When Mico left the partisan camp, and didn't return, Captain Tulio, Vaccaccia and several others questioned Lorenzo again. The Americans were closing in; the war was ending."

"So?"

Carla daubed her eyes, took another sip of water, "Lorenzo mentioned he had a cache of gold and liras hidden and would give them the hiding place if they would spare his life."

Another sip, "Furthermore, Lorenzo vowed to kill you and Mico if they let him live."

Gianni, calming a bit, "An offer greatly appealing to their cowardly wishes. Go on."

The poor woman took a deep breath, "About six weeks ago, the day we argued and you went down to Pavolo to inquire about passports, I walked into the house and found Lorenzo sitting at the kitchen table."

Another lightning bolt struck Gianni; his *Grugno* tightened his stomach; he wanted to vomit. ".... here in the house, at our table and you say nothing..."

Beatrice squeezed her son's shoulder, "Let her finish. Courage Carla, you are doing just fine."

"He was wearing a brown shepherd's cloak and a woolen skiing hat;" she hesitated, "he had a gaunt, haggard face", she looked pleadingly to Gianni, "I really didn't recognize him until he said, "Hello my darling Carla; don't you know your own husband?"

"I was stunned! I just stared at him; I couldn't focus, I just stared at him." Carla was trembling, her head throbbing as she continued, "Then, I noticed he was aiming a pistol at me; I asked him if he had come back to kill me."

Her head spinning, sharp knives cutting her innards, "He pointed the gun at a valise on the table and said, "It's been a long two years, but now I have some of the bread I had hidden in my cantina wall. Your brave partisan friends didn't get all of my savings."

"You mean money you stole."

With another snarl, he said, "Tut! Tut! For all I've been through", then pointing the weapon at the valise, "this is a pittance."

"I told him he had his money and gold and to get the hell out of the house."

Carla beseechingly looked at Beatrice, "Go on Carla; you are doing just fine."

A grateful smile, she continued, "His face reddened, I thought he was going to hit me. In a menacing tone, he growled, "As I remember, this is my house and you are still my wife. I'll leave when I'm ready." Then with a vicious smile he asked, "Where is your lover and his cousin, Mico? Since I now have my money, I want to repay them; if you know what I mean."

"I told him Mico was killed and I asked if he was involved."

He answered, "Ah! What wonderful news. Glad to hear he got his reward. I only wish I had been there to see the big oaf go down."

She stared into Gianni's eyes, "Then he looked at me wild-eyed and maliciously sneered, "What about your lover boy? When does he come home?", she looked down, "he wanted to know when you would return, adding, "That is, when does he come back to my house?"

Gianni sat. He was on the cusp of vomiting, "Go on."

Carla hesitated, folded her hands on her lap, "I yelled, "You bastard! Get out of here!"

Hearing the word "bastard", Beatrice cringed, remained quiet, patted Carla and encouraged her to continue.

In a pliant murmur, "The animal continued, saying, "your boyfriend is the bastard, not me. You make a lovely couple."

Carla again looked at Gianni, her dark eyes pleading.

Brusquely, "Go on, continue; I want to hear it word for word."

A forlorn, woeful gaze, "Then he stood, reached into his pocket, withdrew a one hundred lira note and placed it in front of me saying, "Here is full payment for the lovely years of service you gave me. Frankly, it is too much but I am a generous man. Tell lover-boy the rest of what I owe will be delivered in due time. Have him come down to Lucca; have him ask around about me; we can have a brotherly reunion."

The poor woman once again wistfully looked at Beatrice.

Gianni, with jealousy, rage and resentment eating at his innards, "For weeks you have given me all this crap while at the same time hiding all this! What am I Carla? Tell me..."

Beatrice gave her son a motherly tap, "Gianni quit making it worse!"

Head down, twisting her handkerchief, Carla continued, "He then picked up the satchel, walked to the door saying, "Yea, the bitch and my half-brother bastard; a beautiful love story."

He giggled like a mad man and said, "but, Carla dear, this story is going to have a sad ending because, if I'm not mistaken, I'm not dead and I am still your husband; not Gianni boy!"

The poor woman hunched over, covered her face with her hands, whispered, "Then he said, "Tell my so-called brother, one way or another, I'll see him soon to collect the rental payment he owes me for using my house and my wife."

Lorenzo's words were devastating to all three. Minutes passed before Gianni spoke, "So, for nearly two months you keep this from me? Why?"

A long hesitation and then again, a whispered, "I was afraid you'd go off on a vendetta and this time there would be no stopping you."

Gianni kicked a chair, then silence.

Another whisper, "Gio knows. I talked to her."

Gianni looked at her incredulously; Beatrice in amazement.

Looking up, somewhat bolder, she quickly added, "We both believed Lorenzo would not return to Sasso. He took a risk this time because of the money stashed in the house."

She hurriedly continued, "Gio and I also agreed the viper was not going to risk his life for vengeance sake; his life would be at risk with the Communists in town still hunting for ex-black shirts; especially those, like Lorenzo, who were Fascist big cheeses."

Gianni's hands quivered in anger, "You talk to Gio and say nothing to me?"

Boldly, a bit of rising anger in her tone, "Yes, I talked to Gio for advice and not to you! When you first wanted to go down and avenge Mico's death you gave no thought to how your actions would affect the rest of the family, including how it might hurt your own child. Who would stop you now?"

She paused, regaining more self-composure, wiped her eyes, "And you would ask Nasciente to join you in another vendetta idea and sure as one can be, he'd jump at the opportunity to go hunting Lorenzo with you!"

Carla, now more assertive "Gio is nearly six months pregnant but, just like you, it wouldn't matter to that Brazilian; she hesitated, "and you would have welcomed him."

She turned to Beatrice and quietly said, "I'm sorry Beatrice, but we decided not to upset you or the others. We believed it best if we kept this between the two of us."

Gianni put on his coat and boots and screeched "I can't believe this crap!" and walked out the door.

"Gianni don't…."

"Let him go; I know my son; he needs some time. This is quite a shock, to say the least; he has some thinking to do."

Beatrice pulled up a chair, sat and took Carla's hands. "You should have told him. However, at this point, it is neither here nor there. The question is what we do now?" she tightened her hand clasp, "as a family".

The two women hugged; Carla, with a huge sigh of relief, "Thank you Beatrice; you are an incredible woman."

She hesitated, looked at Beatrice with swollen red eyes, "I love him so much."

CHAPTER 30

IF YOU DON'T WANT ANY MORE WINE—LEAVE YOUR GLASS FULL

June arrived, life for the Carboni clan bettered. The world was righting itself.

The Lorenzo matter had been discussed and discussed, deliberated, argued without a resolution.

Gianni, to his credit, did not talk "vendetta" and Carla appreciated, to an even greater degree, his strength of character and his love for her. Her reoccurring guilt feelings aside, she was grateful for the status quo.

The Brazilian, Nasciente, after a day re-roofing the chicken coop, strolled over to Gianni's house and found him sitting under a small tree sipping a glass of the red. Gianni tipped his glass to the big man, patted the seat of a near-by chair, and took another sip, "Not bad; not bad."

A broad smile, "Too good to waste on some damn Brazilian."

Bruno sat, wiped his forehead with a huge yellow rag. His sweaty shirt clung to sledge-hammer arms as he grabbed for the flask and poured himself a very generous serving of *the red.*

"Geezuz, don't finish the bottle in one attack!"

Bruno saluted with his glass, "You know, besides liking the grape, we have a lot in common."

Gianni smiled; he had genuinely grown to like the big man for his honesty, hard work and, particularly how well he treated his cousin Gio and Aunt Gina. For all his bluster, both families were fortunate having him around; especially with Mico gone.

"Please spare me the details of your keen considerations; I was just enjoying my privacy."

Unperturbed, "Let' see. First, Gio and I are having a baby and we are not married. You and Carla have a baby and you are not married."

Bruno, hoping for a response, failed to elicit one.

"Secondly, we are managing huge parcels of rocks owned by our two, should I say, fiancée's; I figure the two of us are sort of indentured lovers, if you know what I mean."

Gianni studied his glass, raised it towards the sunlight, and took a sip, "So?"

"Gianni I love my woman, but I don't want to hack rocks and milk goats for the rest of my life; and I know you feel the same way."

He emptied the glass as his Brazilian motor began to rumble, "Third, these local yokel Communist are going to be as bad as the Black Shirts. They don't like the idea that we have more rocks to hoe than they do; and, despite the fact we gave part of our lives to help end the war, it ain't gonna matter to them. Our women are land owners and now you and this beautiful son of Brazil are part of the Sasso elite!"

Gianni was amused but kept a serious face.

Another sip of the red, "Ya, I walk proudly on elite chicken shit as I fix elite chicken coops." He wiped his forehead with the stained yellow rag, "They have every reason to envy my social status."

Gianni laughed and attempted to refill the big man's glass; Bruno covered the glass, "No. No more. Gio will be all over me if I go home with a tingle in my tummy", then pointing a finger at his head, "and buzz up here."

With little effort, Gianni pushed Bruno's hand aside, "If you don't want anymore, leave your glass full. Tell Gio I was the culprit."

Tipping his chair back against the tree, "OK, so you and I have problems with the new maestros. What else is bothering you?"

"I'm here, a deserter from the Brazilian army, without a passport; an outsider living among people who do not take to foreigners."

Gianni, "Hell, these new saviors of Italy don't even like their own."

"As I said, we do have quite a bit in common."

Another sip; then, his right index finger finished stroking back both sides of his moustache, "More importantly, Gianni, I'm worried about this Lorenzo nut coming back here. Gio doesn't say much but I know she and Carla are on edge. They are trying to hide their anxiety but Gio, in her delicate condition, is getting especially fearful and apprehensive; and, you know, that is not very much like her."

Gianni looked at his friend, sat up, picked up a twig and started drawing circles on the ground.

"Bruno, I have been drawing circles like these in my mind since Lorenzo showed here. And, you know what I've been able to accomplish?"

He dropped the stick and erased the circles with his shoe. "I'll tell you what", he leaned back, finished his *red* and laughingly said, "I've accomplished zero! Going after him is out of the question. Moving from Sasso is not the solution; it is also out of the question."

He grinned, "The entire family thinks my *"L'America"* idea is a wine-laced pipedream so, in my opinin, all that is left is exactly what we have been doing. We continue to be on alert and pray he doesn't show again. What else is there? You tell me."

"Well, everyone is afraid of something."

"Even Brazilian military heroes?"

"I have very private personal fears beyond Lorenzo."

"Heroes are devoid of fear. Tell me what scares you."

"I'd never admit it to anyone. Not you. And, with our new baby about to arrive...."

"Being sent back to Brazil as a deserter?"

Bruno picked up his glass, extended his brawny arm, "My glass is empty."

They clinked their glasses knowing it was 1947, but well-aware the war still affected their lives.

CHAPTER 31

AN ORDINARY DAY

On the first day of August, 1947 Gio gave birth to a ten-pound baby boy whom they named after Gio's deceased brother, Mico. The child was absolutely beautiful and more than one person in the family wondered how these two less than attractive people had produced such an angel.

Little Domenico, per his father, "had the color of a bronzed Brazilian god and would be sought after by every pretty girl walking Copacabana Beach."

To which Gio immediately replied, "Ya, but only if one those pretty things comes over to Italy."

A month later, on a spectacular Sunday morning, the church's newly assigned Father Matteo, finished with little Mico's baptismal ceremony, approached the child's parents and the new God-parents, Gianni and Carla.

"Congratulations! He is a beautiful baby; may he and you always be blessed."

Gianni, uncomfortable, as he and Carla hadn't gone to mass for quite a while but, since his mother was a regular attendee, he played his best card, "I'm Gianni Carboni, Beatrice's son; I'm sure you have met her."

The young priest, his dusty black cassock contrasting a snow-white collar, removed his tasseled black hat, wiped his brow and quietly said, "Yes, we have had a few conversations about you and actually, it is because of her concern, I have waited for an opportunity to talk to you."

The four, concluding Beatrice must have said something about Lorenzo, remained silent for a few uncomfortable moments. Gianni recovered, bowed his head towards his mother, smiled and in a mocking tone asked, "And what are my dear mother's worries?"

Beatrice, dressed in a flamboyant red dress she had made for herself, walked up behind Gianni, with a broad grin, "Your mother has had plenty of worries over the years and you have been the one most responsible for my anxieties."

She then took the newly christened baby from Carla, "Why don't you four listen to what Father has to say. I'll go back to *La Rimessa* with the others and we'll start our little celebration; you shouldn't be too long. Right, Father?"

With an affirmative nod from the good Father, Beatrice walked towards the path leading up the mountain, turned and said, "You are invited too, Father; roast chicken, some rather good ravioli, Nilde's best angel food cake and a good supply of the *red* awaits you. It's the least we can do." And away she went, leaving the four bemused and amused.

The good Father, "Beatrice is a woman of few words and much action." He smiled, turned towards the church entrance, "Why don't we go inside?"

The Brazilian winked at Gianni, smirked and shrugged his shoulders. Gio rewarded the gesture with a jab into the big man's rib cage.

Father Matteo invited the four to sit, then in a soft mild voice, "After several conversations with Beatrice, followed with a bit of research regarding your situations, I think I can offer some sound advice. Not as a man of the cloth but rather as a friend of Beatrice and your family."

Gianni shifted in his chair but remained quiet.

"I am going to suggest you consider marriage", he hesitated, looked at Gianni, smiled at Nasciente, "I'm not going to preach, pass judgment or give advice, however, I believe I have a few ideas you might want to think about."

Earning a "wait 'til were alone" look from Gio, Bruno turned a laugh into a cough. Gianni shuffled his feet, kept his head down and suppressed a laugh.

The good priest ignored the reactions, placed his hands on the table in prayer mode and continued undeterred, "In any event, Beatrice thought you might be interested."

Again, not a single response.

Impervious, the young priest continued, "Let's consider Bruno and Gio's situation first."

Bruno was about to interrupt, Gio interjected, "Father, Bruno is a non-believer..."

"So was Tomaso; hear me out."

He tugged at his collar and continued, "Bruno you are a deserter from the Brazilian army; you cannot go back home and, sooner or later, the Italian authorities will come looking for you."

Pointing his finger at the big Brazilian, "And given your status with the neighbors running this town at present, I would not be surprised to see a government visitor sooner than later."

"So?"

A soft smile, "So, should you marry an Italian citizen and if you are the father of an Italian citizen, the situation dramatically improves your chances of remaining here."

In a moment, the value of Father Matteo's stock soared; the Brazilian stroked his moustache, grinned and looked at Gio, "Padre Matteo, your comments place a commitment to marriage into an altogether different light."

Gio's acerbic answer, "Jerk!", drew laughs from the others.

Turning to Gianni and Carla, Fr. Matteo continued, "From what Beatrice told me, your situation is a bit more difficult."

Gianni shifted, straightened in his chair, a touch of anger surfaced, wondering just how much his mother had revealed to this stranger.

"Your mother has mentioned the possibility Lorenzo Grandi may be alive."

Gianni's face reddened, anger surface, "I don't think it is ...."

Fr. Matteo, seeing Gianni's face, immediately interrupted, "I'm originally from down river and I vividly remember a huge *Alpini* gathering in my town; Lorenzo, was the star attraction. From a platform, he screamed Fascist platitudes at the crowd; there was music, singing of Fascist songs and from every throat roared "Viva Il Duce! Viva Il Duce! Viva Il Duce!"

The good padre hesitated, "I was seventeen years old."

"So?"

Carla patted her husband's hands, "Gianni, let him finish."

"Unlike Cain, who slew his brother Abel out of jealousy and anger, Lorenzo, like his Fascist brothers, killed for power and greed," he hesitated, "and now they are reaping their rewards."

He looked directly at Gianni, “Lorenzo was an evil man then and, if he is alive, he is an evil man now.”

“Rather unpriestly comments”, thought Gianni.

The good man took a sip of water and continued, “If alive, for over two years Lorenzo has been experiencing daily punishment. First, he cannot return here as the Reds will have him immediately digging his own grave. Secondly, because of the individuals he killed or sent to the camps, he will need to hide from the authorities or he’ll be jailed for years. Third, there is no one in these parts that will help him without putting their own skin at risk.”

The priest now had Gianni’s complete attention.

“You must not let this imbroglio affect your child; everything else is secondary.”

“Priest, what the are you talking about?”

Carla sat up, “Gianni please stop interrupting” then, turning to the priest, “Father, forgive Gianni but this is an excruciating problem for us and …”

The man of the cloth interrupted, “I know, I know. But please let me continue.”

He looked at Gianni, then touched Carla’s hand, “Many Italian wives lost their husbands to Russian winters and to German and Fascist atrocities; their men never returned home and, in many cases, no one has been able to ascertain how, where or when they died.”

He took another sip of water and hesitatingly continued, “I am told many women are filing legal “presumption of death” notices and I further understand many such requests are being expedited and granted.”

Complete silence.

Fr. Matteo waited a few moments then took Carla’s hand, “Carla, I suggest you go down to the authorities in Pavolo and file a presumption of death notice.”

He hesitated again, smiled, released Carla’s hand, “He has been missing for a long period. He was a Fascist and the authorities in Pavolo and/or Modena are Communist to the core. They surely will be helpful.”

He opened his palms, “Once approved, you two could marry.”

Gianni stood, shook the padre’s hand, “Thank you Father, we appreciate your advice; we will discuss the matter. However, for the moment I think its best we get ourselves to the baptismal party.” He walked out of the room.

The others stood, shook the man's hand, Carla saying, "Forgive him Father, this is a most difficult situation for us." A tear glistened, "I'll talk to him."

As they began their climb up the mountainside, Gianni, his temper now under control, "I wonder what the Vatican would say about our friend's advice? He is well meaning and has some good ideas, however there is some wishful thinking involved, probably driven by my mother's urging. I wish she would…"

Gio interrupted, "Well, he was right regarding Bruno and me. I am going get more information."

"That's for you two to decide. But, insofar as Carla and me, there is a helluva lot more involved."

"Like what?"

"Like "*la busta*".

"What's that?"

"The envelope under the table."

"A bribe?"

"Remember the old saying?" Gianni mimicked playing the violin, saying, "The strings need a bit of rosin and furthermore, who knows how the courts would react if someone challenges?"

"Lorenzo?", asked Gio.

Gianni, still harboring intense feelings brought on by Lorenzo's appearance in Sasso a few months back, looked at Carla, "He'll be back to claim what he thinks is his."

Bitterness seeping from every pore, 'He has a hate and an ego that eclipse the sun; he'll show even if it kills him."

Carla, lips trembling, put her hand to her mouth, remained silent. Gio began to speak but Gianni, oblivious to Carla's reaction, interrupted "I don't think my mother told the priest about Lorenzo's recent appearance."

Even justifiable jealousy is a bitter poison.

CHAPTER 32

IT'S A LONG WAY TO TEXAS— JULY 1948

In 1946, "The Russian Stooge", Palmiro Togliati, led the largest Communist party in Europe – over 2,000,000 members; many living in the provinces surrounding Sasso. However, with help from the United States and the Vatican, by 1948, the number had been halved as Aldo De Gasperi's Christian Democratic Party led the way to the signing of a new Constitution.

Those with allegiance to the hammer and sickle, continued their bitter and virulent vendettas. Party members living in the "Red Cities" (Modena-Reggio Emilia-Bologna) were among the most fanatic. Vendettas were so commonplace the area became known as "The Triangle of Death".

Personal feuds continued unabated; jealousy, wounded egos and an "eye for an eye" mentality whetted the appetites of many who had been politically active or held personal grudges.

Sasso remained in the "Red Camp" and families owning the larger properties in the area were at particular risk. The Carboni clan, among those families owning the most property, was at risk. They were considered "outsiders", even though the family had lived in Sasso for generations.

The war years faded into the past and, despite the political situation, living conditions improved. Gio and Bruno had married and found a new level of love as the big Brazilian changed baby Mico's diapers, washed dishes and, every month or so, cooked a "real Brazilian meal."

The baby was big and beautiful. Chubby red cheeks, a huge mop of midnight black, curly hair blending into what his father called a "Brazilian bronze" skin. Except for extraordinary loud cries when he was hungry, the child wore a perpetual smile.

Gio's mother Gina continued to remark to Beatrice, "How could two ugly people produce such an Adonis?" Beatrice would scold her for the remark but, inwardly, agreed.

Gianni and Carla, now living in the Berti house, remained unmarried. Their baby boy, flashing dark mischievous eyes, was a little devil, enchanting one and all. Beatrice gave the child the ultimate praise, claiming, "The child was handsome like his father."

Although Gianni appeared to spend less and less time worrying about a Lorenzo re-appearance, he could not ignore the animosity some neighbors directed towards his family. He was uncomfortable in his own town and fretted over his family's safety. The situation reawakened his American dream idea.

Correspondence with his sister Roberta in New York and his cousins in Texas renewed his desire to leave Italy. His American relatives promised work and lodging for all. Roberta, writing to both Gianni and Beatrice, hungering to see her family after so many years, offered to pay their sailing fares.

Gianni continued conversations with the men in the family and found them enthusiastically receptive to the trip idea. Nilde's husband continued to express strong interest in immigrating.

But Gianni knew the votes that mattered wore skirts; to succeed, he must convince the ladies.

"Thanks for lunch, Ma; your pasta is still the best."

"Stop with the compliments; it was warmed over from last night."

"Your second day pasta is better than most ..."

"Stop it with the compliments, what are you casting for this time?"

Gianni smiled at his mother's quick perception, "I'm taking the bus down to Pavolo tomorrow", he looked at his mother and sister, "either of you interested in coming along?"

"Pavolo? Why Pavolo now? You know someone tried to assassinate Togliatti a couple of days ago. The Reds are on strike throughout the country and you can bet there is plenty of trouble in Modena and Pavolo. I wouldn't be surprised to soon hear one of the local idiots banging on our door."

"But..."

"Don't be so stupid! You can wait a few days. Let things calm down."

"Last week they stopped milking their cows, let their udders burst because they wanted higher milk prices. Tomorrow it will be something else. They lost the national election and instead of accepting the defeat they come up with every excuse to upset the country."

Gianni was livid, "They are not going to control my family's life; neither here in Sasso nor anywhere else in Italy. The Communist take-over of Czechoslovakia has whetted their appetite and, just like Mussolini's black shirts, they won't quit until they swallow the entire boot!"

The two women remained silent; Beatrice feeling an intense sense of pride in her son.

In a gruff commanding manner, "I received another letter from Roberta yesterday, she says she also wrote you both regarding a trip to New York. Frankly, I'd like to make tentative plans…"

Beatrice, trying to ease the tension gave a light elbow into Nilde's ribcage, "So, my favorite and only son, I assume you are going to Pavolo to buy a suitcase?"

"No, no. There is a man in Pavolo who arranges these trips. I'm told he would help me obtain passport applications, immigration forms and whatever else is needed. He can provide transportation costs, schedules, etc. Of course, we would buy our tickets through him."

A chuckle, "Naturally."

Gianni ignored the mocking remark, "Once I have all of the information, we can have a family meeting to seriously discuss the trip possibility."

"Let's forget the Communist; more importantly, does your wife know why you are going to Pavolo?"

"She read the letter from Roberta without comment. I think it best I get all of the information before…"

"Nasciente know about this?"

"No, not about going to Pavolo. He would tell Gio and my wife would know it before I boarded the bus." He hesitated, "I want to keep this low key this time. You are the only two I have talked to."

He looked at his mother and sister, "So, anyone here interested in going with me?"

Beatrice, "This has nothing to do with national politics but, for your own good and for Nilde and me, I suggest you keep both of us out of your trip preparations. I very, very much want to see Roberta and her husband but not at a price creating family problems."

She looked at her handsome son, thinning hair or not, he was so beautiful in her eyes, "Gianni, it really should not appear as if I was urging you to make the trip."

"You mean Carla?"

"I mean Carla."

The trip to Pavolo was uneventful; Gianni was given various application forms and all sorts of information regarding the contemplated trip. He spoke to all the family members, including his wife who, to his surprise and delight, expressed no hostility to the trip idea. So much so, she agreed to host a family dinner on the Feast of the Assumption so Gianni's could present and discuss the travel ideas afterwards.

The days leading up to August 15th were busy ones for the families. Hay had been cut and stored, animals sold and gardens harvested. It was also a festive and happy period. Weekend evenings, local musicians met at the town square to entertain for hours. The red flowed freely as couples danced while an erstwhile Carusos sang the new post-war songs of lost love and tender kisses in the moonlight.

The Brazilian was an excellent dancer and happily shared his wine-enhanced exuberance with the young ladies and old widows, alike. Gio, after an initial spin with her husband, a dance she named "The Obligation Waltz", was grateful for being relieved of having to "jump and stomp around like a bitch in heat."

Gio sat on one of the piazza benches chatting with various neighbors while watching her husband twirl himself into a glob of sweat, "Look at that big oaf; even his moustache is sagging", she commented to no one. She smiled, looked to her left and noticed a man staring at her. It was dark and the piazza lights were weak but she thought he looked familiar. "Who in the hell is he? And, what is he staring at? Holy Bacchus I hope he is not going to ask me to dance."

The dancers surrounded the make-shift stage as the best tenor in the mountains began to sing a favorite ballad, "*Vivere*". A few bars into song, four or five wine-laced voices joined in and formed a chorus hitting a variety of high notes making the mountain shudder. By the end of the song, most of the crowd, inspired by the music and stimulated by *the red,* joined the chorus, bringing the evening to a joyful close.

Gio stood and approached her husband who, using a half-filled glass of the *red* as a baton, had been conducting the musicians in the grand finale, "Come on Toscanini, I think your debut is a rousing success and …"

She glanced at the back of the crowd and saw the stranger again, "Good Lord, he is smiling at me. What the hell..."

Lightning struck, she no longer heard the music, bile gurgled and a fearful shudder collapsed her knees. She grabbed her husband's arm, "What's the matter? Too much wine, my love?" the Brazilian mocked.

"Bruno take me home", she whispered.

He looked at Gio's ashen color and immediately understood there was a serious problem. He half carried her out of the piazza and began the climb up the mountain path. Nasciente put his big arm around her waist, "Feeling better? Did you eat..."

"Lorenzo is here."

The big man abruptly stopped, "What?"

Gio, trembling, "I saw Lorenzo in the piazza."

The big man had never seen his wife so fearful, "Nonsense. No way."

She bristled, then regained composure, "Damn it, shut up! I saw the son-of-a-bitch and we've got to alert Gianni and Carla. I should have told them immediately..."

"It's damn near midnight…"

"I don't give a damn, we've got to alert them; who in the hell knows what our dear Lorenzo has in mind," She stopped, "so sober up and stop the jawing. That maniac has nothing but jealousy and revenge on his mind. Let's go! Now!"

Quietly, soberly, "I don't think you saw Lorenzo but if you are right, he is here for a vendetta of some sort and Carla, Gianni", he hesitated, "and their baby, will be his first targets."

They ran to *Casa Berti,* saw a kitchen light peeking through a small curtained window, "Good, someone is still awake."

Bruno banged on the door and was greeted by a bare-chested Gianni. "What has happened?"

Before they could answer, an alarmed Carla, dressed in a blue robe, ran in to the room, grabbed at Gio's arm, a near scream, "What is the matter?"

Bruno, "Calm down, calm down. Gio thinks she saw Lorenzo down at the piazza."

"I think he was there and we thought it best to alert you", a hesitation, "even at this late hour."

A nervous giggle, "No way! It's your imagination. Yes, that's it; you probably saw someone you thought looked like Lorenzo. The *red* will do that every so often."

"It's possible I was mistaken but it wasn't because of the *red*." A stern, serious look, "Gianni, I saw what I saw."

Gianni, putting on an undershirt, "I'm sorry Gio, let's sit down. What did you see?"

They sat at a long wooden table as Gio described the piazza sighting. She finished; no one said a word. After a few moments, Carla softly said to no one in particular, "If it was Lorenzo there is no doubt he will come here."

"How was he dressed?"

"Shabbily. He appeared to be hiding in the semi-dark behind the band stand. I think I noticed him because he was wearing a wool hat pulled down over his ears", a wry smile, "as if he was going skiing. I wonder why he would show up at the piazza? Putting himself at risk?"

"Right. Unless he has gone a bit off his noggin that coward would never dare endanger himself, even for a vendetta."

Gio, "But, he might take the risk for money. The Grandi house is unoccupied; easy to enter. And who knows what else is hidden there ..." She didn't finish the sentence.

They sat in silence for a few moments then Gianni stood, "Gio, Bruno thank you for your concern. You are the best. Rest assured we will stay on alert", then giving Gio a hug, "but this time it wasn't Lorenzo."

"Gianni I ..."

"Gio it's late. We will be watchful and prepared. Now get back your little Brazilian ... it's past everyone's bedtime."

Bruno took Gio's arm, "Gianni, just in case, I can sleep here and ..."

"No! We will be ok. I'll keep my pistol ready, but I don't think we need to worry."

Bruno stood, turned towards Gio, "Come on love, we'll talk about this tomorrow."

The ladies embraced one another for several minutes, each fighting tears. Bruno gently pulled Gio away and walked her out the door. As the door closed, Carla turned and hugged Gianni.

She held him tightly.

CHAPTER 33

KILL THE DEVIL TWICE

The August 15th, The Feast of the Assumption holiday arrived without incident. The entire family had been in alert mode but, as each day passed, the tension lessened as all believed Gio was mistaken. Gio did not relent but, after a few days, to everyone's relief, she stopped insisting she had seen Lorenzo.

The entire clan attended mass and returned to Beatrice's house to celebrate the holiday together. Bruno, Gianni and Michelle and his father, Emilio, were sitting outdoors at the large wooden banquet table Emilio had made.

It was a serene setting. The leaves of a huge oak tree, with the aid of a soft breeze and the brilliant August sun, produced a ballet of shadows and light on the table. A happy silence with background music from an old Victrola.

The men, sipping their first glass of the day, were having conversation while savoring the aroma of fresh bread baking in the nearby outdoor fireplace. The heavenly tang of simmering heady sauces emanating from inside *La Rimessa* added to the festive air.

Michelle, lifting his second glass, "Here is to the 15th of August. After all, this is our most important holiday. Right?"

"Don't let your mother see you drinking ..."

Gianni, who had been very quiet, interrupted, "If Lorenzo was at the dance, we would have had a visit by now. He couldn't afford to linger up here and be seen. He is no dummy; he knows a vendetta works two ways. If Gio was right and he was at the *festa*, I think he probably went to his house, took whatever and is back in hiding in Tuscany or in some large city further south."

The Brazilian quickly responded, "You are right Gianni; I think my wife was seeing ghosts. If he wanted to do harm, he would have acted by now."

Bruno, wearing a bright red silk-like handkerchief around his neck, adjusted his jaunty black cap smartly changed the subject, "My wife will crucify me if she comes out and sees me having a second glass before the noon church bell has been heard."

Michelle, "I'm never getting married."

"Oh! That's what I said not too long ago. Then, in the middle of the war, I find myself kissing a lady wearing boots. The next thing you know, good-bye Brazil, good-bye Copacabana beach, so-long pretty girls and hello sheep, Italy, rocks, fatherhood and, I repeat, a woman who will kill me if she sees me with this second glass of what is the best part of this damn country."

The Brazilian finished the glass, wiped his moustache and extended his glass for a re-fill.

Michelle, "I'll make sure I avoid girls wearing boots."

Gianni interrupted, "What's the bulge in your pocket?"

Michelle, face reddening, put his glass on the table and patted his side, hesitated, and proudly claimed, "It's my Lugar. The German officer's goodbye gift to me."

A defiant smile, "It's my war trophy."

Emilio, addressing his son in an unusually stern voice, "Damn it Michelle, put that thing away before Beatrice or your mother see you are carrying…"

"Baloney, Pa, I'm keeping this honey. The German officer would be very disappointed in me if he knew I gave his gift away. Right?"

Another sip of the nectar, "Furthermore, the war may be over but it won't be long before a new one starts. You are a nice man but, in case you forgot, there are a few of our dear neighbors who..."

A heavy female voice thundered from behind the fireplace, "Give me that damn gun!"

Beatrice, wiping her hands on her bright yellow apron, charged the five men, "Have you been carrying this weapon right along? What the hell is the matter with you?"

"Nonna…"

"Nonna, my butt! I've told you more than once to put the gun away", she approached her grandson, "Give it to me or you'll be sleeping with the cows?"

The lad did not move until his father, in his quiet reserved way, patted the boy on the shoulder and said, "Give the gun to Nonna. Let's have a nice dinner and tomorrow we can discuss the gun."

Gianni interjected, "Come on, Michelle, let's not anger the cook and, anyway, you are not going to need the piece today. Right?"

Michelle, gave his uncle an unpleasant smile, extracted the weapon and, without looking at his grandmother, surrendered the Lugar.

"Is it loaded?"

A subdued, "Yea, but the safety is on."

"Geezuz!" She stuffed the gun in her apron pocket, shook her head and scolded, "I swear I'm living with a bunch of donkeys!", turned and headed back towards the fireplace.

Once she was out of earshot, the three older men laughed. Bruno, refilling Michelle's glass, "Here, have some more medication; don't worry, she'll return the gun in a few days."

A stroke of the moustache, a sip, "Frankly, I think your grandmother is a bit self-medicated, herself. Tomorrow you'll be her favorite again. Now, what the hell were we talking about?"

Seminal moments in one's life arrive for us all. How one reacts in these seconds can, and most often, affect us for a lifetime. Around 8:00 PM on Assumption Day the entire Carboni clan faced such a challenge.

With the meal finished, dishes washed, more wine sampled and the two babies safely sleeping in Beatrice's second floor bedroom, the group gathered around the huge table and awaited deserts and coffee.

The Brazilian, with great ceremony, placed a bottle of anisette and a bottle of cognac on the table, "Now, Gianni, your guitar, it's time to sing a few verses of "Amapola."

Giggling, "No, no! I haven't played since the war. I hid the thing from the Germans; I don't even know where it is."

A much-lubricated Michelle stumbled towards the stairs, "I know where it is! I'll get it."

Nilde was about to admonish her son, looked at her husband and had to laugh. Her poor, quiet Emilio, who hardly drank more than one glass of wine at a sitting, was looking at her with a stupid grin on his face. He put his hand up and mouthed "I love you." He was higher than their son. She didn't know if she should throw the glass or a kiss.

Gio and Carla came from the kitchen with real coffee and trays of anise biscotti, *fritelle* (fried dough with cane sugar sprinkle) and crispy almond cookies.

Gianni strummed his guitar as Nilde served coffee. Beatrice, happy and thankful, remained in the kitchen putting the finishing touches to the climax of the wonderful meal, her amply laced sweet pudding named "English Soup".

She was in a state of complete euphoria; the family together in a circle profound trust and friendship, celebrating together and all in good health were gifts from above. She lifted her glass towards the dessert, "and this *red* isn't bad!"

"Gianni and Bruno, well into the second verse of "On the Isle of Capri", saw the front door slowly open and, suddenly the music stopped; Bam! In a microsecond, the world changed.

A tall man, dressed in black and sporting a woolen ski hat pulled down over his ears, closed the door, "My, what a lovely gathering. I'm so happy to have been invited."

The sneer was as disturbing as the weapon he waved from left to right.

From the stunned silence, Nilde's panicked scream, "Lorenzo! It's Lorenzo! Oh No! No!"

The Devil had joined the celebration.

Carla's entire body began to shake, hands trembling as tears gushed down her cheek. Gio immediately hugged her, placing her body between the fiend and Carla.

Gianni stood and took a step towards Carla, "Sit down Gianni-boy or I'll shoot you here and now."

Bruno tugged at Gianni's sleeve and pulled him back into the chair.

"How appropriate! Music, much wine, a grand dinner and, best of all, being greeted by your entire clan after such a long time. I am so honored."

"You bastard!"

An ominous giggle, "Oh, no my dear half-brother", Lorenzo pointed the pistol at Gianni, "you are, always have been and always will be, the bastard."

He hesitated, pointed the weapon at Carla, "I understand you and my wife have fornicated yourselves into making a little bastard of your own."

He again turned toward Gianni, "That is so sweet."

Michelle came out of his chair, Lorenzo spun, aimed his gun at the lad's head, "Sit down little boy or I will make you a hero forever."

Gianni and Nilde simultaneously screamed, "Sit down! Sit down!"

Venom spit out of the lad's mouth, "You are still the coward you always …."

An anguished Emilio, "Please Michelle, please!"

The boy looked at his father, hesitated and dejectedly sat down.

The man's eyes appeared to bulge as he spoke. The glare echoed evil personified; his voice hissed and oozed hatred, "I've taken a great risk to attend our family get-together. It's been a long time since… "

"This is not your family, Renzo. Your family is …"

"Shut up Gianni", the gun quivering in the fiend's hand.

"I've come all the way from Tuscany; Porretta to be exact", he turned and faced Carla, "Remember our vacation there so many years ago? We were so in love, you and I were two … "

A scream, "It's a lie! I never loved you! I hated you with every ounce of venom in my soul. You were and are …"

"Oh! My, my!"

Gio hugged a convulsing Carla as the fiend turned to Gianni, "You should have been there oh step-brother of mine. We lounged in the mineral baths, listened to beautiful Tuscan *stornelli*, drank the finest wines…"

"You are insane…"

"Maybe, Gianni-boy. But not then." He returned his attention to Carla, "Should I describe our love-making for Gianni?"

"You are the Devil!"

He ignored the remark, laughingly, "That should about do it for my lovely wife. Now to the matter at hand."

He faced Gianni, "I have taken a great risk for one purpose and that purpose is called Gianni Carboni. It is time to settle several problems you caused for me."

The women gasped as Lorenzo turned and pointed the weapon at Gio and Carla, "Carla, my bride, I've waited a long time for this moment."

He removed his cap, stuffed it into a pocket, "I thought about including you in my celebration but you'll suffer enough thinking about your dead lover each time you look at your bastard baby!"

Carla raised her head, saw a wild-eyed scruffy manifestation of evil, repeated, "You are insane..."

"If so, your lover-boy", he turned to Gio, "and your brother Mico, were the cause."

The devil laughed, turned and again pointed the weapon directly at Gianni's head, "Gianni-boy, you and Mico killed me more than once. Mico felt the agony of a just Tuscan vendetta and now, from Porretta, I am going to deliver my version of the same promise; it's your turn to feel the pain you gave me."

Gianni, "We let you live at the risk of our own lives! Let you live when we should have …"

"Enough of this! Get up Gianni, wave goodbye and start praying as you go out the door. We are going to take a little walk; I don't to wake up your little bastard and we don't want the joy of my vendetta to pass too quickly. Do we?"

A wave of the weapon, "Start walking …"

"Lorenzo, you need help. Let me ..."

A high-pitched scream, "Get up now! Or you'll leave for paradise with your family watching and waving good-bye! I said, get up!"

Bruno was about to leap at the intruder when a terrifying explosion pounded his ear drum!

He saw Lorenzo falling backwards and sliding down the wall. Before he could react, a second roar deafened him.

Through an acrid smelling haze, he could see *Il Diavolo* sitting on the floor, his back to a blood splattered wall; a very dead Lorenzo with a face minus its left eye.

The shock immobilized the others for a brief unreal, dreamlike moment.

Then reality!

A matronly figure stood immobile in the kitchen doorway, arms rigidly pointing at the opposite wall. Powdered sugar covered her face and festive yellow apron, a bit of grey hair escaping her kerchief. Transfixed, she held a Lugar in both hands.

She began shaking as Bruno, ears ringing, managed to relieve her of the gun and helped her to a chair. She took a sip of *the red,* then Beatrice asked, "Is he dead?"

"The Devil is dead twice, Nonna!", howled Michelle.

"You killed him twice, Nonna!

One in his stomach for Gianni and Carla and one in his head for Mico!"

The old girl looked at her handsome grandson and smiled, "I would have acted sooner but it took me a few minutes to unlock the safety on your damn Luger."

CHAPTER 34

SUMMER'S END

Ah! Peace! So wonderful. Or was it?

Throughout history, tyrants rose and tyrants fell. The new replaced the old but the same music thundered from the new maestros' self-constructed pedestals. Different colored flags, different military march steps, new anthems, new promises flooded the front pages of newspapers, world-wide. It is almost comical the way we repeatedly listen, read, believe and accept each new "symphony of promises." Although the music may wear different clothing and speak in different languages, tyranny existed; tyranny exists; tyranny will continue to exist.

Every generation apparently must re-learn the lesson.

Beatrice, because of her actions, became a favorite in the entire province, even the Communist sympathizers paid their compliments. She had killed the worst of the Fascist. A man who had helped the Germans kill and/or send many of their friends and relatives to the camps. A man deserving punishment no matter who or how retribution was administered.

There was no trial, no hearing. It was an honorable vendetta and anyone objecting would do so at one's own risk. Even the post-mistress who, since the war's end, had been most critical of the clan, changed her tune, saying, "It is an honor to deliver mail to Beatrice Carboni."

To which Michelle, sotto-voce, answered, "We are the only family in all of Italy receiving daily air mail via a red broomstick!"

Winter passed and a new half-century began. While political tempers continued to flare in Italy and on a world-wide basis, Sasso was calm and, despite many shortages, living conditions slowly improved and a degree of pre-war normality returned to this tight-knit world. Life revolved around family, hard work and a hope for the future. Except for a handful of zealots, political conversations were avoided. The past was the past and tomorrow will be better became the new mindset.

Packages and letters from Roberta continued to arrive on a regular basis from New York. In each letter, she asked about possible visits or immigration possibilities for family members.

Gianni raised the subject from time to time but, with a few exceptions, his efforts met with unenthusiastic responses.

"Why doesn't your sister visit us? Her husband has all sorts of money, doesn't he?"

"Carla, I've told you, he has a business to run and Roberta will find it impossible to come alone. He is one tough monkey. I know him well. I am sure she wouldn't dare bring up the idea."

"Well, count me out of any travel plans you may have for me. There is no way I'm taking the baby on any long trip."

Gianni remained silent.

"And stop talking to Bruno about a trip. Gio feels as I do. She is not going to take her baby to any New York. All you do is stir up trouble with your continuing talk about *L'America.* Furthermore, in case you have forgotten, for nearly five years Bruno is still living here without papers."

Gianni looked at his wife and finally realized his dream of returning to *L'America* was just that – a dream. He shook his head in silence, smiled, "You are right; I'll drop the subject. You won't hear another word from me regarding the matter."

And so, a dream died.

The warmth of a pristine June sky arrived in the central Apennines. Children played in the piazza, women made cherry schnapps while their men sat on benches discussing the possibility of a Communist inspired agricultural strike, local soccer matches or the just completed 2,500 mile *Giro del'Italia* where biker, Fausto Coppi, defeated national hero, Bartali.

After attending mass of the feast of Corpus Christie, Beatrice and Nilde put the finishing touches on another celebratory meal. The entire clan had been invited to partake in an outdoor back-of-the-house *"peek-neek"*. The mother and daughter saying they were going to make a "surprise special announcement".

The guesswork as to "the surprise" became the choice banter around the old wooden table.

Gio, "Nilde is pregnant, right Pasqua?"

Emilio merely smiled while Michelle snickered.

The Brazilian, "Beatrice are you finally going to see Rome?"

"Farther."

"Farther?"

The tone of Beatrice's voice alerted Gianni, "What do you mean? What are you talking about?"

Nilde stood next to her mother, "Roberta is sending the money for a trip to New York."

Gasps around the table.

"Mamma, Michelle, Emilio and little old me are going."

An obviously stunned Gianni, "How could you …"

"Gianni, calm down. Let me explain", a very composed Nilde interrupted her brother. "We are quite serious about immigrating. Emilio is sick of Italy and we think our Michelle will have a better future over there. We will take a trip, see if we like it and then make a decision."

A profound silence; so deep one could hear the soft sound of the breeze caressing the leaves.

Nilde, center stage, continued, "We have been corresponding with Roberta and have been following her advice as to papers, passports, etc. We will be going as visitors, but Roberta's husband will sponsor Emilio and file immigration papers for him."

A giggle, "As you know, Berto is very successful, he now owns three s*alumeria* (deli) and he needs butchers and butchers fall under the "immigration skills" quota.

"The American authorities will fall for that? Emilio has never…"

Emilio, quietly but firmly, "I think I will more than qualify, I have slaughtered dozens and dozens of sheep, calves, pigs here at *La Rimessa* and…"

"What about Michelle?"

"Oh! I'm a butcher, too!"

Gianni smiled for the first time since Nilde's announcement, "You a butcher? It's a complete lie." He poked his index finger into the lad's ribs, "The only meat you've butchered was served to you on your dinner plate."

Michelle, "But I am also very handsome."

Gianni stopped, looked at his nephew, thinking "Good Lord he sounds just like Mico on our long-ago trip to America. He silenced a melancholy sigh as he momentarily reflected upon the so long ago.

Nilde interrupted, "It will be a long process but we want to try. If it doesn't work, we will have had a nice vacation." A smile, "Right?"

Gianni, after the initial shock, clearly pleased with his sister and brother-in-law's decision, asked, "And how does Ma fit into your plans?"

"I'm going over to see my daughter; I haven't seen her in ten years and this is my chance to spend some time with her before I die."

Gianni, "Ma, quit talking like that."

He took his mother's hand, "Why did you keep all this planning from the rest of us?"

Nilde, "Because we knew…."

Beatrice interrupted, "Because you and Bruno belong here with your families; Carla and Gio are right."

"Meaning?"

"Meaning you can't take two babies on a trip like this. And you can't and shouldn't badger your wives into something they do not want to do. You belong here with them. Period!"

The Brazilian looked at Gio and saluted her with his pipe. Gianni remained silent.

Gio, "Thanks Aunt Beatrice. How long will you be gone?"

"Not sure. A couple of months, maybe. Hopefully, Nilde, Michelle and Emilio will be able to stay on. I hope to sail home alone."

The sun dropped behind the mountains, night approached. Gianni rose, embraced his mother, and thanked her. He shook Emilio's hand and offered his congratulations. He then approached his sister, kissed her on the cheek, "I'm so happy for you Nilde. After all you have been through, you deserve your every wish to come true."

He held her tenderly in his arms, "Whatever I can do, Sis. Whatever I can do; just ask."

It sounded like a last goodbye.

FINALE

HOLY NAME CEMETERY—NEW YORK CITY—THE YEAR 1961

It is a huge cemetery. Surrounded by a steel rod fence which gives the appearance of black spears planted side by side in such a manner one immediately senses an ominous aura, a presence of severity and finality. I always felt a sense of foreboding approaching the massive gate leading to the interior. It was the Tower of London without the tower.

This is where they had buried her. Not in that small cemetery back in the old country. The little serene resting place high in the Apennines; a place where she would have been laid to rest with people she knew; her friends, her family. No. Instead she lay among strangers, in a strange land she never understood and had no interest in understanding.

I am thirty years old now and some memories have been filed away for reviewing in my old age. Not hidden, are those vividly remembered Sunday rides to the depressing resting places of decayed bones and bronze caskets.

Instead of playing Sunday basketball or baseball with my school buddies, I was obligated to sit in the back of my uncle's new green Plymouth for the thirty-minute ride to this ground adorned with headstones decked with faded flowers nourished only by the tears shed upon them.

We entered through the massive iron gates and were immediately greeted by colossal memorial houses and gigantic stone monuments. Family names proudly proclaimed title over this property owned by the dead. We were awed by the competition for attention; my Ma said "not even Cristoforo Colombo's tomb in Genoa could compete."

We drove past "the rich" granite jungle section and stopped at the burial sites of the less affluent. Markers in this section lay flat on the ground. In the bitter, damp winters, plastic flower vases stoically guarded the remains of the dead, while summer weekends brought a changing of the guard; fresh flowers brightening the field with expressions of love and loss.

The routine was always the same. In winter, we placed a green plastic wreath on the grave; in the spring and summer, my Uncle Berto clipped the grass around the grave while my mother and Aunt Roberta placed fresh flowers on the flat grey head stone.

My task was to fetch water from a fountain, then clean the head stone. We knelt and prayed over the etched stone indicating the last resting place of my grandmother; it read:

BEATRICE MARTINELLI CARBONI
1870-1949

Most of my people are gone and now I am standing at her gravesite holding my own little boy's hand, hoping Nonna Beatrice is looking down at her great grandson, Gianni Michelle Pasqua.

If she is listening, I want her to know I will tell my little Gianni all about her. I will explain how she died suddenly in a strange land she never knew. I will recount the tale of her years of suffering through the hardships of two wars, tragic losses of close relatives and friends. With great feeling, I will tell him how she gave so much of herself to others. I will tell him how much better the world would be if we had more Beatrice-like people living among us.

What I will hold within is the question of fairness from above; about a favor, a small favor not granted—her wish to see her only son one more time and to die in Italy. I ask the head stone "Why wasn't the wonderful way she lived her life payment enough for just that one small request? There is no answer, of course.

It's getting late, my little guy is getting a bit antsy, and so I say a quick Our Father and a fast Hail Mary, take my child's hand and head for our car.

I give a last glance at the huge oak tree guarding her grave; I'm smiling, I look up to heaven and apologize, "Nonna, I know it isn't as beautiful as your favorite tree, *la faggia,* back in Italy but, you've got to admit, it is a pretty good substitute."

I'm smiling. No, I'm laughing! A full-blown laugh, I look up again "Nonna, I know that when we meet again you'll tell me I'm full of baloney."

My little boy is also laughing and suddenly I have the urge for a sip of *the red.*

MICHELLE CARBONI PASQUA

AUTHOR'S NOTES

(1) Introduction – *Although there were some early breaches of the mountain line and advances in the flat lands and larger cities, the final breakthrough in the northern Apennine Mountains did not take place until April of 1945. Americans, Brits, Polish, Canadian, Brazilian and other countries' troops charged bunkers, machine gun nests and other German positions in the rain, mud and cold. Casualties on both sides were staggering and thousands of civilians were killed as the Allies drove towards the Po Valley and the end of the war.*

(2) Chapter 19 – *No better example of Benito Mussolini's betrayal of the Italian people was his decision, against Hitler's wishes, to send ill equipped and ill trained Italian soldiers to support German troops in Hitler's savage Russian campaign. Little has been written about the role of "L'Armata Italiana in Russia"; of their suffering, humiliation and losses. Less is known of those innocent souls who never saw their "Beautiful Italia" again and those few who managed to return, scarred for life. It is estimated that of the 235,000 soldiers Mussolini sent to Russia, 115,000 were wounded and over 88,000 were killed.*

In mid-November 1942, the Russians began their counter-offensive against the invaders. The Red Army began a two-pronged offensive, including a drive to free the city of Stalingrad. The offensive was successful and led to the annihilation of the German 6th Army Corps, Hitler's greatest defeat of the war.

In the early phase of the offensive, the ill-equipped Italian 35th Corps (Il Corpo di Spedizione in Russia) was also attacked with overwhelming force. The Italians were left to defend themselves and attempt a retreat through hostile territory without ammunition, proper clothing or leadership. No supplies nor vehicles to transport them, they were degraded to foot marching in 20 below zero temperatures through some of the most treacherous and desolate parts of the world. Of the 30,000 who began the march, only 4,000 lived to walk the rest of the way home.

Then, after the Ally/Italian September 1943 armistice, the Germans turned on many of their former allies, sending thousands to a series of German slave camps. About 3,500 Italian veterans, including survivors of the Russian debacle, were enslaved at Buchenwald; where at least 1,200 died. ***The author was a friend of one of the survivors.***

(3) Chapter 22 – *Éclaireurs Israelites de France, (EIF, the Jewish boy scouts in France) rescued and saved the lives of thousands of Jews (and others) during the Second World War. After France fell in mid-1940 the movement went underground in Paris, while many of its members moved south into the area of the new puppet Vichy government.*

When the Germans started the deportation of French Jews in the early spring of 1942, the EIF morphed into a rescue operation; establishing "safe houses", supplying forged papers and helping these poor people escape France. Early in 1943 the EIF became part of the underground movement and became actively involved in liberation of southern France.

ACKNOWLEDGEMENTS

My first novel, The Reluctant Patriot, was based upon firsthand accounts of difficult World War II events experienced by friends and family members who lived through the difficulties of two world wars. This second novel continues the narrative.

One of the relatives I interviewed was my cousin, Cesare Bernardi. Many of my discussions with Cesare pertained to his November 1944 flight from German held territory to the American lines at the Tuscan town of Cutigliano. Thank you, Cesare.

Thanks also to friends or relatives here in the USA and in Italy who shared their family experiences with me. The walk back from Stalingrad, Buchenwald and the vendetta aspect of my novel are based on actual events.

Many thanks to Pauline Mohr, Roger Mohr and Lary (one r) Larsen who critiqued, edited and contributed so much to my continuing this project. One of my characters has some of Roger's predilections.

And a HUGE thanks to my wife, Mary Silvia, who encouraged me to continue with a project delayed by illness and doubt.

E.P.B.